FLURRY

ALISON RHYMES

Editors: Zainab M. at the blue couch edits
Cover Design: Ben | Pilcrow
Cover Photo by: Ren Saliba
Formatting: Sunshine Tucker

A NOTE FROM ALISON RHYMES

Any trigger or content warnings for Flurry, or any of my other titles, can be found on my website: alisonrhymes.com

To those that don't fit.

The ones who break all the molds.

Live in your power.

1

WILLA

"Are you going to be obnoxiously obsessive over his neck tonight?" Kit, my best friend, asks.

"I mean, yeah, maybe," I answer as we stride into the arena. "Probably."

Tonight is the night that Alexander Fane plays his first professional hockey game. It's an enormous night for him, and though he doesn't see me as anything but his best friend's little sister, I'm here brimming with excitement for him. Zander has been Isla's friend since the day he showed up to play Junior hockey for the team my dad coached. Dad now coaches the NHL's newest team, the Seattle Blades, and a couple of years back, they drafted Zan, but he's been playing down on the farm team all this time.

Due to a player's season-ending injury last game, they called up Zan. *And his big neck.* Kit and Isla always tease me about my odd infatuation with it, but I don't care. The man has the thickest neck I've ever seen. I want to trail my fingers down it, lick it, taste it.

Pipe dreams, that's what I call them. He doesn't know I know this, but Zander is gay. When I'm not in class or studying, I work as a bartender at The Chapel, a popular gay bar. I take fewer shifts these days, as my schooling takes up so much more of my time. However, during one of my shifts, I saw him there and he wasn't alone. Later, he'd come over to the condo I shared with Isla, and when it came up in conversation that I'd started working there, a strained look passed over his features. I never saw him there again.

His sexuality hasn't dampened my feelings. I've been a little in love with him since the first night Isla dragged him home with her. He was young, only eighteen at the time, when he plopped down on the living room floor and tried teaching my toddler niece how to build a house of cards. The feelings only grew from there. My sister has excellent taste in best friends. He's kind, generous with the little time he has, unimaginably sexy, and one of the scrappiest hockey players I've ever seen.

"You are so strange," Kit says, laughing. "I want to grab one of those poke bowls before we head up to the seats."

"Yeah, definitely. And a beer or two, I'm nervous."

"Why? You aren't the one playing."

"Shut up," I say, grimacing at her playfully. "I'm nervous *for* him."

"Hockey is his whole life. He'll be fine," Kit reassures. I'm sure she's right, but the NHL is different. All the players are bigger and faster. Besides, rookies get a lot of shit from other players.

Zan wasn't the biggest guy when he showed up as a teenager to play for my dad. He worked hard to gain some bulk, but even when he was shipped off to California, he wasn't big by NHL standards. Despite wanting to, I could only attend couple of his games these past few years. I thought it was weird to go without Isla and she's been busy. I'm not trying to be a clingy stalker type or anything.

My sister works in fan development for the Blades. She's also married to one of the team's star players, Cillian Wylder. Plus, she's a mom… finding time to go see her best friend play hockey in other states has been hard. She's probably more excited than me to have him back in Seattle. Well, maybe not more than me. But it's close.

Zan and I are friendly, but we're not that close. Like, I can text him on holidays or congratulate him on big moments. Anything beyond that feels forced somehow. He keeps me at arm's length, and I can only imagine it's because he's aware of my crush, which isn't reciprocated. Because... vagina.

"You have it bad, my friend," Kit says when she notices me succumbing to thoughts of the unrequited. "We need to find you a good dick attached to an available man."

"Yes, please," I say with another solemn moan. It's not as if I don't date. I do on rare occasions, when a guy catches my attention either from good looks or a great personality. None holds up to the inevitable comparison. "You're right. I need to get ahold of my schoolgirl crush and stomp into the dirt."

"Atta girl," Kit says, beaming. "You know Seattle is the top city in the United States for single people. And men are plentiful. They outnumber the single women by almost twenty percent. Finding you a dick to ride shouldn't be a hardship."

I laugh at how easily she spits out data. Kit is a statistician with a head full of these sorts of random numbers. Often, I've wondered what it must be like inside her head. She's always happy and energetic, moving a mile a minute, I bet her brain is the same, constantly on the move from one sub-ject to the next and the next. Unlike me, she doesn't date. We became fast friends when we met on our first day on campus. I'd gotten through my lectures and stopped at Molly's, a coffee shop on campus. When my order of an oat milk dirty spiced chai was called, someone else's hand reached for the drink. It turned out to be my bubbly friend. It was love at first identical coffee order. Or chai, whatever. She'd moved from Maine to attend school.

I found that so brave, as I only lived a five-minute walk from the university property and only a handful of miles from where I'd grown up.

We're opposites in a lot of ways. Kit never had a great family life, while I have a close knit, although small, family. She's always been on her own in so many ways. I, on the other hand, have been practically coddled in comparison. Mom and Dad don't mean to do that, but growing up as the daughter of a former NHL player naturally comes with certain privileges.

Kit's past with men hasn't been any better than her family life. She's sworn them off completely. It doesn't stop her from appreciating the male specimen, but she doesn't want anything to do with one romantically. At least for now.

Kit has been continuously tested in life. Being so close to her has taught me a lot; she grounds me, and I love her to death. I wish life had thrown us in each other's way years earlier.

"I don't know why I can't just get over this crush. It's not like I'm twelve and still figuring my way through puberty or something. I'm an intelligent woman, on her way to a PhD no less. Being hung up on a man that doesn't think twice about me is embarrassing."

"Stop that," she chides. "He likes you more than you pretend. But I agree that he's not a sensible choice. Hot, yes, absolutely. Available? Apparently not. Because you're a catch, a dream woman. And since he hasn't snatched you up by now, fuck his dumb ass."

"I'd love to do just that," I tease. "Maybe that would get it out of my system, and I could hop on the next dreamy man to come along."

We reach the vendor that serves salmon or ahi poke as I say the words. The lady working the counter, a retiree just taking a part-time job for something to do, if I had to guess, smiles at us and then winks.

"You young women enjoy your night," she sings happily as she hands us our food and beer. Seems even this stranger understands my need to get laid. It's been a while. I like sex, but it hasn't been a priority of mine lately. I just entered the doctoral program for feminist studies at the University of Washington, it's a big course load and I don't plan on fucking it up.

Besides, men are just so... well, ridiculous. Even here in one of the more liberal cities in the country, I meet plenty of incel types who want little more than to go head-to-head with me on my chosen studies. Too many men live to try and knock a strong woman down a notch or two. Especially a woman with a semi-famous father and brother-in-law.

Men, or boys rather, are equal parts jealous of my family's talent, envious of their lifestyle, and hateful that they don't have the same. All of that somehow leads them to want to fuck me but also make me feel inferior to them. As if I have anything to do with my dad or Cillian's success. Like saying they fucked the coach's daughter and came all over her face gives them some sort of street credit and the other bros will look up to them.

Hard fucking pass.

I learned a long time ago that I don't let a guy finish until he's finished me off first. And if he doesn't automatically go there, he isn't given a second chance. It's a huge red flag. I know I'm more than the holes I offer for their pleasure, as crass as that sounds.

Kit and I head to our allotted seats in the designated family section, seeing my sister and niece already there as we approach. Isla is speaking to a man I've never seen before. Granted, I don't come to many games these days, but the family faces usually only change with player trades. Or if one of the players finally gets serious enough with a woman to invite her to sit with this lot. It's not something most guys' do lightly. Sometimes they'll date a woman for months before they allow her into the circle of wives and girlfriends.

"Hey, Sadie," I greet my niece.

"Hi, Auntie Willa," she says, excitedly. I used to live with her and Isla since we're close, but like with most things in my life right now, I don't see her as often as I'd like. "You sit there." She points to the seat directly behind her own and next to the stranger my sister is still talking to.

He's broad but doesn't seem bulky under his black peacoat and dark jeans. I surreptitiously give him a once-over as I settle into my seat. He's got expensive black boots on, and upon closer inspection, I can tell his coat is also a high-end brand. The cost of his apparel isn't what grabs my attention though; it's his thick dark hair, and the ink painted over his skin. Markings show on the back of his hand, bleeding down to his fingers. It's wrapped around a paper coffee cup so I can't get a great look at the image, but the art is deeply shaded. It screams of something dark and ominous.

The man himself, dressed unlike any regular hockey fan, is intriguing. Especially with his deep voice that sounds as rich as the clothing he wears.

"I know very little about the game. I hope you don't mind my questions while I learn," he says to Isla.

"You're in the right section for that. We're all basically experts here. Ask away," she answers.

"I can teach you; I know everything about hockey," Sadie says. The man grins at her, probably not believing her. But she does know just about everything, even though she's only six years old and is missing a front tooth.

"You sure do," I agree with her.

"Willa, Kit, this is Damian March," Isla introduces us, pointing her finger at each of us, as she says our names.

"Nice to meet you both," he says in a voice that sounds like he finishes his nights with a glass of bourbon.

"Likewise," Kit says.

"Always nice to meet a new hockey fan," I tell him as he unabashedly ogles me. Excitement shines in his dark eyes, as if he's been waiting for this moment. I blink away my astonishment before turning back to my sister. "How's the head WaG?"

"Shut up," my sister whispers with a nervous laugh. She's been asked to take charge of the wives and girlfriends this season. The wife that did it previously, divorced her player and moved back to the East Coast. Isla hates it and can't wait to pass it off. But the stubborn control freak in her won't let her hand it away if it might make her look weak to others, like she can't handle it. She can, of course, but planning baby showers and the like isn't something she has much experience with.

"What's a wag," Damian asks.

"Wives and girlfriends," I say.

"There is a head wife?"

"Yeah, it's a whole thing," I tell him.

"Subject change, please," Isla demands, making my grin grow.

"Who do you belong to, Mr. March? And why do you look vaguely familiar?"

"He goes to UW, too," Isla says. "Maybe you've seen each other."

"I'm certain I wouldn't have forgotten such a meeting," he says, the silkiness of his words sending sensation to places that haven't been excited in a long while. Though something tells me he isn't being entirely truthful. *Interesting.*

"What do you study?"

"I'm in the sociology PhD program. Group behavior and cults, specifically."

"Wow, impressive," I say, turning to face him slightly. Our knees bump, but he doesn't pull away.

"It was a hobby that grew into something more," he says, shrugging. "What's your path?"

"Feminist studies."

"She's going to change the world for women," Kit chimes in, always so confident in me.

"Hopefully," I say. "That's the dream anyway."

"Admirable," he says. "To answer your other question, I'm a friend of Alexander's."

"Alexander? As in, Zander Fane?" Nobody that knows him calls him by his full name, it throws me off. Though the formality somehow fits coming from this man.

"Yes," he says, offering no other explanation as to how he knows Zan. Immediately, I know it's more than just a friendship and that tiny spark of heat I felt a moment ago snuffs itself out.

Stupid vaginas.

"Is his mother here," I ask Isla.

"Couldn't make it," she answers, shaking her head with some remorse. Zander comes from a small town in Minnesota and has a sister much younger than him, I know money was always tight for his family. I also know my sister would have offered to fly his mom out. "His dad is ill."

Ah, that explains it more. He's never said anything in my presence, but I've caught on to the fact that his father is an alcoholic.

"That's unfortunate," I say. "I'm sure she would have loved to be here."

The pregame clock keeps ticking down, and it's almost time for warmups. More family members trickle in, and we make our greetings. Damian is introduced to everyone. He politely says hello but doesn't seem too eager to converse with any of the new arrivals. I'm oddly tuned in to all things Damian March now. Registering every sip of his coffee, every infinitesimal shift of his body. The way he leans closer to me when another player's wife takes the seat next to him.

I hate how much I like the heat of his arm pressed against mine. Even more, I hate that I can only seem to be attracted to homosexual men. Maybe I'm doomed to singlehood. Maybe I'm doomed to singlehood because I was meant to be a man but was born in a woman's body. No, that's not right. I love being a woman, even when life seems like it would be so much easier if only I had a cock.

"You keep shyly looking my way, Ms. Cole. What is it you'd like to see? Be direct," he whispers into the curtain of hair at my ear.

"Oh my god, am I being that obvious?" Embarrassed, I try to laugh it away. He doesn't seem bothered by my attention, rather, more intrigued. "I'm so sorry."

"Only obvious to me," Damian reassures with a smile. "Probably because I'm paying so much attention."

"Well, I'm trying to place where I've seen you before and get a better look at the tattoos," I say, motioning to his hand. "Now that you know my reasons, what are yours?"

"You're fucking gorgeous," he says bluntly, switching his cup to the other hand so he can splay the one with the art on his knee for my inspection. Ignoring that stupid flutter deep in my belly, I look at what he's displayed for me. The florals bloom over his hand, vines and buds trailing up his wrist and winding around his ring and pinkie fingers.

"Garden Spirit?"

"Wedding Piano, but they are quite similar."

"You know roses, Mr. March," I say with a raised eyebrow.

"So do you, Ms. Cole," he says, once again using my last name.

"My grandmother had a large rose garden, one of her few obsessions. If we wanted to spend time with her, it was often in the midst of thorns and blooms," I explain. "How do you know I'm a Cole, by the way?"

"You and Isla look alike. Besides, Alexander has spoken of you."

We do look quite a bit alike, both taking after our mother in many ways. Though I got my mom's coloring with fair skin and honey hair, Isla takes after Dad with her darker curls and skin that always looks like it has a healthy sunglow to it.

"Has he?"

"Don't be surprised. He's quite fond of your family."

Right, my family. Not me, specifically.

"We feel the same; he's practically an honorary Cole."

"There's time for one more before warmups," Kit says to Sadie. They have a game they play where Sadie rattles off a subject and Kit tells her whatever random stat or fact she knows about it. If she knows nothing, they look it up together.

"Um, pineapples!" Her "s" comes out in a lisp due to the hole in her front teeth.

"Good one," Kit says. "I don't know much, but one third of all pineapples come from Hawaii."

"Mom, can we go to Hawaii?"

"Someday, maybe. Ask your dad."

"Okay."

"She loves pineapple," I explain to Damian.

"Alexander says she's a vegetarian."

"She is. She's an animal lover. Especially cats."

"I, too, love pussies," he says quietly along the shell of my ear. I burst out laughing at his bold statement. Damian winks, his eyes gleaming.

Maybe my vagina isn't so useless, after all.

2

ZANDER

"I think I might puke."

"If that's what you need, now's the time," Cillian tells me calmly, but a smile ghosts over his lips.

"It's not funny, asshole."

"You're right, Rook," Oliver Lehtinen says, as he tightens the laces of his breezers. I hate the nickname the team gave me as soon as I stepped on the ice at yesterday's practice, but I am the rookie, so I let it slide. "It's fucking hilarious."

A few other guys laugh, and I ignore that too.

"You'll be fine, Zan. We've all been there; just remember you've been playing this game your whole life. Tonight is no different, it's just new ice."

Easy for Cillian to say. He's been in the league for years now, having been drafted straight out of junior hockey. He didn't spend any time in the minors fighting to be seen by an NHL general manager or coach. Cillian Wylder was hotshot since he was fourteen. I've been more a steady grinder, not a standout.

Most of the guys on the team are exceptional talents. But I was called up for a reason and I need to remember that. More importantly, I need to earn my damned spot on this team and make sure they never have a reason to send me back down. Or trade me off. I like it here in Seattle. Despite my family being back in Minnesota, Western Washington feels like home.

In large part because of the Coles. When I first moved here to play for the Timberwolves, Coach and his family took me under their wing. He kept a close eye on all his transplant players. But Isla befriended me, and that part was special. She didn't let many people get close to her back then, because of trust issues. But there was something kindred between the two of us, one damaged and determined soul finding another. Or some shit like that.

Because of her, Cillian and I have grown a friendship of sorts. Maybe even a mentorship that I can't complain about. He's probably the closest thing to Gretsky in the league right now.

"Just new ice," I repeat.

"Yep, now get the fuck out of your head and finish taping your stick," he says, knocking a fist to my shoulder. "We have warmups in five."

Every player has their pregame rituals, some stranger than others. Mine is taping my sticks in a very specific and precise way. Everyone tapes their own stick and in their own way. I can get obsessive about it, though. If the tape isn't exactly right, I'll rip it all off and start over until it's perfect.

"You got this, Rook. You're going to love it; this crowd goes wild for us. You'll have a host of new pussy lined up by the end of game," Lehtinen says, leering like a creep from the stall next me.

"Give the kid a break, Olly," Vaughn says, throwing a towel at him. Oliver is the clown; I quickly picked up on that.

Cillian eyes me with understanding before shrugging. It's his way of telling me to let the comment slide off my back. Because Cillian Wylder is married to my best friend, he knows I'm bisexual. A fact I've always kept quiet. Hockey frowns on anything that deviates from wholesome family values. An NHL player with a boyfriend would be frowned upon greatly.

Not that I have a boyfriend. I have Damian, whatever he is. The thought of him reminds me that he's here tonight. Watching me play and probably meeting Isla as we speak. *And Willa.*

Fuck, I can't wait to see them all. It's been a mad rush since I got the call that I'd be playing. I was booked on a flight five hours later and shuttled to practice at the Iceplex as soon as I landed. After that, I crashed hard at my hotel because today is game day and I needed to be ready. There hasn't been time for catching up with old friends. Or new, which is technically what Damian is.

We met online a few years ago. Not long before he moved to Seattle to finish school. And, unfortunately, just before I was sent to California. We've kept in contact but other than one time I met up with him when I was here visiting Isla, we don't see each other.

I grew up in the small town of Ely, Minnesota, playing hockey in the shadow of the U.S. Hockey Hall of Fame, which was only an hour away. The sport runs deep in those parts and the pressure rivals what I'm feeling tonight.

The dream was always the NHL. Never could I have guessed I'd have a filthy talking pen pal in the stands watching me play. Let alone that he'd be sitting next to the only women I've ever loved. The Cole women are special, each in their own way. Isla is the best friend I've ever had, but her sister… Fuck, the things Willa makes me crave.

But I can't think about that now, it will fuck too much with my head. Not to mention other parts, and this sure as hell isn't the time or place for that. Thankfully, I excel at compartmentalizing my shit through a game. It was something I had to learn as soon as I acknowledged that I wasn't quite the same as all the other guys I was growing up with.

Being bisexual in a Midwestern small town and being an elite hockey player? Yeah, it was fucking hard. It still is. I've resigned myself to the idea that it always will be. This sport isn't changing any time soon.

"Let's go, Fane," Cillian says, tapping my knee with his stick and waiting for me to rise. "You good?"

"For sure," I answer.

"Good. Get out there and work out any last nerves."

Once I hit the ice, I realize how right Cillian was. It doesn't feel different than any other game I've played. Other than the noise level, anyway. It's just warmups so the seats aren't full yet, but fans crowd the plexiglass and cheer while holding up various signs. Still, it's going to be so loud when the stands are full. Thousands of people cheering you on does something to your ego and adrenaline. So, I follow Cillian's instructions and work out any remaining nerves by following the exact same warmup routine I've been doing for fifteen years.

I'm a creature of habit. I love my routines. They keep me sane. Circling our side of the ice a few times, I then move into lunges and hip stretches before I start taking some shots with pucks. My body feels good, my skates are sharpened just how I like, my stick is taped to perfection.

And my head is clear of bullshit and ready to fucking play.

After warmups, we head back to the locker room to change into our game jerseys and get some final words from the coach before puck drop. I've played with two of the guys on our opposing team before. Their goalie, Meadows, grew up near me and was in the WHL the same time as I was. We've always circled one another's careers. One of their defensemen, Burke, was on the same AHL team as me for a year. It helps knowing how they work, how they play, how they move.

On the bench, I'm sandwiched between Gavin Vaughn and Axel Wallin, both veterans in the league, as we wait for our turn while eagerly watching the play in front of us. Axel is vocal, yelling at anything and everything, as one of our livelier players. Vaughn is more like me, silently taking in the play before us.

"Show us what you got, Rook," Wallin says as we hop the boards to switch out with the line coming off the ice. Cillian controls the puck at the other end of the ice, giving us plenty of time to position up. As soon as we do, he passes it to Vaughn who skates around a player and heads toward the net being defended by Meadows. Another of their players swerves in to try and snag the puck from Vaughn. The move leaves me wide open.

They may underestimate me as the newest player, but Vaughn doesn't. He passes it cleanly and the puck lands at the heel of my stick. Burke is there quickly, having anticipated the pass. He's not the fastest skater, instead he relies on his size. The man is massive and often uses his body to dislodge the puck from players.

He forgets I know him. He hits high. Never aiming for the head but upper body for sure. I, on the other hand, am small in comparison. A handful of inches shorter than his enormous six-seven. When he moves to rush me against the boards, I lunge deep, turning with the puck still on my stick. He side-swipes me some, but the momentum only helps me maneuver around him and get a shot on goal. Meadows blocks it with his left leg, and it bounces just inches in front of the net. Right to where Wallin is waiting for the rebound, elevating the puck just enough to sail into the net under Meadows's arm.

I just got my first NHL assist.

I'm dazed for a half second until Wallin and Vaughn slam into me, patting me on my helmet.

"Fuck yeah, Fane," Wallin says. Not Rook, *Fane*. Damnit, that feels better than just about anything in my life ever has. Skating to the bench, I get variations of the same congratulations from everyone there. Cillian wears a huge smile for us all. Coach, who is notoriously tight-lipped and stoic, lifts his chin and slaps my shoulder.

My chest hitches. With a dad like mine back home, Coach Cole is the father figure I always needed. His small acknowledgment of my accomplishment is all the parental pride I could dream of.

Houston's team ties it up in the second period and neither of us can land a puck in the net during the third. We immediately head into overtime, and still the score doesn't change.

Some players love a shoot-out. Some hate them.

Me?

I love them. They excite me like it's my birthday and I'm about the get the best blow job of my life. There's little hope Coach will send me in unless we have to go down the whole line of players, but I don't mind.

"Meadows is weak on his right side. He'll fall for a fake on the left more often than not," I say.

"You're up first, Fane," Coach says, and I still.

"Seriously?"

"Olly is number two. Wylder, you play clean up. He'll fall for a fake out on the left, so aim top right," Coach says, repeating my words and sending me a raised eyebrow. "Go get it, Rook."

For fucking sure.

Two hours later, I walk into the family room to another round of congratulations. I don't know most of the people telling me it was a great game, but I accept it all graciously. I scored the game a winning goal, at the top right of the net. Just like Coach told me to.

Scanning the room, I see Isla's dark curls and start through the maze of people waiting for their players to come out.

"Hey, hotshot," she yells, jumping into my arms for a big hug. "Way to make a debut."

"Thanks, friend," I say, squeezing her and lifting my head to wink at Sadie, who's trying to climb me like a tree.

"Great game, Uncle Zan!"

"Thanks, kiddo," I tell her, swapping her for her mom.

"You won it," she says loudly in my ear.

"Ah, team effort," I say.

"Whatever," Sadie says with an eye roll. I place her down on her feet, and a hand lands on my shoulder.

"That was a perfect fake, Zander." I turn to Willa, her voice always sounding shy when she's speaking to me. Only with me. With everyone else, she's confident, direct, but still kind and playful.

That's not the Willa I get.

I hate it and love it all the same. Because I'm a little in love with her and hate that I can't just take what feels like it should already be mine.

"Thank you," I say, wrapping her in a hug as well. I inhale her, breathe her deep into my lungs. "Thanks for being here."

"I wouldn't have missed it," she tells me, her arms wrapping around my shoulders. I lift her slightly off her feet and hear the small gasp she makes. "I'm so proud of you."

Giving her a final squeeze, I set her feet back on the floor but keep one arm casually around her shoulders. I'm not ready to let go. Everything about Willa Cole works me up, forcing me to remind myself of who she is and why I can't have her the way I want.

Coach's daughter.

Best friend's sister.

A woman who deserves more than a stubborn man, who refuses to compromise just now.

"Thank you," I repeat, dropping my arm and taking a step back.

"Kit asked me to congratulate you. Your friend didn't stay, either," she says, her berry-stained lips turning into a half-smile. "We tried."

"Not surprising," I admit. Looking to Isla, I ask, "What did you think of him?"

"He seemed nice, but you should be asking Willa. They were thick as thieves."

"Oh, really?" I ask Willa, raising a brow at her. An unfamiliar feeling prickles as it comes to life in my chest. *Jealousy maybe?*

"He was fun," she says, shrugging, as she turns her face downward so I can't gauge the expression she wears under her blushing cheeks.

Fun isn't the first word that comes to mind when I think of Damian March. Mysterious, maybe. Quiet and direct? Definitely. Insanely sexy with his dark looks and sly smiles, for sure.

We started chatting through an exclusive online app at a time we were both looking for connections. He wanted to meet people of a like mind here in Seattle before he relocated, while I was desperate for male interaction that wasn't heterosexual. There have been some sexual escapades. That type of vulnerable intimacy took months of building up trust.

I don't work as hard as I do to throw it away for a little virtual booty call. And Damian… well, he's even more reserved with his sex life.

Damian's very much aware of Willa Cole and who she is to me. He made a point of orbiting her on campus, keeping an eye on her for me, in a sense. Any day he saw her, he'd relay to me what she was doing, what she wore, who she was with. It made me less lonely, less homesick.

Probably made me *more* of a creep. But I am what I am.

It's not a shock that Damian would have taken the opportunity to get to know Willa tonight. Although it's surprising that Willa is responding like she has a new crush. Like how she has always responded to *me*.

I'm not at all sure how I feel about this development.

3

DAMIAN

"**Y**our schedule is pure insanity."

Alexander hums in agreement, running his hand over a few hangers. He has a rare two days off. Which is basically a lie. He still had morning training and skate both today and tomorrow. Plus, some promotional shoot tomorrow afternoon at a local pet shelter. But he doesn't have games and needs to take advantage of every spare second.

Apparently, that means new suits befitting an NHL player and finding a place to live that isn't a hotel room.

"What about this one," he asks, pointing to a navy-blue suit with thick off-white pinstripes.

"How very *farm boy's day in the big city* of you," I reply with the hint of disdain it deserves.

"Asshole," he says, chuckling. "I'm overthinking this, aren't I?"

"Yes. Keep the suits classic. Pair it with flashier items. Trust me."

"I do. That's why I brought your silver spoon ass along."

"Then stand aside and let me pick for you, Alexander," I say, and he steps back with raised hands. I was born with the privilege he teases me about. I have more money than I could ever know what to do with, yet not a single dollar of it was earned by me. My privilege is a circumstance of birth that I've done exactly nothing to deserve. The March family is what they mean when people say *old money*. I come from a long line of men who only procreate to carry on the tradition of passing enormous amounts of money to offspring that they only interact with for special occasion photo ops. Not because they enjoy their children, or child in my case. My father said one and done after me.

For how different Alexander and I are, in some ways, we're quite the same. A complicated family life being one of them. Neither of us received the level of love and emotional support all children should get. My life was cold and stoic, his was more toxic turmoil. The end results were much the same, we both fiercely depend on ourselves. Which only makes navigating new relationships more difficult.

I wave to the sales associate who has been distantly attentive.

"We'll need a fitting room," I tell him, choosing a few clean-lined pants and jackets. "I'll get him started with a few options and let you know when we're ready for measurements."

"I'll get a room started for you," the man says, sizing up Alexander. Not in a leering way, more just gauging his suit and shirt size. Well, perhaps in an appreciative way as well, he is quite an eyeful after all. "Let me know when you are ready for assistance."

The shop is small and only has one associate. Luckily, we're currently the only customers. I select a few more pieces and usher Alexander toward the fitting rooms in the back of the store.

"That's it?" he asks.

"From here, yes. You should have let me call you a tailor."

I'm still making minor league money, custom suits can wait until I know I won't be sent right back down to California."

"Slim chance of that happening with the way you played last night," I tell him.

"One good game doesn't seal the deal. Or makes you an expert," he says, playfully. He knows I've tried to watch games on television before; learn the sport and be supportive of my friend. It moved too fast for me to grasp it all. Something that greatly annoyed me since I like to think I'm a reasonably intelligent human. The ladies last night were a huge help to my effort of understanding rules like 'icing'.

"You sat me in the middle of hockey savants. I'm probably an expert now."

"It's in their blood," he says, opening the fitting room door. "Isla said you got on well with Willa."

Of course, I got along with her. Willa Cole has a natural gravitational pull as strong as the moon itself. She's fun in an easy way, it's not forced or loud. The way she exudes confident sexiness even while being bundled up in a puffer coat was enough to endear me, if not attract me, though it did that, too. Not to mention her patience with me, or how she matched my flirting with a sweetness I rarely see. She reminds me of a friend back home in New Orleans. Delilah never knew the effect she had on those around her either.

For some, beauty is everything and their attitude about it only makes them shine less. For others, people like Willa, Delilah, and even the man standing in front of me, beauty isn't what they strive for in life, yet seeing them is like waking up to sunshine warming your whole body.

"Impossible not to," I tell him, raising a brow. "Now strip for me, Fane."

His mouth, those perfect lips that have only been wrapped around my cock one time, part in awe.

"We're in public," he whispers.

Yes, we are. The fear of it is written all over his face. I understand it but can't relate. Being afraid isn't ingrained in us from birth because we never risked anything. It's easy when you're filthy rich. I've never experienced poverty, hunger, or even general survival from living in the wrong part of town or with the wrong sort of parents. Mine are horrible because of absence, even when in the same room. Not because they were abusive or neglected my basic needs. I was always given shelter, food, and care in the form of nannies and tutors. I was afforded the best of everything with all the necessary precautions to keep the March heir healthy and safe.

"Hardly," I say. "Besides, that man likely thinks I'm your stylist, not the man you dream of fucking you every night."

"I think you have that backward," he says, mouth still tight even though he takes a small step forward and pulls his tee over his head in one quick move.

"Do you now?"

The thing about Alexander and I is that neither of us makes for a very good bottom. Not with my born superiority complex and his innate cocky dominance nurtured from years of elite sports. It's made for an interesting dynamic between us, both grappling for a position we've become accustomed to.

But with him standing here in front of me, that sculpted body on display, a feast for my hungry eyes, I'm ready to drop to my knees without a second thought.

"That look on your face tells me I'm right," he gloats.

"Fuck you, Fane."

"You only call me that when you're… in a mood."

Horny is what he means. It's difficult not to be when I'm in the same room as him.

"I'm in the mood to get you some suits and get the fuck out of here. Focus," I tell him to do what I can't as I reach to unbutton his jeans. The rippling abs under my fingers are an indication that Alexander is as worked up as I am.

Sex is not something I take lightly. It's not something I have often. I'm a picky asshole about who gets near my dick. I always have been. There needs to be something more than fleeting lust for me.

That doesn't mean I won't watch and get myself off though.

My friend in New Orleans, Fig, called me the Voyeur Extraordinaire, a name I embraced. He never minded having me in the room as he fucked his way through the city. I don't have a Fig in Seattle, though. But now I have an Alexander Fane and a Willa Cole.

"That is not how you're going to get me to focus," he clips out. He grasps my jaw and collars my neck, stopping me from coming any closer than arm's length.

"This is going to get very awkward for you when he comes in to take your inseam."

"Then quit helping me." He laughs lightly, but it's tinged with the same heat I feel rushing to places that don't need encouragement just now. Alexander brushes my hands away and finishes undressing.

"Fine. I'll just watch."

"Your preference," he says. *Exactly.*

Somehow, we manage to get through the rest of the ordeal without further incident. How, I'm not sure. His body is exceptional. With how much I know he trains; it shouldn't be surprising. Except I've mostly only seen it through a screen while sexting. In the flesh, it's fucking spectacular. He's bulked up since I last saw him, his chest thick and thinly covered with hair. I like that he doesn't shave it like so many men do now.

I can get soft and smooth from a woman. From Alexander, I want his version of rugged masculinity. It's what initially attracted me to him. He's polite and personable, exactly what you'd expect from someone who grew up with a big family in a tiny town. Only when he's feeling aroused or on the ice does he let the other part of him show. The big ego alpha male side. Even then, it's always with an edge of care and control of himself.

Alexander is a rare find. Our relationship is not defined in any substantial way, but I aim to hold on to it. To develop it into more. Whatever that looks like between the pressures of his career.

"Where is the apartment you're going to look at," I ask him when we stop at a favorite restaurant of mine for dinner. An unassuming hole in the wall with a small, but excellent, menu and an abundance of privacy. I've ordered a carb lover's dream meal, while he's having sensible high protein with vegetables on the side meal. I know he carb loads on some days, today must not be one of them.

"It's a condo for rent in the building Isla used to live in." He takes a drink of water and averts his gaze.

"And," I prompt, confused at his nervous reaction.

"Willa still lives there with her roommate, Kit."

"Is that a situation we need to discuss?"

"No."

"Alexander..."

"No, Damian. She's a friend, nothing more."

Lie. No matter how many times he says it, it's no less false. He once told me all his reasons for never pursuing a more *personal* situation with Willa, but after meeting her, I don't know that I understand his reasoning anymore.

"I quite liked her. She's very amusing, not to mention beautiful." He hums and takes another sip of his water. I take a drink of my gin, mirroring his movements. "Alexander."

"I know, March. I fucking know how great she is without your reminders."

"I'm March now," I ask, as amused with him as I was with Willa last night.

"You are when you push me, I guess," he admits.

"I'll make a point to push you more often then."

"I bet you will," he says.

"Bet you'll like it, too," I tell him with a smile.

"Bet you'll like it more."

"You're awfully confident in your knowledge of me, Alexander."

"We've been friends for over three years," he says. While true, I didn't give him much of myself at first. Like him, I kept my cards close. We both still do in too many ways, the most intimate ways.

"Are we friends, Alexander?"

"You know I can't offer much more," he says, stopping abruptly as the server makes his way to our table. The poor guy. I don't mean that teasingly, he does have a real dilemma. I've never been anything but obnoxiously and abundantly myself. While he's spent so much of his life suppressing who he is for his first love. Hockey.

"No, I guess that's true," I say when we're alone again, and he's taken a few bites of broccoli. "As I've said before, we'll work through it. Or around it, rather."

"And as I've said, I appreciate that, but I'm also not putting parameters on this." He waves his knife between us. I roll my eyes at him.

It's a discussion we had once; how he can't give exclusivity to me. Not that I ever asked for it. Alexander made it clear that there is no other man in his life, for obvious reasons. But there are no rules for him with women. If a woman catches his eye on a day he needs physical release, he wants the freedom to fuck her without guilt.

Unlike me, he has urges for physical affection.

Because he likes things to be fair, he hasn't asked for me not to fuck women. We're complicated enough separately, but together, we're practically a dumpster fire.

Except, I like him more than I've liked anyone my entire adult life, and I know he feels the same. With the exception of one honey-haired little sister to his best friend that he really doesn't want to talk about. But that's an obstacle that we can tackle at a later date.

Tonight, I want to make things easier for him, not harder. He's got plenty on his plate as it is and it's not my job to be any sort of burden to him.

"Eat your food so we can get you tucked in for some beauty rest before you have to be back up at the ass crack of dawn," I say, dropping the subject altogether.

"Are you coming up," Alexander asks me when I near his hotel. I'd planned on dropping him off and heading home, expecting that's what he'd want. "I have a little time before I need to crash out."

"Invitation accepted. I won't stay long," I say. Long enough to get us both off and then let him focus. Besides, I have a paper I need to be working on as well.

"Long enough, though."

"Yes, Alexander." I laugh. "Long enough."

We both need to finish whatever it was we started in that dressing room earlier. But I sense he needs some general affection, too. Something I'm not so great at giving.

There are a few drunk women in the elevator ride with us, considering their giggling and side-eyeing. We both stifle laughs of our own and bid them a goodnight when we exit two floors before their own.

"Did you see how thick that one was?" one of them comments as the doors begin to close, making me laugh more.

"You sure you don't want to follow them up, sounds like you could have had a great time," I ask him when we enter his room. It's nice, but small. No wonder he wants to find a place to rent so quickly. He'd practically bounce off the walls in here. The hotel room door thuds close behind me at the same time as Alexander's hand snakes up under one arm and to my throat. He pulls my back against his firm chest, his groin grinding into my ass. We're nearly the exact height, landing his already hard cock in the perfect spot.

"You know that's not what I want," he says, his voice guttural. "Are we touching tonight, or do you only want to watch?"

"A little of both," I answer, stretching my neck under his fingers and swallowing hard. Nothing about this is uncomfortable for me. I can only guess it's because of him. Because of the way he understands my limits due to how many he has as well. That doesn't mean I'm ready to push myself, though. "Get naked. Don't rush it."

I spin to face him, taking a few steps back until I can sit on the only chair the room has to offer. It's a small armchair, pushed into a corner by the window. However, it offers a clear view to the entire room, specifi-cally Alexander.

"You looking for a strip tease," he asks, humor flashing across his high cheekbones.

"No, Alexander. I just don't want to miss an inch. Now do as you were told."

Unbuttoning a few buttons of my own shirt, I watch as he removes his jacket and hangs it neatly in the closet that's only large enough to hold a handful of items. My belt is the next thing I unfasten, while he removes his tee, giving me another look at his magnificent chest.

If men were built like him back in the day, I imagine Italy would be full of Alexander statues instead of the likes of David. He's goddamn perfect.

We kick off our shoes in our slow dance, removing item for item until he's in nothing but snug boxer briefs that highlight how incredibly hard he is. and I've only my unbuttoned pants on. Bare underneath of course.

"Let me see you," I tell him, leaning forward, elbows resting on my knees. His briefs drop, and again, I swallow hard. This is so much better in the flesh than through a screen. His long dick juts out in front of him, and he strokes it, eyes glazing over slightly. They never leave mine, though. When his thumb circles the tip to catch a drop of pre-cum, I lick my lips and stand. "You like to touch yourself for me."

Alexander tips his chin up in agreement. We've done this often enough, but tonight, just watching isn't enough for either of us. His Adam's apple bobs as I kick my pants away. As I step forward his mouth drops open and his eyes dart down to my cock. Another area we match, our dicks are very comparable. I don't know why the fact excites me as much as it does, but it is what it is.

I move closer, careful not to touch him when I lean forward and drag my tongue up from his collarbone, along the column of his neck and to the corner of his mouth.

"Kiss me, Fane."

His spare hand tangles in my dark hair, angling my head so we're eye to eye. Nose to nose, staring at each other with the heat of a hundred bonfires. He battles himself for a moment; not wanting to give up full control to me. I decide to throw him a net and nibble on his lower lip. Instantly, his mouth seals to mine, and we groan. It's been so long. His hand tightens when I step closer, bringing our bodies together. Our cocks jumping to life as they nestle between us. That's all it takes for my pre-cum to spill, slickening us in the process.

My hand pushes his away from where it still works at his dick and I take over, wrapping my palm around us both. It's a stretch, but when his fingers tangle with mine and our rhythm matches... Holy fuck.

"Damian..."

"I know. Fuck our hands, Fane. Come on my cock."

"Fucking hell," he moans before thrusting his tongue into my mouth. His hips start to roll, his heart beating harder under his warming chest. A minute later, he erupts, pulling me over the edge with him. His hand tightens at my scalp until he's spent and everything about him softens. "Thank you."

"Always so polite," I say, humorously.

"Fuck you, March." He rolls his eyes at me. "Shower?"

"No, just let me have a minute." I head to the bathroom, equally as small as the rest of the room. While cleaning myself, I stare at the mirror. Alexander makes me feel so different that I study myself for any changes I can see. Surely, it's apparent through relaxed features or something.

Because Damian March has never wanted certain things in life. Until now.

4

WILLA

"How infuriating," I mumble as I read yet another new article about the limiting of women's rights in our country. I toss the last of my chicken sandwich down, my appetite lost.

I've never been very passionate about anything in my life. Hockey is a great love, but not at the level of my dad. Or even my sister, who always wanted a career in the sport. She works in fan development for the Seattle Blades but has even greater ambitions there. She always knew what she wanted whereas I didn't.

My path wasn't clear, and I had probably chosen a dozen different career paths before I graduated high school.

Everything changed for me when I moved in with my sister after I graduated. She found out she was pregnant the day she found out the love of her life had been unfaithful. Her mental health took a sharp decline due to several circumstances. And then her physical health did as well.

She almost lost her baby from going into pre-term labor much too early. There's no way to be sure, but we assume it was stress induced due to the turmoil her life was in because of her then-ex and the woman who was in his life at the time.

It was terrifying and I worried over her every day until she delivered my niece. Only then, she had postpartum depression, and we had a whole new set of problems.

Isla overcame it all because she had me and our parents. But what if she hadn't? Her situation placed a seed inside me that grew into a passion. I want to help women.

"I'll buy you a new one if it will help," a vaguely familiar voice says, and I look up.

Damian March stands at my table, looking amused.

"What?"

"Your sandwich. Not good?"

"Oh," I say with a wave of my hand. "It was fine. My newsfeed, however, sucks dried up cat shit. Have a seat?"

"Sure," he says with a laugh. "Taking a break or are you done for the day?"

"A break. I have a lecture in a couple of hours and didn't want to go home. It's too hard to leave again once I'm settled in, you know?" My routine is to pop into an on-campus coffee shop, grab a chai, and a snack while digging into some reading or starting on a paper. Damian nods as if he understands but doesn't say anything. "And you?"

"Done for the day, just lurking."

"Is it coincidence that we're running into each other only after a formal introduction a few days ago?"

"It's said that coincidence is an explanation used only by liars," he says.

"Let me guess? You're not a liar."

"Never," he confirms.

"So, you knew I'd be here?"

"No. But I have noticed you. Maybe I made a concerted effort to notice you," he says with a shrug, as if it's not weird at all.

"And why is that? Better yet, why should I not be freaked out by it?" I'm not worried about him, which should be worrying in itself.

"Alexander mentioned you often, said you studied here. I liked checking up on you."

"I don't need a babysitter," I tell him, resting my chin in my hands while I try to study his features, his reactions. Damian isn't hard to look at. His dark hair falls low, almost hiding one of his equally dark eyebrows. His eyes contrast them in a light hazel shade. He's handsome, clean cut, but with an edge that portrays danger with all the black tattoos that peek out around the hems of his expensive clothing. Today, he's dressed down in a hoody, but even that screams pricey to a trained eye.

"No, you don't. I didn't do it for you, anyway."

I tilt my head at his words. Does that mean Zander wanted him to check up on me?

"Why do you call him Alexander?"

"Because nobody else does," he says with a wide smile. His teeth are bright and perfect. I wonder if this man has any physical flaw.

"You're one of those," I tease.

"One of what, Ms. Cole?"

"Someone who likes to stand out."

"Not even remotely. I prefer to keep quietly to myself in the shadows." The way he says it sounds ominously sexual, and like the other night at the game, I have to tell my lady parts to settle down.

"That's... unexpected. What made you decide to study cults," I ask, changing the subject so I can watch his thick black lashes blink at me.

"I met a woman."

"Ooh, cliché much, Mr. March?"

He laughs. "I was already very interested in group behavior and was deep diving into both extremes with religion and the military. But then I met Delilah, a survivor of a polygamist cult. My focus shifted there; it wasn't much of a stretch."

"I can see that," I agree. "All three use similar tactics. How did you meet her?"

"She's my best friend's little sister's best friend," he says, smiling again at his convoluted description. "She's practically their third sibling, so we all grew very close."

"This is back in Louisiana, that's where you said you were from, right?"

"You cannot tell by accent, ma chérie?" he asks, exaggerating the words with a Creole lilt.

"You don't speak with an accent. Why not?"

"You're inquisitive."

"And you're something like a stalker. I think I've earned my questions," I snark, but with a smile.

"Touché," he concedes. "An accent was discouraged in my family. They thought it was below them. I wasn't allowed one inside our home."

"Eww, that's harsh. What year are you in here?"

"You jump subjects a lot," he says, blinking in surprise once more.

"I can't really get to know you if we only talk about one thing," I tell him, enjoying that I'm keeping him on his toes.

"Is that what we're doing? Getting to know each other."

"I think I'd like to," I muse. "Besides, I'm sure that's why you walked up to my table today."

"You'd be right," he says, draining the last of whatever is in his cup. Coffee? Or is he a tea drinker? Something tells me he might be, only because he doesn't look like he'd drink anything but coffee and maybe whiskey and I should expect the unexpected with him. "This is my final year."

"What are you writing your dissertation on?"

"Fundamentalist religion's grasp on modern day American politics," he answers.

"Fuck, for real?"

"Why do you sound so surprised," he asks.

"Because it's not all that different from what I'm writing mine on. Though I have another year after this," I tell him.

"And what's that?"

"Oh, a whole thing about how purity culture is rape culture and the systems in place that protect it."

"I think you and I are going to get along well, Ms. Cole," Damian says. "Are you going to the game tonight?"

"No. I don't get to that many. I prefer to watch from the comfort of my couch," I answer. "That way, if I want to yell and curse, it doesn't offend anyone."

"By anyone, do you mean the sea of blonde women we were seated in the midst of?"

"You noticed that, huh." I laugh. "There are a few brunettes, but they do tend to be outnumbered. For the most part, all of the wags are great, though. I think professional athletes have a type. It's not just the NHL."

"Can I be honest?" He mimics my pose, leaning his elbows on the table so he can settle his chin into his hands.

"Of course, Damian."

"I know absolutely nothing about any other sport. Let alone hockey."

"You were catching on quickly enough. A few more games and you'll have it down." Casual conversation continues as I pepper him with more questions. Some, he dodges but most he answers candidly. In return, he asks me a laundry list of his own.

When the time comes for me to walk to my next lecture, I feel like I've got a good idea about the man.

"Is it too forward if I ask for your number," he asks after he's walked me out the café door. The weather is mild today. A light breeze blows a few of the colorful leaves along the sidewalk.

"No more forward than outright stalking me," I suggest, stepping on a few and hearing the familiar crunching sound under my feet.

"I'm not going to live that down, am I?"

"Not likely."

"Maybe I can take you to dinner some time to make up for it."

"A date?" I didn't expect this. We've got on well today and that night at the game, but I still suspected Damian's in a relationship with Zander.

"A something." He shrugs. "Call it atonement. We can discuss more on the evils done to women. Or hockey, if you prefer."

"Yes, you can have my number," I say, holding my hand out for his phone. "Maybe, to dinner. A definite yes to further discussion on the evils of the world. We may be able to help each other out there."

"I'll take what I can get," he says, taking his phone back from me after I've programed myself in under the contact name 'Unwitting Prey'. When he sees it, he laughs louder than he has any other time, as if he's suddenly more at ease with me. "For now, anyway, Ms. Cole."

"So maybe he's not gay," Kit muses when we settle in front of the TV at home later. The game is about to start, and I've made a pot of chili for dinner. It's Kit's favorite out of the dozen or so things I cook regularly. We take turns, and between the two of us, we eat healthily enough. Especially by college student standards. Though Kit has already graduated, she stopped at her master's degree, not wanting to wrack up more student debt. Which is rather sizeable.

Dad pays for my schooling. Or what's left after the scholarships and grants I've managed to land. I'm grateful for his generosity and don't like it all the same. I want to be self-sufficient, though I may not be headed down the right career path for that. But those are problems for future days. I need to finish the PhD program first.

"Honestly, I don't know. I didn't want to ask what his relationship with Zan is, and he never offered up any information there. But why would he flirt and ask me out if there *is* a romance between them?"

"I don't know, Willa, but be careful. You don't need to be crushing on two men you can't have."

"Oh god, right?"

"Right. I could still hook you up with Will from my work," Kit teases.

"Fuck off," I say, sending her a look of pure terror. "Will and Willa, can you imagine? Plus, the guy couldn't even look me in the eye when you introduced him at your company Christmas party last year. Like my mere presence flustered him."

"That's charming," she protests.

"Then you date him."

"No, thank you," Kit says primly.

The game starts with little excitement. Ten minutes into the first period, neither team has scored, though both have gotten decent shots on goal in. "Does Isla still talk to Tyson?"

Tyson Murphy plays for the Vancouver team and was the only man my sister seriously dated before marrying Cillian. The two men have something like an on-ice rivalry, even though I don't think they have real hard feelings toward each other. Or at least I know Cillian doesn't.

It's good for the crowds though, each team's star player play fighting over a woman. They tend to be chippier with one another than what's necessary. But that's hockey, it's a weird sport.

"They're still friendly when they run into each other. But I don't think there's much contact past that."

"I'll never get over the fact that she's had two of the best-looking men in the sport," Kit says, then takes another large bite of chili.

"Lucky bitch."

"Lucky bitch," she repeats, appreciating the men on the ice, even if she's sworn off all things related to penises.

Tyson takes the puck into our end and shoots, but our goalie, Hugo Blom, blocks it. Tyson tries for a rebound which also gets blocked. Now, there's a traffic jam in front of the net as both teams scramble for the puck in the middle of the scrum. The whistle blows, stopping the play, but Tyson and Cillian are still shoving each other. It's Zander who gets in the middle and skates off with Cillian in tow before it can become penalty worthy.

My phone dings with a notification, pulling my attention away from the game. Isla's contact shows with a new text message.

SESTRA:

Zander is renting a condo in your building. Don't be fucking weird about it.

Oh fuck!

"What," Kit asks.

ME:

I make no promises.

SESTRA:

Of course, you don't. But please try.

"Zan is renting in this building."

"Oh shit. You're going to be weird about it, aren't you?"

"Why does everyone think that," I protest, but Kit gives me a knowing look.

"I'm sure he just wanted somewhere familiar. After all, he was here so often when Isla lived here. "

"Sure, sure," I say. "But how am I supposed to move on from him when I have to see him all the time?"

"By getting yourself some dick."

The image of Damian immediately comes to mind. I'm in a real pickle here, I fear. All my own making, of course. Well, that's not entirely true. It's not as if I've forced Damian's flirting or Zander's consistence in my life.

If there's a higher power, maybe she hates me, and this is all a funny joke to her. Except I'm a good person, dammit. I don't deserve torture the likes of this. Except, maybe Damian isn't gay and therefore completely available.

Ugh, I'm being a stupid woman.

"How about we don't speak of men for the rest of the week," I offer.

"It's only Monday."

"I know." I sigh.

"Deal."

"How isn't this a bigger issue? Especially with so many younger members in congress now?" Emma, a fellow student, asks. We're in the café again, tablets out as we research for a group project we're brainstorming ideas on.

"Like us, they probably don't know about it. These are all old statutes, and, in most states, they've never been contested, from what I can find," I say, skimming another page of the current website. "Our state is one of ten that has no minimum age for marriage. Every other state range between fourteen and eighteen."

"Insanity," Emma says, disgusted. "This says, eighty-six percent of children married off are girls. Fucking of course."

"The numbers have drastically decreased over the years. But how is this even possible to begin with?"

"Because men," Emma groans. "Crap, I need to run. This is our subject though, yeah? And once we finish it, we march straight to Olympia."

"Agreed," I tell her. "Have a good one. See you Tuesday."

"Bye, Willa, have a great night."

Emma shoves her belongings into her oversized bag and rushes off with a wave just as my phone springs to life on the table. It's on vibrate and quickly trying to commit suicide off the edge. Rescuing it before its inevitable demise, I come across a text from an unknown number.

At the counter ordering, what's your poison, it reads. Craning my neck, I see an expensive dark hoodie in line to order.

ME:

Dirty oat milk chai latte.

I program his name in as 'Ted Bundy' as his reply comes in. Nobody gets their normal names on my phone, a silly habit I started as a teen and haven't abandoned.

TED BUNDY:

Coming right up.

"Oat milk, huh," he asks, setting my drink in front of me.

"Mhm, cow's milk is for baby cows. Besides, you should see the studies about what a plant-based diet does for your body. Especially, when it comes to sexual organs."

"What benefit does it give sexual organs," he asks, his eyes glinting with humor as he takes a seat across from me. "Please be specific."

"Several hundred percent increase in blood flow to the nether region, causing erections to be harder and more frequent," I say, matter-of-factly, trying not to flirt back with the dangerously beautiful man opposite me.

"You're telling me all these old men popping penis pills could just stop eating meat?"

"Maybe. I don't think that study has been done yet, but the way medicine treats an erection like it's a golden calf, it won't be long," I answer. His smile widens, but he doesn't say anything else as he looks at me. I wonder if he's trying to figure me out just like I'm trying to figure him out. "Are you stalking me again, Damian?"

"Is it stalking if we're friends?"

"Is that what we are?"

"I'd like to think so. You're"—he hesitates for a moment—"easy to be around."

There's more to the statement than he's telling, adding another layer of mystery to the man and ramping up my curiosity. But you know what they say about curiosity.

"Am I?"

"I'm helping Alexander move into his new place this weekend. Will you be around?"

"I'll be around." *Come what may.*

5

ZANDER

"**F**ane," Coach hollers. "Back office after you're changed."

"Yes, Coach," I say, trying to sound far less amped than I am. The back office means someone higher up the chain wants to talk to me. Which may mean I'm being dropped to the minors.

And wouldn't that be my luck the day before I'm supposed to move into my own place.

Fuck.

"Settle down, Rook. Could mean anything," Vaughn says. He pats my shoulder as he turns the corner of the locker room to the showers.

Admittedly, I've been romanticizing the idea of my own apartment. A safe place where I can be myself. Privacy is a dream I don't always get. It felt so close, my fingertips nearly touching it. I roomed with another player in California. Ben is a solid guy, but I couldn't have brought Damian home there. While he isn't homophobic, he's not necessarily trustworthy enough to keep his mouth shut either.

I only want a place that I can walk into, shut the door, and not feel like I still need to hide something. I like dick from time to time, it shouldn't be such a big fucking deal. It's nobody's business who I choose to spend time with, and I wish the sport, the league, would catch up to that. Because, damn, I love this game. It's my passion. I can't be the only player with this same dilemma in the NHL. Or any other league, for that matter. Out of all the football, baseball, basketball teams, there must be plenty of men hiding their sexual preferences. It's just not possible that they're all perfectly straight. Or that they all fi t into the box society requires of us.

Maybe I'm overreacting, but my gut tells me I'm not. Something the higher-ups have to say to me is going to sideline my plans. I'm sure of it as I take the stairs to the upper level of the Iceplex.

The general manager, Jonathon Markel, waits for me along with two women I recognize from my quick meetings when I was brought up, though I can't recall their names just now. I don't know why they're here, but meet-ing with GM is a good sign I'm headed back to California.

"Hey, Zander," he greets. "Come on in and have a seat."

"Yes, sir." I follow him inside the offi ce. One woman, Audrey, I think, sits next to me, while the other stands to the side.

"You looked great at practice this morning. How are you doing with the move?"

"Good," I say, a bit confused. "I start moving into my own place today."

"That's good news, Zander."

"I'm sorry. Am I not being sent back down, sir?"

"No, Rook. That's not why we're meeting today. Audrey?"

"Right," the woman says. "We want to make it very clear that this isn't an issue with the team."

Audrey opens a file folder and pulls out a sheet of paper, handing it to me. It's a printout from a website, a blog. One where the author has writ-ten a post about their theory on my sex life based on an encounter while suit shopping.

Motherfucker.

I read it as quickly as I can. It's not long, but I'm a ball of tense rage by the time I finish.

"Frankly, it's not the team's business," I grit out.

"We feel the same," Markel says. "It was the League that brought it to our attention."

"We're sharing it with you because you have a right to know," Audrey adds. "Your personal life is your business."

"But if it starts to affect the team…" I ask, because that's what it always comes down to in sports. They'll drop me if it's good for the franchise.

"I think if we all work together, we can keep that from happening. Legal team will see if they can get the page removed. We'll do whatever we can to help you, Zander." Markel has always seemed a stand-up GM to me, this bolsters my opinion, even if my instinct is to not fully trust what he says. "If you want help navigating anything, Audrey will help with PR."

"The four of us and Legal are the only ones aware of this within the organization," the other woman says. I think she's from Human Resource, if memory serves.

"Coach doesn't know?"

"We haven't told him," Audrey says.

"I appreciate the candor," I say. "Any suggestions on what I should do?"

"Ignore it, for now. No comments. It's a small blog, it may gain no traction at all. It does, however, have the potential to spread locally, at least. We can wait and see if it dies off by itself."

But if it gains traction, not only will my career be on the line, but the relationship with my family as well. I've never come out to any of them. For good reason. My father isn't a good man, and for all my mother tries to be, she's still incredibly conservative. Not to mention, easily influenced by my father's tirades.

The best thing to do would be to defuse the rumor altogether.

"Would it help if I was seen with a woman publicly?"

"We won't ask you to do that, Zander," Markel says emphatically.

"I'm not…" I start, then pause to take a steadying breath. These people are here to help me, and I need to take advantage of that. "I'm not gay. I'm bisexual. My personal life is never something I've highlighted, but if it would help, I can take a woman to a function or two."

"It couldn't hurt," Audrey says. "But again, to be clear, we're not asking you to do that."

"Understood," I tell her.

"We're with you on this, Zander. If you need help, reach out," Markel says, standing to let us all know we're done here.

"Thank you, sir."

My mood only sours further as the day goes on. I made a trip to Ikea to buy essentials for my new place. What a fucking nightmare that place is, but I had such few possessions, since I was only renting a room from Ben in California. At least, I need to be able to cook some basics and dry my ass after a shower.

Then I stopped at one of those grocery stores that has a home department attached so I could grab both a coffee pot and coffee. As well as some other food and cleaning products. Between those excursions and the furniture that is now getting delivered, I should be set. I'll have a bed anyway, along with a sofa and television.

I'm rarely home for more than a night's sleep. What more does a guy with my schedule need?

Some motherfucking privacy, that's what.

I knew we were pushing it that day we were shopping. Damian doesn't understand that even though I don't have paparazzi trailing my every move, I'm still a recognizable figure. Probably more so when I'm with him, because he stands out in all his expensive, dark glory.

While paying the delivery guys, I feel Damian's piercing stare into my back. As promised, he came over to help me get settled. After the day I had, I'm not the best company, but I haven't had the opportunity to explain why. He's been glaring at me with gaining interest for the past forty-five minutes, obviously picking up on my sour mood.

"What's up with you," he asks as soon as the movers walk out the door.

"My day took a shit on me this morning after practice," I say, moving to the kitchen to unpack my coffee pot. The contraption is more confusing than it needs to be. I should have just bought a plain damn pot, not one with a grinder and different brew strengths. "What the fuck?"

"Talk to me, Alexander." Damian brushes me aside and takes over.

"The guy at the suit shop wrote a blog post about me. About me being gay, more fucking specifically." I lean back on the counter and watch Damian's shoulders sag.

"I'm sorry, I didn't expect anything like that."

"Yeah, well, I did. It's why I'm as careful as I am," I tell him, my anger rising again. Not at him, necessarily, just at…everything. "Now, the League knows."

"How did you find out?"

"When the GM called me in to talk with him, Human Resources, and Public Relations. When they handed me a printout of the blog post headlined, *Is the Seattle Blades New Defenseman Playing for the Other Team*," I rage. "They didn't tell Coach, but I'm sure it's going to get around that I'm queer."

"Knock, knock," Willa says, and I turn to see her grimacing in my doorway. "Sorry, the door was open. I didn't mean to interrupt."

"It's fine." Damian rushes to her, ushering her in and firmly closing the door behind her.

"It's not fucking fine," I admonish. "Nothing is fine. And you are interrupting."

Willa pales, and I instantly feel horrible.

"So… sorry. Damian said… Well, anyway, I thought you might like dinner. I'll just leave it." She hands him a dish I didn't even notice she was holding and quickly retreats out the door.

"Willa," I call at the same time Damian hisses my name.

"What the fuck, Alexander? None of this is her fault."

"I fucking know that." I rub at the growing tension in the back of my neck. "She caught me off guard is all."

Fuck this day. Willa fully deflated when I snapped, her shoulders and chin both dropping by inches. It's like a million needles to my heart knowing that I'm the one that put it there. And now I have one more problem I need to fix.

"This smells delicious, but I don't think you deserve to eat any of it," Damian says, lifting the foil off the dish and taking another sniff.

"What is it?"

"Pasta. Looks like chicken and broccoli," he says. He's right, it smells mouthwatering, and I feel like an even bigger asshole.

"I'm a dick."

"Yes," Damian says.

"I'll go apologize, see if I can get her to come down and eat with us."

"Least you can do," Damian mumbles when I walk out of my apartment.

I let her expression replay in my mind the whole way upstairs to Willa's. It's only a floor, but I'm properly pouting by the time I reach her unit. Snapping at her was rash and rude. It's not her fault I'm dealing with this shit, nor is it her fault she walked in on me practically admitting being queer.

Isla could have told her, being as close as they are. Except, Isla's not the type to break a confidence like that. She didn't even tell Cillian when they got back together. I had to tell her it was okay to fill him in because I knew it made her uncomfortable having conversations with me like we were speaking code in front of him.

If Willa ever caught on, I never guessed. Truth is, I've never wanted her to lose that lustful-tinged-affectionate look. It's one of my favorite things in the world. It nearly trumps hockey.

She opens the door a moment after I knock, tears streaming down her face.

"Ah, fuck, Willa. I didn't mean to make you cry," I tell her, wrapping my arms around her and pulling her in for a hug.

"I'm not crying because of *you*," she contests. "I don't cry over boys."

She called me a boy. *That stings.*

"I don't believe you," I say, tilting her chin up with a finger so she has to look me in the eyes. I wipe away a few tears.

"Fuck you, Fane. I'm crying over the documentary I was watching. When it got too depressing, I took a break to cook an asshole I know some dinner."

"But he was rude, so you came back up and started watching again," I guess, seeing that the television is paused.

"Yeah, he's an arrogant prick," she says, causing me to burst with laughter.

"He is," I agree. "But he's very sorry." I lift her off her feet and kick her door shut behind me. I carry her to the sofa, and she wraps her arms around my neck.

"I'm sorry I overheard something so personal. But I hope you know I'd never judge you." She speaks the words softly against my neck. Her soft breath tingles down my spine, and I repress a shiver.

"I know, Willa. It's not something I talk about. It's not personal that I didn't tell you."

"I understand," she says.

"Will you come eat dinner with us and tell me what your documentary is about?"

"I don't want to intrude, Zan," she starts to argue. Wrapping my fingers gently in her hair, I tilt her face back to mine again, pressing a kiss to her forehead.

"You're never an intruder, Willa. I'm sorry I made you feel like one. Come downstairs?"

"Okay," she relents after bouncing her eyes all over my features. "I really like Damian; he seems like a good guy."

"He is," I agree. "Come on."

This isn't the way I'd have planned on telling Willa that I'm not straight, but I know I can trust her with it. Trust was never my issue with her. She's as loyal as her sister. Coach raised honest, trustworthy women.

Willa is a door ajar. One that I have always been too afraid to open wide or shut tight.

I still am.

That doesn't mean I can't open my door a little to her though. I remember the first time I met her. Isla asked me to come have dinner with her, meet her sister and her daughter. I walked into the apartment to Willa dancing with Sadie as if they had no cares in the world and no audience to judge. They were joyously free, and I wanted to capture it like a butterfly in a net and keep it for myself.

Then Willa turned at Isla's introduction of me and my heart missed a beat. She has the most genuine smile, reminding me of every movie I'd ever seen with a girl next door. Natural, real, shining, like the light of a thousand moons. Bright but soft—that's Willa.

I wish I could offer her everything she deserves.

Damian waits for us in my living room where he's set up the television and is signing into a streaming service. He looks up when he hears us enter and beelines to her.

"Hey, you okay?" He runs the pad of his thumb over her tear-stained cheek, sending me a glare over her shoulder.

"I'm okay," she says.

"You sure? It was bad timing."

"I know, and as I told Zan, I'm not upset over that."

"She was watching a sad documentary," I say in my defense. "It's not *all* my fault."

"It's not your fault at all," she says. "Do you have dishes?"

"Yeah, somewhere. Let me find them."

The three of us work together to find what we need, wash what's new, and plate dinner. I'm struck with how easy we function in such a small galley kitchen. As if we're a cohesive unit, no one is in another's way, moving around on instinct. Like we anticipate the other's moves.

Willa chatters on about the new project she's working on and how the documentary she was watching was part of her research.

"She was being raped by a youth pastor from the age of nine and got pregnant at ten. TEN! Her family forced her to marry her rapist and it's all completely fucking legal in more states than you could imagine. Including Washington, if you can fucking believe that. As long as a court signs off, we have no legal age of marriage here," she rants. And yeah, I can see why she is so upset.

"That's... I don't even have the word. Can we watch it," he asks her.

"Is that really how you guys want to spend your night?" Her nose scrunches up with skepticism.

"Yes," Damian agrees immediately.

"I've got about two hours before I'm going to pass out. I don't care what we watch as long as I get to lounge on that couch while we're doing it." I look over at it longingly. It's the most expensive thing I've ever bought and I'm hoping it's worth every damn penny.

"Okay, then. But don't say I didn't warn you; it's going to make you mad."

An hour later, every bite of pasta is gone, and Willa is snuggled up between Damian and me on my oversized and overstuffed sofa. Damian has his arm wrapped around her shoulders, her head resting on his chest. Fresh tears fall from her eyes.

It's our legs that hold my attention most. All three of us are tangled together as if it's the most natural thing in the world. I'm not sure how or when we ended up like this. My instinct is to get up, create the distance I always do.

A glance at my lounge mates stops me. Damian twines a strand of Willa's hair around his finger. He's comfortable with her, maybe even comforted by her in the same way I am. She's a balm to every wound. A personality that instantly eases moods and tensions. Though I've resigned myself to the torture of never being with her, I don't want to take that away from Damian.

He notices my perusal and raises a brow in question. I shake of my head and ease further down in the cushions, enjoying the way her foot rubs against my calf.

6

WILLA

"**Z**ander says you've been over for dinner a couple of times," Isla says. We're at our parents' since Dad called a family dinner because the team just got back from an eight-day road trip, and he missed all his girls. Mom and Dad are cooking together, Sadie is rolling around on the floor with their dog, Curly, and Cillian's watching hockey on the television. All the while my sister grills me.

"I made him some food, yeah. He hardly had anything. I thought he'd like some home cooking." I shrug, keeping my sight trained on the TV. Though, I'm not registering any of the plays.

"That was nice of you," she says, but I know she wants to say more.

"What?"

"Do you still obsess over his neck?" Cillian laughs at his wife's question.

"That's bizarre, Willa. Even for you," he says.

"It is not," I protest to his growing laughter. "He has a very exceptional neck."

"Please don't get your hopes up."

"I know, Isla. I know about him, and I understand that we're only ever going to be friends." She sends a look to Cillian that I don't understand. "It's nice to have another friend in the building though. And I have fun with him, always have. Damian, too."

Damian has come over to watch the games with me twice while Zander was gone. And another time, he found me at the café and refreshed my chai latte. He still flirts with me, but I've come to understand that's just who he is. He's fun, and while my lady parts still get excited over both men, my head is just happy to have a new friend.

"Okay." She scoots closer to me and wraps an arm around me. "I just worry about my kid sister. I kind of like you, you know?"

"You love her," Sadie yells from the floor. "Because she's badass, you always say."

"Shh, don't let your grandma here you say that word," Cillian warns her, and they both grin at each other.

"Okay, I'll be careful, Daddy."

"How's school," my father asks when we finally gather at the table for dinner.

"Good. Working on a team project that I'm feeling passionate about."

"You okay on money?"

"Yes, I haven't even touched what you gave me at Christmas. Stop asking."

"Make me," he teases.

The man would give us anything we asked for. Yet he also raised us to not be greedy or materialistic, so we never took him up on it much. He had a humble upbringing and wanted the same for us, despite the paychecks he brought in. I'm frugal because of it.

"I'm okay for a while. And I can always pick up shifts at The Chapel, they told me to come back whenever I needed hours." I haven't been working because my workload at school is so heavy, but I left on great terms.

"All right, you know I have to check."

"I know, Dad. But I'm okay, I promise."

Sadie grabs a few olives from the dish in the middle of the table, popping them on her little fingers and wiggling them. I grab a couple and copy her, making her giggle in that little girl laugh she hasn't lost yet. I'll be sad the day I can't make her smile with such ease; she's growing up far too quickly for my liking.

"Willa, stop encouraging bad habits," my mother chastises, playfully.

"Bad habits are the most fun, Mom."

THE NECK:

You home tonight?

ME:

Just getting back from family dinner.

THE NECK:

Want to come up and watch a movie?

ME:

I'll bring the popcorn.

I pop two bags so there is enough for three of us and dump it into a big bowl. The first night I had dinner with them was great. It was comforting. Every gal should have gay guy friends that they can cuddle up with. That level of physical touch was something I didn't realize I had been missing. How much I enjoyed it made me remember that I haven't had that in years. Not since my high school boyfriend. Since then, my relationships haven't made it to the cuddling stage.

Maybe having their sexuality out on the table has added a layer of security between us as well. I don't know, but I like getting the benefit without all the work of having to date a bunch of random losers before finding one I want to snuggle with.

I quickly change into pajama shorts and a T-shirt and shove my feet into my fuzzy slippers before I make my way to Zander's apartment. He opens the door on my first knock, as if he was waiting on the other side.

"Hi," I say, surprised.

"Hey." His voice is quiet, and his eyes drag down my body like he's thirsty and I'm a drink of water. Blinking rapidly, I try to clear my head, because that can't be what I'm seeing. It must be my silly fantasies still at play. He takes the bowl from me and pulls me inside by the hand. Dropping the bowl on the coffee table, he turns to wrap me in a hug, lifting me off my feet like always. "Missed you."

"I missed you, too. You guys played great, though," I tell him, my words muffled against his chest until he sets me back on my feet. I watched every game on their road trip. They won more than they lost, which is about all you can hope for on a road trip. "You racked up three more assists and your plus-minus is outstanding."

"Thanks, Coach," he says, laughing.

"Sorry."

"No worries, I like that you keep up with me," he says with a cheeky grin.

Umm, okay then.

"Where's Damian?"

"Not sure. Haven't talked to him in a couple of days."

"Oh. Is everything okay between you?"

"Everything's fine," he says nonchalantly. "There's a new thriller streaming, you good with that?"

"Sure," I answer and follow him to his divine couch. The thing is seriously too comfortable for its own good. It would probably fit eight of me with extra room to spare. Zander drops onto the chaise part of it, sprawling his legs out and pulling me into his lap.

Oh.

"I only have one blanket," he says, in way of explanation. He grabs it from the back of the sofa and tosses it over our laps. "And we only have one bowl."

With one hand wrapped around my abdomen, he leans us forward so he can reach the remote. He hands that to me, then grabs the bowl, then… to my utter confusion, arranges us comfortably with me still sitting on what strangely feels like a burgeoning hard-on.

Zan has always been a hugger, but this is new. Way new. Way unexpected. As the movie plays, he becomes more relaxed. My body is aware of every move he makes, every big muscle that stretches and flexes against me. And man, are they moving a lot.

Not to mention, his roaming hands. One has been on me, touching or gently petting the entire time. It's distracting as hell.

The movie, from what I can gather is about a domestic violence survivor still in hiding from her ex when she meets a new man. I think he's a serial killer. He's hot though, so there's that.

"Damn," I whisper in awe. The guy stares at the heroine with carnal hunger, stalking closer to her, inch by inch, her chest quickens with anticipation. "Slam her against the wall, homeboy. Take her."

Zander chokes on a piece of popcorn.

"Jesus, Willa."

"Look! He's doing it. You can't tell me that's not hot?" I say, shoving a few more pieces into my mouth. The man yanks up the woman's skirt and rips her panties off. They don't come off cleanly, because… reality check. He has to yank a few times before they come apart, his frustration palpable. "There you go, big guy. Get some."

Zander shifts under me. I slide off him, my ass now next to his thigh but my legs still over his lap.

"Sorry, was I getting heavy," I ask.

"No," he blurts, not looking away from the movie and the couple fucking now.

"Movie sex is so much better than porn sex."

"I'm sorry, what?" Zander chuckles. I like his deep and contagious laughter.

"I mean, from a woman's perspective anyway," I explain. "In movies, the woman, at least usually, is an active participant in pleasure. In most porn, she's nothing but a hole. She could be reading a book, and I don't think the guys would care as long as she keeps making ridiculous sounds for his benefit. Or rather, for the viewer's benefit. Some viewers anyway. I usually watch without sound."

"Holy shit."

"What? Like you don't watch porn."

"I watch porn. Of course, I watch porn. I don't typically have conversations about it."

"Sorry."

"Stop apologizing to me. I'm not upset, just surprised. You normally aren't so… I don't know, blunt."

"To be fair, my niece is around whenever we're together." It's true. There have been times when Zander's schedule aligned and he'd go out with Isla, Kit, and me. However, the time we've spent in each other's presence has been more G-rated than R.

"Good point. I guess this is the first time we've ever been alone, isn't it?"

"It is? I guess you're right. Is it weird?"

"Why would it be weird," he asks, his brow furrowing.

"Because Isla isn't with us. Or even Damian."

"I knew they wouldn't be here when I invited you over," he says, moving the popcorn bowl to the coffee table and rearranging us so that I'm cradled in the crook of his arm.

"How long have you known him?"

"Damian? A few years."

"Can I pry a little bit," I ask, not wanting to overstep any unspoken boundaries.

"You can try," he says into my hair.

"How did you meet?"

"Online. We were both looking for a connection, I guess. The timing was wrong though, he moved here around the same time I moved to California."

"You stayed in touch while you were there," I say. "Did you get to visit each other often?"

"No, but that was more by preference. I wanted to stay focused on getting called up."

"You sports guys," I say with an amused sigh. "You all must have really small attention spans or something."

"Fuck you, Cole." He tickles my sides, sending me into a fit of laughter.

"Oh my god, stop! I didn't mean it!"

"Bullshit, you didn't," he says when he finally stops attacking my sensitive skin. My shirt's ridden up a little, leaving a patch bare under his fingers. He hovers over me, nose to nose. If I were a silly woman, I'd think my dreams were about to come true. "Enough about me. Are you dating?"

"Meh." I scrunch up my nose at him, the tip of mine grazing his. "There's a guy at school that's been asking me out a lot."

"Is his name Damian March?" Zander winks, making me smile.

"Pauly."

"No, you can't date a *Pauly*."

"That's what I said!"

"Ooh, Pauly, fuck me harder," he mocks in a high-pitched voice. My brain malfunctions for a half second when he says *fuck me*. Luckily, I'm quick to reboot.

"Right? Nothing sexy about 'shove that big dick in my mouth until you come, *Pauly*'."

Everything slows. As if the world has ceased to move at normal speed. Or like in the movies where the camera stays focused on one thing, unmoving, while everything else speeds up. Zander and I no longer align with anything else. His forehead drops to mine, and he lets out a slow breath.

"Debatable," he mumbles. Now I feel a tickle in my vagina, that dumb ho. "I think we're missing the movie."

"I think he's about to murder her," I whisper dramatically, widening my eyes in horror. Zander rearranges us yet again; this time we're lying on our sides. My back to his front, the blanket pulled up to my chin. The woman figures out that she's fallen in love with a murderer and can't seem to care.

Waking with drool running down your cheek is never great. Doing it all while your gay friend-slash-man crush has one hand on your boob and one slightly tucked into your pajama shorts is downright mortifying.

We fell asleep watching movies. It must be early still as there is no sunlight streaming through the windows, but it isn't pitch black either. My guess is dawn is just about on us. I know the team has the day off today, so I want to let Zander sleep in. Does he sleep in on his off days? Does he wake up and workout? He gets morning wood; I can answer that much since it's digging into my back. I try to shift down with ease, not wanting him to wake up until I've at least dislodged from his hold on me. Maybe we can avoid some embarrassment here.

Zander groans, and I freeze in place, holding my breath to help keep me still. After a minute, I try again. An inch is all I need for his hands so they aren't down my pants and playing with my nipple.

"Willa," he says, sleepily. The palm at my abdomen presses to hold me in place.

Shit.

Maybe my best move is to just jump up and quickly rush out? Rude, maybe, but less awkward than this, surely. Then Zander moves again, his leg curling over my hip. It's so warm and cozy here, I mean, everywhere except my head which is utter chaos.

Because what the actual fuck is happening right now?

"Mmm, you're soft," he mumbles.

You decidedly are not, Alexander Fane.

"Are you awake," I whisper so very quietly.

"Hardly," he says. "Did I molest you in your sleep?"

I snort. "You kind of still are, big guy."

"Fuck, sorry." His hands move away from all my lady parts, but not far. I'm almost sad I said anything. "You're warm."

"So are you," I say, snuggling deeper under the blanket. "Is it weird yet?"

"Not the word I'd use."

"What word would be better?"

"Perfect," he says, then falls back to sleep.

I wake up some time later and once again Zander has his hand on my chest. Snoring softly in my ear. Again, I'm cradled against a giant boner. Except now, after a little more sleep, my body is ready to react to it.

Which is bad. Even if he was sleep-flirting with me earlier, it's bad. Because Zander is gay and I'm pretty sure Damian is his boyfriend. I like Damian, a lot. And I adore Zander. I don't want to be someone who gets in between them.

Well, not in that way. If things were different, I'd happily be… something in the middle.

I need to get out of here.

Deciding this time easing off the sofa isn't the best idea, I jump up. Zander makes a noise of protest, but I ignore it, shoving my feet into my slippers and digging in the cushions for my cellphone.

"Willa?"

Damn it, why does he sound even sexier when he's sleepy?

"Gotta go," I blurt. Finding my phone, I use it to wave at him. "See you later. Uh, thanks, bye!"

I rush out his door and make my way straight to the stairwell, not stopping until I'm at my own door. Kit is already awake. She's making herself breakfast and coffee when I enter. She's a morning person, perky and ready for the day as soon as her eyes pop open. I, on the other hand, require caffeine before my brain can even contemplate conversation.

Zander's hard dick must have served like a shot straight to my bloodline though, because I'm surprisingly alert.

"Hey there," she says with a sly smile, her dark curls falling over one eye. "You look like a hot mess. Do tell?"

"I slept with Zander."

"Fuck off, you did not."

"I did," I argue. "In the actual REM kind of way, not in the sexy times way. But he was feeling me up when we woke up. With a huge hard-on. What the fuck is that about, Kit?"

"Morning wood?"

"Sure, but that doesn't explain his hand working my boob."

"He was asleep, plus boobs are soft and comforting. I'm not sure it has to be something to freak out about."

"Then why am I freaking out?"

"Because you've had a crush on the guy for five years. Isn't it established that he's gay?"

"Not with direct words," I say, running through everything I know about him. Each conversation. He never said, I just assumed.

"You think he's bi or pan?" Kit's eyebrows perk in interest.

"I don't know. But what if?"

What if?

7

DAMIAN

"This all started with The Moral Majority," Melissa says.

"Religion has been in politics for much longer, but sure, that's when Fundie's were a lot more in your face about it," I tell her. Melissa is a regular study partner of mine. Her interest is more on theology than occults, but often, our work aligns.

I'm not a big fan of working with others, but Melissa doesn't take no easy. After trying to study with me a handful of times, all with me rejecting the idea, she finally found the way to my agreement. Bring me snacks. Preferably homemade.

Today, it's lemon poppyseed muffins.

I let her keep hanging around because she's a great baker and she understands that I'm not so talkative. Melissa is a mother; married and pregnant before she graduated with her BA. She took time off until her son started school. Then she came back. She told me once that she likes to work with me because I'm not a stuffy asshole, just a regular asshole.

"This part here," she points to a page. "This is really good, Damian."

She's going over some of my dissertation notes. We're at a table at the front of the library, against a wall of windows that give me a view of the café next door. I haven't seen my new friend for a spell, and I miss her.

That night at Alexander's was eye opening for me, to say the least. I've never been the type of guy to offer comfort to others. In return, people don't seek it from me. Willa did, though. And I liked it more than I could have dreamed. She sought me out for emotional protection when she curled into my side and hid her face in my shoulder to cry for the women in the documentary. It's a new role for me, one I don't hate. Quite the opposite.

For the past few days, I've dreamed of what a relationship between the three of us could look like. I've known for a long time that Alexander is in love with Willa. He makes it evident with the revery in which he speaks about her. All it took was one hockey game with Willa to know the feelings are reciprocated.

Then there's me. I know Alexander has feelings for me and vice versa. Every new conversation with Willa deepens my affection for her. I want them both.

I wonder if they feel the same.

My fantasies about it make me feel almost childish. But I can't deny that I want to come home at the end of the day to a house with both in it. Where we could spend evenings cooking together and relaxing with stimulating conversations. My mother would never believe that I could have intellectual interest in an athlete, but she'd be very wrong. Alexander, especially for someone whose schooling was fragmented and often on the road, isn't stupid. His perspective is refreshingly different than mine on nearly everything.

"This all looks great," Melissa says. "You're off to a good start."

"Thanks, Mel. Only another hundred and fifty pages or so to go."

"You'll get there." She stands and starts packing away her belongings. "You take the rest of the muffins, you're too skinny."

She tells me that all the time and it always makes me smile as the mom in her peeks its head out to say hello.

"Thank you. See you later, Melissa."

Just as she leaves, Willa enters the café with a couple of other women. Not wanting to crash her party right away, I work on my laptop for a while longer. This is another noticeable thing that's changed since Alexander and Willa entered my life. My selfishness is much decreased. Setting aside my own wants and desires for someone else's benefit isn't how I was raised. I no longer feel like I'm the star of the show, I'd rather be a background player in theirs. A supporting act, ready to prop them up or catch their fall if ever they need either.

Maybe it's age, or that I'm nearly done with nine years of schooling, but my goals are shifting. I can't help but believe that they play a role in that.

I get a few thousand words written, then call it a day. When I walk into the coffee shop, I don't have to scan the space to find Willa. I hear her immediately.

"I'm just saying women have the same rights as men," some guy says to her.

"That's because you're only looking at it from the point of view of rights," she's saying to the guy who looks like he was pulled right out of a fraternity catalog. "I'm not that close-minded on the subject. Until being a woman is as easy as being a man, I'll be here arguing with assholes like you."

"How is it easier to be a man," he argues.

"In nearly every way. Skipping over obvious things like the ability to make medical decisions with a doctor instead of the state, there are examples in everyday life. You'd probably call a woman a whore if she slept around, but you'd high-five your buddy for the same behavior. Men want men's clubs and 'man caves' in their homes, but if a woman wants a space free of men, she must be a man-hating feminist lesbian. Men can have leg and armpit hair, and no one bats a pretty eyelash, whereas a woman doesn't shave and she's unhygienic. A woman with a family is considered a liability by employers, but a 'family man' is looked upon favorably," she rattles off her points quickly and directly. "Not to mention the thousands of other ways. Your willful ignorance on the subject is just that, *Chad*."

"You know my names Derek, Willa."

"Same thing," she dismisses him with a wave, and he walks away in a huff.

"Well done, Ms. Cole," I say, stepping up behind her and getting a whiff of whatever sweet-scented shampoo she uses.

"That guy lives to come in here and push our buttons." She looks over her shoulder at me and winks. "Emma, Jennifer, this is Damian."

"Nice to meet you," they both say in unison.

"Likewise," I say to them. "Hey, you free tonight?"

"What did you have in mind," she asks, turning her eyes down almost shyly, something she's never been with me before.

"Dinner upstairs." I keep it cryptic, for Alexander's sake. Emma and Jennifer don't need to know that I'm having dinner with the city's new hockey stud.

"Mmm, you may want to ask if that's a good idea," she says carefully. "Let me know."

"Okay, I'll do that. Talk to you later, Willa."

"Bye, Mr. March," she sings as I walk away.

What the fuck was that about?

"Have you seen Willa?" It's the first thing I say after hello when I get to Alexander's later in the day.

"Yeah, she was here last night," he says.

"What for?"

"We watched a movie," he says, shifting in his seat to turn his body from me. He's being cagey, only confirming that I've missed something.

"What happened?"

"Nothing," he answers too quickly.

"Don't fucking lie to me." I sit on the other side of the sofa from him. "If you're not going to have a real conversation, I can go pry one out of her."

"Fucking hell." He leans forward, resting his elbows on his knees and dropping his head into his hands. "We fell asleep on the couch, and I got handsy during the night."

"Handsy how?" He'd never hurt her intentionally, I know this, so I keep my temper in check. Besides, he looks beat up about it all.

"We woke up with one of my hands on her tit and one playing with her waistband."

"Did you apologize?"

"Of course, I fucking did, and she seemed okay. Except when we really woke up, she ran out of here like her ass was on fire."

"I'm going to go see if she's home," I say, standing back up.

"Maybe I should go," he argues. "I don't want her to feel weird about it."

"You going to tell her how you feel about her?" I've hinted at this so many times. He always brushes it off, and I expect no less now.

"No. It's not productive. I can't offer her the life she needs. And where does that put you?"

Maybe exactly where I want to be.

"Maybe you don't know what she needs," I say instead. "Maybe instead of making up scenarios in your head, we could have actual conversations about this."

"Why are you so concerned about this," Alexander asks, stepping into my personal space. One of the qualities I like most about him is how quickly he shifts. From casual to heated in the blink of an eye. I think it's the hockey in his blood. A moment ago, he was focused on his issue with Willa, and now, he's stalking me like I'm his next meal.

"I like her," I say, backing up against the wall. Not retreating, only positioning myself where I know he wants me. Alexander is frustrated and needs a bit of control. For him, I'll give what I've never given anyone else.

"How much?" His palm stretches over my throat, running around it to the back of my skull so he can pull at my nape. Dragging his nose along the column, he breathes me in, then nips my jaw.

"Maybe not as much as you do. Yet." It's a taunt, and we both know it. He takes the bait, anyway.

"She's my coach's daughter. Willa isn't for us." He yanks my hair harder.

"She can be. She can be mine."

"And me," he asks, his jaw tense.

"You can be there," I say, reaching down to cup his cock through his sweats. "You can watch."

His cock lengthens, his fingers tighten their hold, and his collarbone becomes more pronounced at the thought. Alexander releases an uncomfortable sigh, bringing us nose to nose. The ideal situation is to be the one watching the two of them, we both know it. Dropping little ideas like this in his head is only to make the idea of the three of us more enticing.

"No."

"Why are you fighting it, Alexander? We both know the truth."

"She's too good for that. She deserves more." This is the Midwestern farm boy talking now. The one that came from a conservative nuclear family and hasn't seen anything different. It's ridiculous, but I understand the struggle to fight your upbringing all too well.

"We can give her more, Alexander. We could give her everything."

"We? You and I aren't even defined," he argues.

"Not by words, no," I agree. Though there are plenty of other things that define our relationship. This, too, he knows.

We're unconventional; rarely spending time together, even less rarely having sex. It's a partnership though. A trust we've built over years of sharing thoughts and feelings. It's more than lust and not at all mere infatuation. I can see a life with this man, something real that runs the distance. We've never been urgent or rushed.

There's no reason to be with Willa, either. Maybe a polyamorous relationship isn't what she wants. Or maybe she'd be open to it but apprehensive. There's no way to know until we talk about it.

"I don't want to hurt her, Damian. I never want her in pain." He softens, only some, but enough for me to see.

"Nor do I," I say. "I also don't want her downstairs alone when she should be up here with us. Let me go talk to her."

Leaning in, I kiss him. Slowly, softly, and intimately, I taste his mouth with my tongue in way of a promise. A vow to never hurt him or anyone he loves.

We're both struggling with the newness of this. Neither of us have experience with relationships between two people, let alone three. Yet I can't get past the urgency inside that tells me Willa is meant to be here just as much as we are. Fate is a bullshit concept, but it's the closest word I can find to make sense of what I feel. I barely know Willa, but she's a magnet that draws me in.

It's not like me to stake a claim, but I want to make them both mine. Hide them away in a gilded cage of my own, making every night where we fuck each other blind. I want to wake up tangled with them every morning. I want to care for them, protect them, grow with them.

I push all those thoughts into this kiss until he can feel it too.

"Okay" he relents, the idea finally settling over him. "We can feel it out."

I smile against his lips.

"We'll go easy. If she seems disinterested, we back off."

"Agreed," he says. "My head says this won't work."

"It can, *if* she wants it," I tell him.

"If she doesn't?"

"We'll figure it out. Together."

Alexander may not be able to envision a life for the three of us, but a vivid picture forms in my own head as I walk to Willa's place. I've spent my existence without many life goals, outside of my degree, anyway. Once

I have that, what do I do next? It's a question that's played in the corners of my mind for so long. Now, I can almost see the answer formed with definition.

I want a family, even if it's as unconventional as they come. I want a home to settle into at the end of every day that isn't as lonely as the one I currently own.

Honestly, it's a strange feeling. Like I'm the grinch who just grew a heart or some shit.

I knock on Willa's door. There's noise from the other side, but no answer. I lean against the doorjamb, listening more closely as I knock again, this time louder. Finally, she answers, pulling an earbud out of one ear.

"Damian. Hi," she says as if I've caught her off guard.

"What are you up to, Ms. Cole?"

"I was cleaning," she says, matching my smile as she looks up at me through her eyelashes. "I listen to music and dance around while I do it, makes it less mundane."

Nothing about this woman is mundane.

"Can you take a break for dinner?"

"Did you clear it with the big guy?"

"Is that what we're calling him," I ask, laughing. She only shrugs. "He knows I'm down here trying to get you to come up."

Willa ushers me inside, taking the second bud out of her ear and setting down the rag I hadn't even noticed she was holding. Her face is enough to hold my attention, but as I watch her move around her space in tight yoga shorts and a cropped T-shirt, my focus goes to her ample ass and the bare patch of skin showing just above it. She's beautiful regardless, her fantastic body is a bonus. What Alexander's kiss started; Willa threatens to finish.

"Did he tell you what happened this morning?"

"He did. Are you okay," I ask. She blinks rapidly at my question, surprised by it. "What?"

"I didn't expect that, I guess."

"Why? You think I'm some kind of asshole Chad who doesn't care about boundaries?"

"Actually, it hadn't crossed my mind to be offended by where Zander's hands were. I'm surprised by my reaction more than yours."

"You liked it, did you, Ms. Cole?"

"I'm not the one who's gay. Besides, he's hot as hell. You can hardly blame a gal."

"Gay?" Who does she think is…Oh fuck. "Alexander isn't gay, Willa."

"What?"

"He's bisexual. We both are."

"Oh fuck," she says, leaning her body against the kitchen counter. "I thought… well, I assumed a lot. You know what they say about that."

"You are not an ass, Willa. He didn't spell it out for you?"

"No, he didn't say much about it. I jumped to my own conclusions," she says. Not surprising, knowing Alexander. He's the most tight-lipped person I've ever known, especially about his sexuality. I know he'd been friends with Isla for nearly a year before he finally told her. "I spent half the day feeling like I had some sort of womanly superpower that could give gay men hard-ons and the other half hoping it wouldn't cause a rift between the two of you."

Laughter erupts out of me, and I realize I've never been around Willa without it.

"You humor me like no other, Willa," I tell her. "Come have dinner with me and the big guy."

"Let me get changed."

"No. Come as you are, beautiful."

8

ZANDER

I heard once that there is more unhappiness in the world than happiness, and we shouldn't expect to deserve to be one of the happy ones. Not sure where I heard it, but it's been sitting on my shoulder for as long as I can remember. Happiness isn't something I thought obtainable. The NHL, sure. But not happiness.

When Damian said we could give Willa more, give her *everything*, the image of my future changed. Hope is a fucked-up thing, though. I don't believe in hope. Hard work, dedication, determination. Those are the only things I know.

They aren't anything I've applied to personal relationships. Truth is I've never had many. Isla and Damian, that's all. Isla doesn't require work, it's not that type of friendship. We could go weeks without talking and still she'd be there the second I needed her for anything. Damian and I have been as casual as possible. That's something he knew to expect from the start, and something he wanted, too.

But now everything changes. Willa's not a woman to be dated casually. She's the one to be locked down for eternity. Damian is someone to be held on too, as well. I've never known a more loyal guy.

Nerves have me pacing my living room in anticipation of Damian's return with her. They walk in laughing and some of the anxiety eases, only to morph into something else. Willa is in nothing but a small T-shirt and smaller shorts.

"Look who I found," Damian says, stepping behind her he wraps an arm around her stomach and pulls her into him. Every drop of blood in my body rushes to my dick. They look good together. I can't imagine how good they'll look naked and in my bed.

He's so at ease with her, it's astonishing, really. Damian has told me how long it's been since he was with someone before he met me. And we took our time. With Willa, there's little hesitation for him.

"He has his hockey legs out," Willa whispers.

"What does that mean," Damian asks, eyes smiling.

"His quads." Her eyes drop to the hem of my shorts. "He has hockey quads. Aren't they fabulous?"

Both of us laugh, because what the fuck?

"I'm going to start dinner," Damian says, pressing a quick kiss to her temple. "Eggplant lasagna because someone told me vegetables are good for your sex drive."

"He cooks," she asks, tipping her chin up to me as I step in front of her, crowding her close enough to see every last freckle she has.

"Sometimes, he does. Hi," I say, cupping her cheeks. They color the tiniest bit and it's a fucking rush. Why did I fight this for so long? I can't remember a single reason that makes sense. "You okay? You took off quickly this morning."

"I am now. It was unexpected, is all." She turns her head, rubbing her cheek into my palm.

"Guess I'm tired of resisting whatever this is between us," I tell her, being honest with her for maybe the first time ever.

"Are you saying I'm irresistible, Zander," she teases me after a beat or two, her mouth turning into a soft smile.

"Absolutely, gorgeous."

"What *is* this between us?"

"Not sure," I admit. Honestly, I don't know where this will lead, or what I even have to offer. I don't feel like it's enough for anyone, let alone a Cole, a family I hold with such high esteem. Even if I'm successful in hockey, the life brings instability in so many ways. She knows that though, better than most. So why am I trying to talk myself out of trying? Again. "Something that could be explored with the three of us."

"I can get down with some exploration." There is not sexual inflection in her tone, but my man brain goes straight to the idea of exploring her body. Damian said she could be his and I can watch, but fuck that. He's the voyeur, he can watch.

Or maybe we take turns, because damn, that sounds hot as hell too. My dick is ready to jump the gun, but we said we'd take this slow. Ease into the idea, see if this is something that works. So, I take her hand and pull her with me to the kitchen where we can help the third person in this experiment.

"What have you been working on lately," I ask her as I check the noodles boiling on the stove.

"A paper about medical research being predominantly based on men only. Did you know that they only started testing tampons with human blood in 2023?"

"Seriously," I ask.

"What did they use before that," Damian follows up with his own question.

"Water or saltwater, mostly."

"That's ridiculous. I bleed enough to know blood and water absorb differently, and my blood isn't like menstrual blood," I say.

"I know," Willa says with a heavy sigh. "Sorry, it's probably not the best conversation while we're about to eat."

"I don't think either of us are squeamish, beautiful," Damian tells her, and I hum in agreement.

She talks more about the data she's collected until we have the lasagna ready to go in the oven. I'm not a well-educated man so I'm glad Damian can keep up with her in that arena. And her with him. I take it all in though, knowing I can learn a lot from each of them, even though I don't say much.

While dinner bakes, we get comfortable in the living room. Again, Willa ends up between the two of us. Except this time, she's closer to me and Damian keeps a careful distance.

"Can you make it to my game tomorrow?"

"Who," Willa asks.

"Both of you, preferably."

"I don't have classes, which gives me the day to finish up this paper. I can make it," she says.

"I can, too," Damian says.

"Do you want to sit with me again?"

"Yes, a few more games with you lot and maybe I'll finally understand forechecking and backchecking," he tells her.

Willa starts an animated description of each, all while using my coffee table as an ice rink. She uses our cell phones and my remotes as skaters. Damian watches with rapt attention. I sit back and enjoy it because every time she leans down to move a 'player', her ass is in my face.

The oven finally beeps. Damian stands and picks Willa up over his shoulder.

"Thanks for the lesson, Coach," he says, slapping her ass playfully as he hauls her to the kitchen. She lifts her head to see me following behind and sends me a big grin. Maybe Damian is right, and I have no idea what's best for Willa. Maybe this can work, the three of us. Together.

We're playing Vancouver and we're down by one as we take the ice for third period. The entire second period we played like we were down a man, constantly in catch up mode. Coach Cole chewed our asses for the first couple of minutes of intermission. We fucking deserved it.

The team's ready now, though. My stick is freshly taped, Blom had a cup of coffee and took a shit, and the rest of the guys did whatever their routine is. Everyone's is different, but mostly we all end up discussing what needs to change in the period.

Our forechecking was crap and we made it easy for them to bombard Blom at the net. He did great at stopping them, but everyone gets an amazing shot occasionally.

Cill takes the faceoff, winning it and passing it to Lehtinen on the other side of the ice. I move toward the net as he circles a Vancouver player and shoots. Their goalie gets a pad on it, but it wobbles in front of the net. In front of me. I get a rebound shot that sails just under their goalie's arm and lands in the back of the net to tie it up.

Cill and Letty skate over to pat my helmet when one of Vancouver's players moves up behind me.

"How many dicks did you suck in the locker room during break to be able to get that play right?"

"The fuck did you say," Lehtinen growls.

Cillian pushes me toward our bench, while Olly follows close behind.

"Leave it, Zan. I'll take care of it."

"I don't need you to fight my battles, Wylder."

The other guys on the bench perk up at the conversation, a couple asking what happened.

"Nothing," I say.

"Twenty-four," Lehtinen says. "You get the chance, you fuck that kid up." His message is met with smiles and a few sticks tapping the floor.

Jesus.

"Don't get any stupid penalties over it," Cillian tells me.

"No fucking promises."

The following minutes are torture. Adrenaline races through my veins, I want to be back on the ice. It might not be the best response, maybe it makes me look more guilty of his accusation. But this is hockey, and we only take so much shit talk before we throw gloves.

That fucking blog post must be making the rounds. There's no time to stress out about it now though. The game is my only focus and now, even more than before, I want to fucking win it. When my turn comes back around, the asshole isn't on the ice. I keep my focus on the game, my position, the puck, defending our goalie and net. It's not until a few shifts later that he and I are on the ice together. Cillian stays in the guy's orbit as much as possible, making it hard for the kid to get anything done. But then Letty intercepts the puck and takes it down to Vancouver's zone. He doesn't have a clear shot, so he passes it to Cill along the boards. The shit talker is there though, circling him like a shark. I can hear them exchanging words, but I don't know what's being said. Cillian passes it back to Lehtinen, and within seconds, Vancouver's player crashes into Cill, causing my teammate's head to slam into the ice.

Motherfucker.

The whistle blows at the penalty, but I ignore that in favor of taking the guy to the ice. He sees me coming, knows what's about to happen. Instead of taking the lick like a good boy, he drops gloves. I follow suit and then nail him with a right hook to the jaw. He goes down, and I follow, landing on the guy as we continue to trade punches until the officials and a few teammates pull us off each other.

You don't grow up with a drunk dad without learning how to fight. I may not be the biggest guy in the league, but I can take a hit almost as well as I can toss them out.

Of course, I get sent to the box, but it's worth it. He's bleeding from a cut or two on his face, red streaming down into his eye.

Fuck him.

Cillian isn't on the bench when I look across the ice. Vaughn nods his head toward the tunnel, letting me know they took him back, likely for concussion protocol. Willa and Sadie aren't here tonight because Sadie has a cold. I bet they're watching from home worried as hell.

The hit on Cill and my fight only lights a fire under our team's bench. We end up winning five to two. Wylder is chilling with the team medical staff when I make it to the locker room, his feet kicked up.

"Easiest win I ever had," he says to me as I clunk my way to him, not even stopping to drop my skates.

"You good?"

"Doc says I'll be okay, my bucket looked beat up so they're being cautious. I stayed back here to let them pamper me since you guys had it handled," he says, and I'm not sure if I should believe him. "You knocked that shitbrick into next week. Nice job."

"He fucking deserved it."

"Agreed. You okay?"

"I'm fine," I lie. I'm not fine, I'm pissed off. But what the hell can I do about it?

"Whatever you say, Fane. Clean up, press is bound to want a soundbite from you."

Ah, it looks like it's going to be a longer night than I'd hoped for. I'm typically one of the first guys out of the locker room after a game. Everyone wants a piece of me today though. I take a minute to shoot a text off to Willa and Damian, letting them know not to wait around for me.

Even though they're the only people I feel like being with right now.

There was a text from Damian waiting for me when I finally made it out of the arena. He said he was hanging out at Willa's and to let him know when

I was home. It's so late that I should tell him to go home, except I'm tired of being alone every time something shitty happens to me.

So, when I walk into my apartment, I leave the door unlocked and let him know before I drop my ass down on my amazing couch and pull Netflix up on the television.

When my door opens, it's not just Damian. He's holding Willa's hand as she follows him inside. She comes straight to me, dropping his grip, and kneeling next to me.

"That looks nasty, Zan," she says, sounding far more concerned than needed. A bruise has bloomed around my left eye and cheekbone, but it's nothing more. "Do you want some ice?"

"Nah, gorgeous, it's fine."

"You kicked his ass." She gently runs her fingers all over my face, looking for other bruises or wounds. When they drag to the corner of my mouth, I open it and nip at her lightly, making her laugh.

"Fuck that guy," I say. "Did you talk to Isla? Sadie okay?"

"Yeah, they were freaked out, but Cill called them as soon as he could."

"Good."

"What did he say that started it all," she asks. Leave it to a Cole not to miss a single step on the ice.

"Asked how many dicks I sucked during intermission."

"Are you fucking kidding me," Damian asks from his position on the other end of the couch.

"I'm sorry, Zan, that's horrible." I look from him to her and see tears threatening to spill.

"Shh, Willa." I wrap my arm around her and pull her onto my lap. "I paid him back, he'll think twice next time."

"I hope so," she says, staring up at me with sad eyes.

"You want to kiss it better," I tease, expecting her to laugh again. Only, she doesn't. Instead, she nods. "Yeah?"

Willa makes a sound of agreement and looks toward Damian. He gives her the go ahead with a tilt of his chin. Her soft palm lands on my jaw a moment before she moves her lips to mine in the gentlest kiss I've received. It's not rushed or hungry, it's sweet and caring. And far too short.

"How do you think he knew to say such a horrendous thing to you," she says when she pulls away. It's only an inch or two, but the distance feels greater.

"There's a local gossip blog that caught on to something between Damian and I when we were suit shopping," I explain. "I hoped it would get lost, but apparently, it hasn't."

"People suck," Willa says, fresh tears stinging her eyes.

"Amen," Damian agrees.

"I'm figuring it out," I say, then close the distance. I need another taste; I need more of her.

This time, she wraps her arms around my neck and lets me take the lead, deepening the kiss. My tongue runs at the seam of her lips, and she opens for me. Tongue to tongue, we tangle. Willa's kiss is everything she is—light, airy, humor, and goddamned irresistible.

It's everything, and yet not nearly enough.

Cradling her with a hand at the back of her neck and the other under her ass, I lay her down on the couch. I hover over her, staring down at her as she arches her neck to look for Damian. She reaches a hand out to him, beckoning him to join.

"Not yet, beautiful," he tells her, but he clasps her fingers with hers. Not letting go even when she turns her face back to me.

"He likes to watch. You okay with that?"

"As long as you join if you start to feel left out," she answers. Fucking hell, she's perfect.

"Promise," he tells her.

"Is this really happening," she asks.

"Only if you want it to," I say.

"Do you want to talk about it," Damian asks her.

"We can talk later," she teases.

I run a hand under her oversized sweatshirt, feeling the fluttering of her anticipation under my fingers. Normally after a game, I have to handle my excess adrenaline myself or on the rare occasion, find some random woman. It's exhilarating having both Willa and Damian here, but I'm afraid of rushing her, too.

"Stop thinking and kiss me, Zan."

Yeah, right. Get out of your head, Fane.

Willa hooks a leg around my hip. She licks her lips, and my mind clears of anything but making her come. My hand moves up to her breast, feeling her nipple harden instantly. She isn't wearing a bra and she arches her back into my palm and releases a soft moan that forces all my blood to my already hard cock.

I lick a line up her neck, over her chin, and dart my tongue back into her ready mouth, swallowing all the sounds she makes. She's so vocal already and we've only just begun. Her heel digs into my calf and her hips rock, seeking more friction.

"What do you need, Willa?"

"Less clothes. More skin."

Damian chuckles at her admission.

"Done." I sit up, removing my own shirt. Damian pulls Willa's up by the hem and over her head before grasping her hand. Again.

"You truly are gorgeous, Ms. Cole," he says to her. She smiles shyly.

"Shorts too," she tells me, her gaze glazed with desire. I obey, curling my fingers into the waistband of her cotton shorts and slowly pulling them down. She raises her hips to make my job easier.

Finally, she's naked. So beautifully bare between the two of us.

"Taste her, Alexander."

Oh, I fucking will.

9

WILLA

Zander widens the position of my legs. His lightly calloused fingers send shivers down my spine and to my core. They move down my legs, to my apex, where he uses them to spread me open. He leans in, and I expect the wetness of his mouth, but it's his nose I feel as he scents me.

"Goddamn, Willa."

I whimper, needy and more turned on than I've ever even imagined I could be. Damian's fingers are entwined with mine, he squeezes gently, and I look at him.

"Why are you still dressed," I ask Damian, but then Zander's tongue dives into my cunt, and I lose my sanity. "Oh, fuck."

"Is it good," Damian whispers in my ear. "Have you dreamed of this, Willa?"

"Fuck, yes. Yes!"

Zan's tongue swirls inside me once, then he sucks my clit in little pulses, driving me crazy. Damian runs his hand along my collarbone and down to weigh my breast. He massages it for a moment before one of Zander's hand joins his. I stare as their fingers tangle atop my nipple; Damian's other hand still holding mine, connecting us all together.

"Fuck his mouth, beautiful. He wants to taste you when you come," Damian demands.

Zander hums into me, the warm vibration better than any of my arsenal of toys. His thumb settles on my clit and works overtime when his tongue stiffens and fucks me like a wet cock. I wish it was his cock. Visions play behind my eyelids of three bodies, naked and writhing. Shining with exertion as we fuck each other stupid.

My hips pick up pace. Zander doesn't pause for even a second until I'm pulling his hair and screaming his name in bliss.

"You're exquisite when you shatter, Willa," Damian says to me. "Let me taste her."

Releasing me, he moves to kneel beside where Zander's head rests on my bare thigh. Once again, he twines his fingers with mine, this time in the nest of Zan's curls. Pulling him in, he seals his mouth to his in a passionate kiss. I watch, mesmerized and gushing every time they pull away just enough for me to see their tongues lick at each other.

"I think I could come just from watching the two of you," I say. They both turn to me, grinning widely. "You're both insanely hot. But together, you're unfucking real."

"Oh, we're very real, gorgeous," Zander says.

"Show me how real," I tell him, rising up to my elbows. "I'm the only one naked here, after all."

"That's what you want? Us naked," Zan asks, staring up at my body.

"Yes, please."

"Since you asked so nicely," he says, pressing a kiss to my inner thigh before standing next to Damian.

Damian pulls his tee over his head in that one-handed move men make. His chest is dotted with dark ink. I expected as much, but the grayscale art is breathtaking. There are more roses mixed with other flowers and vines, each one placed perfectly to enhance his body. I pause, before reaching out to touch him.

"Can I?"

"Yeah, beautiful."

Tracing the thorns that creep over his hip with my finger, I preen when I feel the twitch of his muscles. Moving my hands slowly, I watch his face to make sure I'm not overstepping any unspoken boundary. When I reach the button of his pants, Damian nods slightly, giving me the permission I seek. When I get them undone, I find him bare. And so damn hard.

I drag my tongue up his shaft as I push his pants down.

"You're beautiful," I tell him, spying even more art on his legs. He's the complete opposite to Zander's virgin skin. When he, too, is naked, I can't help but sit back and compare. Neither of them seems to mind my lazy perusal. Their height is similar, same as their build, though Zan is much more defined. And their cocks? Zan has more girth, but Damian wins in length. "Shit, I might be the luckiest lady in all of Seattle."

"Open that mouth for me and I'll be the luckiest man to ever live," Zander says.

"Well, I wouldn't want to be the reason for you to lose that title," I say. Damian grabs a pillow off the couch and drops it to the floor. It gives my knees a cushion and props me at the right height to be at eye level with their dicks. "Who's first?"

Damian laughs, a soft chuckle that shakes his whole body. Zander isn't laughing, though. He's staring down at me with an unbridled need. I nudge the tip of his cock with the tip of my nose. It bobs, and he wraps his hand around it, stroking it a couple of times. Opening wide, I offer my mouth to him. Without hesitation, he slides in, taking his time, letting me savor him as much as he savors me.

"Goddamn, Willa."

"The only thing prettier would be our cocks in your cunt," Damian says, making me hum with a greedy need.

"Yes, Willa. Like that," Zander says, picking up his pace. He thrusts in and out of my mouth a handful more times before he takes a step back, letting Damian take his place. He's still within reach, so I spread one hand on his hip and the other on Damian's as I let them control the rest. One finds pleasure in my mouth while the other keeps time with his hand, switching back and forth. Never leaving me without the feeling of their cocks. My eyes bounce between them, not able to take it all in, not wanting to miss a thing.

Breathing becomes heavier for us all, the taste of pre-cum stronger the closer they get to their release. I vibrate with anticipation; with the pure fucking power I possess in this moment. I may be the one on my knees, but I'm bringing them to theirs. Together.

I love this.

I want more.

I want it all.

Damian is close now, his chest flush.

"Where do you want it, beautiful?" Damian asks, clenching his jaw.

"You, here," I say, lifting my right breast to him, before lifting the other to Zander. "And you, here."

To my surprise, Zander is the first. He cups my cheek, angling my face to his, not blinking while he explodes exactly where I told him to. When he's done, spent and breathless, I pull his cock back into my mouth, sucking off any remnants.

Damian follows my directions just as well, coming until it's dripping off my nipple like melted icing. For the next twenty minutes, I'm squished between them in a shower definitely not built for two large men, let alone a third person in the mix. They take turns tending to me; washing every inch of my body, shampooing and conditioning my naturally wavy hair.

Then I'm tucked into Zander's bed, him on one side of me while Damian on the other. I sleep better than I have in years.

"I have questions," I say the following morning, bringing three cups of hot coffee into the bedroom. I woke extra early, admittedly a little too warm in the men cocoon. I'm not complaining though. Waking up entwined with two hard bodies, both positioned as if protecting me from the dark, was… well, kind of awesome.

"Shoot," Zander says, his voice scratchy with sleep. He sits up and takes a mug from me. "You put cream in it."

"Of course. I don't know how you take it, though. I left it black," I say to Damian.

"Black is perfect," he says, taking his own mug. I sit cross-legged, facing the two of them as they lean against the headboard. I have to adjust Damian's shirt that I'm wearing from exposing all my lady bits.

"You two are together, yeah?"

"We're undefined," Damian answers, but his eyes stay on Zander, so I know there's explanation to be had.

"Tell me if I'm overstepping here. But what does that mean?" Damian raises an eyebrow at my question and waits for Zander to answer.

"You know the NHL. I wouldn't have this career if I was open about my sexuality. I've never felt like I was able to foster a relationship when I can't be fair to my partner about it," he tries to explain. "This is new for me, being in the same place with the person, *people*, I care about. I'm navigating new waters; it's going to take me time to learn."

"But you have sex?"

"We haven't taken it that far," Zander says, shifting uncomfortably.

"How far have you taken it?" Damian wears a shit-eating grin when I ask this. "I know you kiss."

"We kiss," Damian says. "Sometimes."

"Oral," I ask next.

"There's been a little of that," Zan admits.

"How do I fit into all of this," I ask, point-blank. Last night was wonderful and I can see myself falling as hard for Damian as I have already for Zander. But if this is a one-time thing, or it's casual, I need to know that now. For my own protection. "Was this a one-off threesome type thing? Or more? You two may not be defined, but I need definitions."

"What do you want the definitions to be, Willa," Zander asks.

"I think my questions need to be answered first. Am I a one-night stand? Am I a buffer between you until you're comfortable enough with each other that you don't need me?"

"That's not what you are at all, Willa."

"Why would you think that," Damian asks. He sits up taller and sets his coffee on the nightstand.

Honestly, a better question is why wouldn't I? I've known Zander for years and he never showed much sign of attraction, especially not at this level.

"Why now," I ask, directing the question to Zander.

"What could I offer you? I'm bisexual, Willa. Stubbornly so. I've spent a life repressing who I am, it's not something I'm ready to make compromises on. Damian was the first person that I thought understood my hard lines there."

"For the record, I don't love the rules. I enjoy you enough to stick around while you work it out," Damian says. "But I've been out since I was a teenager."

"You thought I wouldn't understand," I ask.

"More like I would end up hurting you."

"Because you want to have relationships with men, too," I prompt him to continue.

"Because I want to explore that, and yeah, I thought you might not understand that need."

My life has been privileged in many ways. This is one of those ways. Because I've never had to contemplate my sexuality. I like what I like, and I was never worried about anyone disapproving of it. Mom and Dad were always clear about our family being accepting.

Me with two men might not go over so well with my father, but that's neither here nor there at this point.

"I'd never judge you for your sexuality," I finally say. "But I need transparency and honesty. Can we all agree on that?"

"Of course, beautiful," Damian says, and Zander nods.

"What are the rules between you?"

"No other men," Zan says.

"No rules on women?"

"No."

"Well, if you want me, there are no other women either. That's definition number one." I take another sip of my coffee, happy that it has cooled enough to drink it without burning my mouth.

"Done," they say in unison, making me blink in surprise.

"What else," Damian asks.

"Equality," I say after a moment of thoughtfully worrying my bottom lip. "This sort of arrangement won't work if we aren't on equal footing. If anyone ever feels left out, it will ruin it. I'm not saying we need to be together for everything, but some level of balance and respect must be present."

"Have you done this before," Zander asks.

"Only in my dreams," I admit. They laugh, and the mood softens. Perhaps, we can make this work without anyone getting hurt.

"I need to shower and get to the Iceplex for morning skate. Can we talk more later?"

"Yes," I say, crawling up to the head of the bed so I can get back under the covers. I know I'm flashing them both, but it is what it is.

"Fuck, now I'm going to have to beat off while I'm in there."

"Want an audience, big guy?"

"No, you minx," he says, pressing a kiss to my forehead before he gets out of bed in all his naked glory. "I'll never make it on time if you come in with me. Your dad will hammer me with drills if I'm late."

"I think it's a sin or something to talk about my father when you're that nude."

"Wouldn't be the first thing I've done that will send me to hell." The bathroom door shuts behind him, leaving me and Damian alone. He's quiet this morning, but I've come to realize that's not abnormal for him. He's either chatty, or not, there is no in-between. There must be a reason for it that I hope one day he trusts me with.

"What's your plan for the day, Mr. March?"

"It's Saturday, Ms. Cole. I'm typically a sloth on Saturdays."

"That sounds dreamy," I say with a sigh. It's long days being in an PhD program, the occasional lazy one is something to be cherished.

"Would you like to be a sloth with me? We can watch more horrific documentaries while we fill up on carbs and sugar."

"Do you have paranormal powers that allow you to see inside my mind or something?"

"Or something, beautiful," he says with a laugh. "Go home and grab whatever you need for the night. Once you're at my place, I'm not letting you leave for a solid twenty-four hours." He slaps my ass as I start to get out of bed.

"I like the sound of that. You'll tell Zan the plan?"

"Of course, we're transparent around here," he says with a wink.

"Atta boy," I tease and rush off to find where I left my clothes. "I'll be ready in twenty!"

10

DAMIAN

For the first hour Willa is in my house, she noses her way around every nook and cranny the place has. I don't mind, in fact I encouraged it, wanting her to feel safe with me. There's nothing for me to hide, anyhow. Nothing material, that is.

"Just how wealthy are you, Mr. March?" She stands at the door that leads out to my balcony. Straight ahead is a perfect view of the Space Needle bordered by the city skyline. To the right, there's Lake Union, some blocks away. It's one of the best views you can get in Seattle, and I did pay a ridiculous amount to get it.

"Why would you ask such a thing," I tease her.

"This view is probably worth a million dollars even without the house. Though the house is quite impressive too. I imagine this is the best place to be on the Fourth of July and New Year's."

"You're probably right, though I'm usually home in New Orleans for holidays."

"In all my travels, I've yet to get there. It looks like a beautiful city, rich with history and culture."

"It is," I say. "I'll take you some day, show you all the hidden secrets."

"Already making plans to take me home and meet the parents? You move fast, Mr. March."

I laugh. She always makes me laugh. Other than my friend, Fig, nobody makes me laugh like Willa. Yes, I can see taking her home. My parents would love her; pretty, educated, from an interesting family with some money and name recognition.

Not that I give a fuck what my parents think, but it would make it easier for Willa. If there's a future here, and I hope more and more every day that there might be. She's easy to like and I don't like many people.

Last night, she proved that my suspicions about her are far more accurate than Alexander's. The man lives too much in his own head, making assumptions based on his past and his family, rather than what's truly in front of him. Willa laid out without hesitation that she can handle an unconventional relationship. Luckily, he's seeing it now.

For years, I've felt like my life was missing something. A painting that shows me in the middle but bare on either side. I can see the colors filling the blank canvas now. For the first time ever, I feel like I have a found family. Or the beginnings of one, anyway.

"Did you have something you wanted to watch?"

"A new documentary just hit Netflix. It's about that polygamist ranch that was raided a few years back. The Simms family, have you heard of it?"

Have I ever.

"That's the ranch my friend escaped from. She said she was cooperating with production on it, and she's probably in it."

"Oh, wow. We can skip it if it crosses some line. I wouldn't want you to be uncomfortable or anything."

"No, it's fine. Delilah and I have had a lot of conversations about it. I know what to expect."

Turns out there's much more to learn about than what I already knew. Delilah is on screen often, as is her cousin, Lorelai, who I've met a few times. Neither of them speaks in depth about their time on the ranch. Instead, they talk about their efforts to help the survivors after the government raided.

"She comes across so strong," Willa says. "I'm proud of her and I don't even know her."

"She is strong," I confirm. "I think you'd get along well with her."

"I hope to meet her someday," Willa says, turning to me and smiling. She silently looks at me as if she's looking for an answer to an unspoken question.

"What?"

"It's strange how comfortable I am with you when I don't know much about you."

"I'm an open book if you ask the right questions, Ms. Cole."

"And if I ask the wrong one?"

"I might punish you."

"See? That right there could come across so creepy. Somehow you make it endearing," she says, narrowing her eyes. "You're dangerous, Damian."

"Not the first time I've heard that."

"Do you have siblings?"

"Only child," I say. "My father got his heir on the first try so he saw no reason to add more crying babies to the mix."

Willa frowns at that.

"He doesn't like children?"

"He doesn't like anything but money and the things it buys him," I say with a shrug. "No need to be sad about it. I've always understood him and my place in the family." Her nose wrinkles in the cutest way. I like that she cares, but I meant what I said. My parents aren't worth the emotion. They are who they are, and I've accepted it. I press a kiss to the tip of her nose as if it's the most natural thing for me to do.

It isn't. Like so much of my reaction to Willa, it's all abnormal for me. Like her, I'm oddly at ease in her company. Some piece of me thinks I should overanalyze that, to ask the same question she asked of Alexander this morning. *Why now?*

"Next question," I prompt her.

"Did you always live in New Orleans before here?"

"I did, though we traveled extensively. Most of my summers were spent in some random European city."

"Favorite non-American city?"

"Edinburgh, hands down."

"Good answer," she says with a side eye. "Mine too. Favorite flavor of potato chip?"

"What a random question," I say, sending her a wide smile. "I only like them if they're spicy."

"You are not a hot Cheeto man?" Her eyes widen in shock.

"Gross, no. Those are disgustingly messy, and I don't even want to know what they use to get that color. But give me a spicy nacho Dorito when I'm tipsy, and I'll be happy."

This line of questioning goes on for another hour. Finally, she's satiated with quirky facts about me, I think, and the asks become heavier.

"When was the last time you had sex?"

"The answer might surprise you," I say, shifting to rest my back on the armrest of my couch and propping my legs up in between us. It gives me a better view of her. The late afternoon sun shining through the window behind her lights her up like a halo. I'm not a religious person, but if ever I met an angel, it might be Willa Cole with her easygoing and caring nature.

"It might not though," she says, matching my position on the other side of the couch and tangling our legs together. "We won't know unless you answer it."

"Are you giving me the option of not answering?"

"Yes, I won't make you tell me anything. But I don't fuck people without certain understandings. So, it may affect our play dates."

Play dates. Fuck, she's adorable.

"My sex life is an open book to you, Ms. Cole. I haven't had sex with anyone since I moved to Seattle."

"What the fuck, Damian? You've been here for three years."

"Yes."

"And you haven't wanted to have sex with a single person in all that time?"

"That's not what I said." I've wanted to have sex with Alexander, and her, if I'm honest about it. Though maybe I should keep that part to myself since she's already labeled me Ted Bundy.

"Will you explain it to me?" Her eyes soften, concern creeping in. She's far more intuitive than I'd expect from someone as playful as she is.

"I don't like to touch or be touched, in general. I've never seen a therapist about it, but I'd imagine they would tell me it was because I grew up in a cold household. Physical affection isn't something my parents gave. Honestly, I wouldn't be surprised if they quit having sex with each other after my mother became pregnant with me," I tell her. "Not that they didn't have lovers, there were plenty of those. But the family image was to be maintained."

"The image?" Her nose crinkles again.

"Yes, upstanding citizens, free of flaws. It's all bullshit, of course. Everyone in New Orleans society knows it, but they all have their own images to portray so nobody fusses over the details of it."

"I guess it's not so different than hockey life with all of the NHL's unwritten rules," she muses. "I'm sorry you grew up that way. No child should lack affection. Did you have anyone that cared for you properly?"

"I had a nanny or two that I liked, but they became nonexistent when I was around twelve and could be left to my own devices." Angelique is the one I remember best, a sweet Creole woman who would tell me endless stories about the bayou she grew up in. She stayed with me until she fell in love with a man that worked at our corner grocery store. She was ready to start a family of her own and I never blamed her for leaving. I missed her, though.

"You touch me."

"Unexplainable, really. You're disgusting to look at and you smell awful."

"Oh my god, you didn't just say that." She laughs. It's a little like windchimes, soothing in its chaotic tingling. "Do you touch Zander the same way?"

"I do. I've always been at ease with him," I admit.

"Why do you think that is?"

"We understand each other. From the beginning, it was like we could finish each other's sentences. He's not unexpected and there's a security in that. One I didn't know I needed until I met him. I think of Alexander and warmth creeps into my cold heart." I run my foot along her leg, down to her foot, where I try to tickle it with my own.

"That's sweet," she says. "Thank you for sharing that with me."

"You shared yourself with us, it's the least I could do."

"Do you have questions for me? I feel like I've been peppering you with them all day."

"Because you have," I say, playfully rolling my eyes. "First things first. Are you on birth control?"

"Yes."

"What kind?"

"I get a shot and I'm ridiculously punctual about it."

"Good. When was the last time you had sex?"

"It's been close to six months," she says with a dramatic sigh. "I'm not as celibate as you, but it hasn't been a priority since school started back up."

"Summer fling," I ask her, reaching to grab her foot and pulling so she lies flatter on the sofa. I knead under her toes.

"I guess. More just had an itch that needed scratching. He had a big neck."

"Is that code for something?"

"No," she says, her cheeks flushing just a bit.

"You have some explaining to do, Ms. Cole. What's with the big neck?"

"It's just something I like."

"On everyone or certain necks in particular?"

"One in particular," she says confidently. "I won't accept being teased over it."

Then she sticks her tongue out at me, making me burst out in another round of laughter. I hope I'm never unsurprised by her fun sense of humor.

"I won't tease you. Alexander has an exceptional body. He's easy to obsess over," I tell her. "Have you been with multiple partners before?"

"No, have you?"

"Almost exclusively," I admit. "I prefer it, it allows me to only participate to my own comfort level."

"I can understand that. It's nice you've found a way that works for you."

"Do you have worries about it? About being with two people?"

She lays her head back and stares up at my ceiling before answering. "Maybe not worries, but concerns. Like I said before, I don't want anyone of us to feel like they're not as big a part of this relationship. If Zan's on a road trip and we're here together, is he going to feel a certain way? What if we don't know until it happens and then it's too late and someone is upset?"

"We're adults, Willa. We'll work through it."

"I've known adults that fuck up in stupid ways and it causes more hurt than you can imagine. I'd rather avoid any and all of that, please and thank you."

She means her sister and brother-in-law, I'm sure. Alexander has filled me in some on their relationship, enough to know they had a hard time for several years. One of the things he loves most about Willa is how supportive and protective she was when Isla was working through a surprise pregnancy amidst a tumultuous breakup. Loyalty means a great deal to us both, and Willa is that.

"Have some faith in us, beautiful," I tell her just when our phones ping with notifications.

ALEXANDER:

> Done for the day. Heading over shortly, want me to grab food?

"We've reached group text status," Willa says. "This is all moving so fast."

I sit up to see her face and be sure she isn't being serious. She winks at me, setting me at ease.

"What sounds good?"

"I'm not picky unless it has mushrooms. Don't feed me mushrooms, ever."

"Noted. Thai food?"

"Mmm, yes please."

ME:

> Thai food would be great, thank you.

ALEXANDER:

> Got it. I'll order a variety. No mushrooms.

Willa grins when she reads the text.

"It's like he knows you," I say, sending her a wink of my own.

WILLA:

> Thanks, big guy!

"Damian?"

"Yeah," I answer after we've tossed our phones back on the coffee table. She starts to crawl over to my end of the couch but pauses for my permission. I nod to her, and she continues arranging herself atop me, her head resting on my shoulder.

"Thank you."

"For what?"

"For today. For letting me feel safe to be myself with you."

"I'd never want you to be anything but yourself, Willa." I press a kiss to the top of her head, but she turns her face to mine. So, I press one to her strawberry-colored lips, too. "Thank you for understanding my quirks."

"It's not a quirk. Or a flaw. It's just you, and I like you."

"I quite like you, too, beautiful."

11

ZANDER

"Hi, Mom," I answer the phone tentatively. She rarely calls with anything other than bad news or the gripes she's had my whole life.

"Zan, what is going on in Seattle," she asks, sounding far more aghast than anything could warrant.

"I don't know what you mean, Mom. I'm working, and Seattle is my new home. You know this."

"I saw that article on the internet," she hisses into the phone. "What if your sister had seen it?"

"What article," I ask, although I know what she's talking about.

"The one about you being a homosexual, Zander." She's whispering now, as if just saying the word threatens to send her to Hell.

"It's just a cheap gossip site," I explain. The team's legal team hasn't been able to get the post removed. Short of paying off the author, which I was adamant about not doing, we have no grounds to have it pulled. Paying them off only gives the story more credence and I don't want the asshole to win by getting my cash. It sucks that my fourteen-year-old sister might see it. Callie has a tender heart. Someday we'll be able to have a conversation about it, free of our parents' bullshit, and she'll understand. I think, anyway.

"Is it true?"

"Mom." I sigh. "I'll tell you the same thing I'd tell anyone who asked me that. It's not your business."

"Of course, it's my business," she says. I can hear the tears and hysterics kick in. "How do you think that makes your father and I look? If this gets around, we'll be a laughingstock around town. I can't even imagine what Pastor John will say."

This has always been the way of things with my family. Whatever I do, or Callie does, is a direct reflection on them. But only the things we do that they deem bad. Our accomplishments have never mattered much at all. I'm the oldest of two siblings. My sister is a full decade younger than me. A lot changed when Callie came along. There was a time I thought my mom was going to divorce my dad and we'd get away from the toxicity that wafts off him like cheap aftershave. But then she found out she was pregnant. She wasn't the same after that. Besides, I don't know where we could have gone. Seems like half of the town is related to us. Among all my parents' siblings, I have something like twenty-five cousins. It's hard to keep track, even if I tried.

"Would you be this upset about it if you didn't think Dad will go ballistic if he hears about it?"

"Yes, Zander," she says, trying to sound convincing. *Lies.*

"I don't believe that. As far as the townsfolk and your congregation, you could just tell them that your son is a professional hockey player in The Show and how proud you are of that. It's more than any of their sons have accomplished, after all."

She's quiet for a few moments, taking in my admonishment. It won't change anything, but I refuse to bend any more for her benefit. She has options now, she has to want to take them, though. Hockey is second only to God in my hometown, and only barely. Me playing for the Blades should be getting them plenty of accolades to skate by on. Of course, they only focus on what they see as a negative.

"I am proud of you," she whispers. "Callie is too."

"You don't need to keep on like this, Mom. I've told you before, I'll move you both out here. Just say the word." It's an offer I make regularly. Each time is met with an excuse. She's afraid to leave him and I can't convince her that he doesn't matter.

"Your father has been so sick, who would take care of him?"

"Any number of family members can check up on him while he drinks himself to death."

"He's not their responsibility," she argues.

"He's not yours either. This was his choice. Make your own. If not for you, for Callie."

"Callie loves him."

"Callie is terrified of him, Mom. I'll remind you that if he hurts her in any way, I'll fight legally to get her here with me." My father has been known for an occasional drunken fit of rage. When I was younger, he directed them at me. Now, my mother takes the brunt of them. It's surprising Callie hasn't been caught up in one, but I know my mom tries hard to protect her from them.

"She can't go without me."

"Then come with her. You'd both love it here. It's beautiful with the water, the mountain, and all the trees. Plus, we don't get five feet of snow every year here." That gets a small laugh out of her because she hates winters in Minnesota. "Please."

"I'll... I'll try."

It's the best I've ever gotten out of her, even if I don't believe it. The past couple of days have been the best in my life. I'm playing the game I love on the highest level. Outside of work, I have Willa and Damian. I won't let my mother's judgment or her lack of action damper my mood. Not when I know it's all for my father's sake anyway.

When I get to Damian's, food in hand, it's Willa who answers the door.

"Hi," she says with a huge smile brightening her face. It's the kind that makes her eyes sparkle, my favorite kind.

"Hi back," I tell her, then lean down to kiss her. I mean for it to be a small gesture of hello, but she tastes too good, and I step closer, keeping it going. The bag of food is lifted out of my hand, I assume by Damian, but I don't stop to check. Dropping my backpack, I use my free hands to cup her ass and haul her up, while she wraps her legs around my waist.

"I like how you say hello these days," she tells me when I finally let her up for air.

"Good, get used to it."

"Yes, sir," she says and fuck if that doesn't go straight to my cock.

"Hungry," I ask, walking her into the kitchen and dropping her pretty ass on the island.

"Famished. Damian hasn't fed me all day."

"Lies," he protests. "You've ate everything I had in my kitchen."

"Which was an apple and snack pack the size of M&M's," Willa says. "How do you survive?"

"Takeout and delivery, like any civilized college student."

Damian has told me how much he likes Willa and how well they get along, but this is my first time witnessing just how well. There's something comforting about their banter, like they're old friends or a couple that's been together for years.

"How was practice," she asks me as he works on setting out plates and silverware.

"Good. Cill took the ice," I say.

"Oh good, that's a relief," she says. "And also annoying that Isla didn't let me know."

"She was at the Iceplex today with some camp kids, and your mom has Sadie."

"I'll forgive her then, since she had a busy day. Mostly only because I can smell the food and my hangry self is dropping rapidly knowing I'm about to stuff my face," she teases. "The Edmonton game's on if you want to go watch. I can dish you a plate."

"You don't have to do that."

"I offered, big guy. Go, take a load off."

Taking her up on the offer, I kick off my shoes and get comfortable. She knew I'd want to watch this game because Edmonton is only one game ahead of us in the standings and we play them twice in the next few weeks. It's something I'd expect from Isla, she often spent time with me watching other teams play. It shouldn't surprise me that Willa is so in tune with my life, but I didn't expect it.

We watch the game as we eat and it's Willa who gives commentary and hockey lessons to Damian. She also points out player weaknesses to me, in case I've missed them. And some I have. Isla once told me that it's easier for her to see things because she doesn't have to focus on being a player in the game, so maybe it's the same for Willa. Both know their shit, even if Willa has always been quieter about it.

"Offsides. Right," Damian asks.

"Good call, rookie," Willa praises him. When a whistle sounds, she stands and grab our plates, taking them to the kitchen. We both follow her with our eyes.

"Did you have a good day?"

"We did," Damian says. "Hung out here all day, cuddled up on the couch, watching television."

"You're really that comfortable with her, aren't you," I ask.

"She settles me. I can't explain it," Damian says, a touch of awe in his voice.

"No need to, it's just her. She has that effect on people," I tell him. "I have a gala coming up. I thought I'd ask her to go with me."

Here's where things get sticky, because I can't publicly date Damian, or even Damian and Willa. No matter how much that appeals to me. If all my public appearances are with her, how will that make him feel? It's not fair, it's not right. Maybe if I was at the end of my career, I could make a bold statement. But at the beginning? No. I have no prospects outside of hockey, this is it for me.

"Get out of your head, Alexander. I understand," Damian interrupts my intrusive thoughts.

"How do you always know when I'm overthinking?"

"Because you get a little furrow right here," Willa says, touching my forehead when she walks back into the room. "And you rub the back of your neck. What's going on?"

"The team is expected to attend a charity gala next week, and I thought I'd ask you to go with me."

"Oh. Let's talk about that, then." She comes to sit between us again. "How do you feel about the big guy taking me?"

"I give him taking you to public events my full support," Damian answers, he leans back raising his arms behind his head.

"There wouldn't be any hard feelings?" Willa asks him.

"None at all. I can't fill that position in Alexander's life, so I'd be happy if you can," he answers. "I'm not a jealous person. I'm certainly not a selfish one. Your careers are important to you, therefore they're important to me. The suit shopping incident taught me a lot about how the league works. I'm perfectly content being a background player."

"You aren't a background player in my life, though, Damian. You've been the star player for a while now." I know as soon as the words are out, that it may not have been the best choice of words. "That doesn't mean you aren't important too, Willa."

"Stop right there, Zan," she says, holding up a hand. "You two have established a relationship that I'm only just stepping into. Understandably, Damian would be your biggest concern here."

I stand and pace the room because that's not right either. Frustration weighs me down like a brick. I don't know how to navigate this.

"That isn't what I'm trying to say. You aren't less of a concern," I tell her. "How can this work if I can't even get through twenty-four hours without making it more complicated?"

Willa flops down on the couch, putting her head in the spot I just vacated. Her soft curls fall over the edge and tickle the rug.

"You're obsessed with Damian, I'm obsessed with you, he's obsessed with me. What's so complicated about that?"

Is she serious? That's how she sees us? She's not wrong, but I am also obsessed with her. And Damian is obsessed with me, right? When I look at him to ask the question, he appears amused. She must be teasing me and I'm just the bone head that walked right into it.

"Do you think I'm not obsessed with you," I finally ask her.

"I don't know, but I'm not sure how you could be. You and I weren't pen pals or anything while you were in California. But you and Damian were," she says it so easily, as if it doesn't bother her at all. But how can it not? It bothers me that she feels this way.

"That's because I knew starting something with you would lead to more and I wasn't willing to tempt you away from your life here."

"Oh God. Now you sound like Cillian. Remember he had similar thoughts and it led to the worst five years of his life," she says, sitting back up now. "This isn't a romance novel, Zan. We don't need years of miscommunication and misunderstanding. From here on out, we communicate with nothing but openness and honesty. Deal?"

"Deal," Damian says.

"You know that goes both ways, right? You've been just as quiet about your feelings toward me, as I have toward you."

"Because I saw you at work years ago and figured you were gay. As soon as Damian set me straight, I've been an open book."

"Fuck, I didn't think you saw me that night." I remember that night. I hadn't been in Seattle for long and wasn't a top player for the Timberwolves yet. In a moment of rare bravery, I thought I could go to a gay club and meet some random that would never need to know who I was. Willa was working there, and as soon as I saw her, I bailed out.

"Well, I did, and I thought the best thing was to back right off. So, deal or no deal, big guy?"

"You going to quit lying about how good you are at bowling?" The sport was in our regular rotation of activities when I lived here before. I always beat her and Isla, who admittedly sucks, but I know Willa threw every game.

"Fine," she agrees. "But be prepared to lose. Like every time. I'm that good."

"Deal, with the condition that you understand I'm equally obsessed with you as he is," I say, pointing at Damian who's still looking smug in the corner.

"Well, you're going to have to do more than say some words. But, sure," she says, smiling up at me. "So, yes, Alexander Fane, I'll accompany you to your fancy gala. And we won't worry about Damian feeling left out because we're a tripod and we're nothing without all three legs. Or something like that."

"A tripod?" Damian laughs. "Triforce would be better."

"I'm sure there's some sort of copyright infringement there, though," she sasses.

"Triad," I throw out.

"That sounds old and stuffy."

"Throuple?"

"Gross, watch your mouth, Mr. March."

"Triplex," I say, already knowing how dumb it sounds.

"A residential property we are *not*," she says, faking exasperation.

"Triptych."

"Oh, look at the big brain on Damian. I like that one. Triptych, it is."

"I'm not even sure what that means," I grumble.

"It's okay, big guy, we'll teach you." She pats the cushion next to her. "Now come sit, third period is about to start, and I need man-sized pillow to get comfortable with."

"I'm right here, Willa," Damian teases her.

"I fell asleep on you once already today; I don't want to push my luck."

We end up in a pile with Willa's head on my chest and Damian's on her hip. Somehow, it all works.

Somehow, it all just works.

12

DAMIAN

W hen the clock runs down on Edmonton's win, I walk to my bedroom, dropping clothes as I do. I don't have to look back to know they'll follow. We've had a good evening, after an even better day with Willa. The more relaxed we got while watching the game, the more aware we became of each other though. So, I know without a doubt, they're both ready to shed clothing too.

Despite how I feel about them, despite how badly I want to sink my dick into something warm and soft, there's something I want more right now.

I want to watch.

Naked, I drop into the large chair I placed in the corner for this very reason. It wasn't needed, but tonight, that changes. Tonight, I want the perfect view of Alexander's divine cock sliding in and out of Willa's pink pussy.

He walks through the doorway carrying Willa in his arms, and her eyes find me immediately. The heat between us making my skin tingle with anticipation. She holds herself back from me. It's appreciated as much as it is maddening.

Willa Cole is the most unexpected thing in my life. There's a feeling I get when I look at her, as if I have met her before and I should have been spending my life finding her again. Only I hadn't remembered. Maybe she and I were connected in a past life? Maybe all of us were, because she looks at him the way I look at her. With a recognition that goes deeper than this life.

"Take her clothes off," I say when he places her bare feet on the carpet. They're halfway between me and the bed. If I lean forward, I could touch her. I don't though. I won't, because I want her to be needy and I don't want to miss any bit of that. "Good, now show me that thick ass while you undress him, beautiful."

She turns, wiggling her ass a few times because she wouldn't be here if she wasn't always a little playful. When she has him as bare as the both of us, she faces me again. Alexander pulls her into his chest with his large palm placed low on her stomach. They're quite a pair. His rippling, defined muscles would be enough to make Michelangelo weep with desire. All the while, she's petite, soft, relaxed and ready.

Remembering the first time I sought her out on campus, I would have never guessed she was deliciously naughty. She carries herself with an almost puritanical classiness. Puritanical is the last thing she is and it's never been more evident than right now as she places her hand over his and pushes it down ever so slightly. She stops only when his fingertips rest an inch above where I know she wants them.

They both drag their gazes all over me. I'm not hard yet, but I've never had a reason to be insecure about my body or the size of my dick, even when it's just waking up.

"Did you know she's never been with two men before, Alexander?"

"Only in my dreams every night for the last… however long has it been since we met, Mr. March," she purrs.

She's fucking amazing.

"What happened in these dreams," Alexander asks softly, before he turns her head to take her mouth in a long, slow kiss.

"I think a lady needs a few secrets in life," she answers only when he allows the air.

"Are you afraid of anything," he asks.

"With you two? No. I trust you'll take care of me."

"Are you excited," I ask.

"Maybe Zan can answer that for you," she says and slides his fingers lower. Alexander curses as he feels her wetness.

"Her thighs are already slick; she's so ready."

"Add a finger," I tell him, taking my cock in my hand now as it takes more interest in what's happening. Willa gasps. It's almost enough to get me to stand up and feel for myself.

"Fucking hell, you're tight."

"You'll fit," she says, making him chuckle in her ear. She raises the fingers that have been tangled with his to her mouth, sucking two of them in. Her eyes never leave my face, except for the occasional dip to my hand slowly stroking myself.

Alexander wraps his other arm around her, lifting her and dropping her down closer to me.

"Lean forward, hands on the armrests," he tells her. She follows without hesitation. So close now, I can smell her. Still, I don't touch her. Alexander kneels behind her, and spreading her wide, he starts to lap her cunt. Willa's shoulders droop and her eyes roll up to the ceiling.

"Oh fuck." She sighs, her sweet air mixing with mine.

"What's he doing to you, Willa?"

"Fucking me with that devil tongue of his."

"Open your mouth," I tell her, then wet two of my fingers with her saliva before I move them to play with her nipple that hangs heavy above my full cock. "Is his tongue enough?"

"No," she nearly whimpers.

"What else do you need, beautiful?"

"I need him to fuck me," she says.

Alexander hums. I know how long he's waited for this, how long he's dreamed of her. He's more than ready.

"You don't want to come one time before he does that?" I tease her.

"I'd rather come on his cock."

Unable to stop myself, I grasp her chin and seal my mouth to hers, diving my tongue in to slide against hers. Alexander moves away and finds a condom wrapper.

"You ready," he asks. Her only answer is a moan that I swallow down. When he enters her, I move my hand to the side of her head, keeping her where I want her. My other hand still on my dick that's now more than ready for some equal participation. "Damn, Willa. I've wanted this for… ever."

She moans again, her fingers digging into the upholstery.

"Did you know that, beautiful," I ask her, pulling away to see the ecstasy she wears. "That he's dreamed of you, too?"

"No," she says on a pleased sigh.

"I have, too." I rub my nose against hers. "I'd find you in the coffee shop, studying and unaware of me. Watch you just long enough to have no choice but to rush home and imagine it was your mouth I was fucking in the shower instead of my hand."

"Damian."

"Fuck," Alexander says. Gathering her hair in his hand, he tugs gently, forcing her head back.

"Does that scare you, Willa?"

"It makes her hot, I can feel it," he says.

"Is that true, you dirty thing?"

"Yes," she says. "But next time, I want to watch."

"You're so fucking perfect," I tell her. She lights up with pride. Sliding my hand between her breasts, down her stomach, and a bit further, I play with her clit as Alexander's cock nudges my fingertips. I meet his eyes over Willa's shoulder and find him staring at me. Gently, I cradle his dick in the vee of my index and ring finger, simultaneously applying pressure on her clit with the heel of my hand. His eyes glaze over, and Willa mewls in my ear.

He pushes in harder, and Willa's head hangs to rest on my shoulder. A sweet kiss presses into my neck. A simple gesture that keeps us connected, like last night when she wouldn't let go of my hand as Alexander made her come. She may already be in love with him, but she always lets me know that I'm wanted here, too.

"Are you ready to come, baby," Alexander asks her between grunts as he pounds into her. I slide my fingers back to her clit, circling it until I find exactly what drives her crazy. She nips at my ear in her frustration, wanting to come, wanting it to last.

"Let go, Willa. There's plenty more waiting."

"I'm sorry," she cries when she digs her hands into my hair, anchoring herself only a moment before she falls apart. Face-to-face, I see everything she feels. Pre-cum drips down my cock, her reaction nearly enough to set me off. It's not real, but I swear I can see a thousand tiny fireworks explode in her brilliant eyes.

Without hesitation, I pull her in for another kiss, swallowing down the last sounds of her release until she's quiet, sated, and trembling between Alexander and me. About to collapse, I carry her to the bed.

"That was exquisite," I tell her, laying her down on the edge. Turning to Alexander, I slide the condom off his still hard cock and toss it in the bin nearby. How she didn't pull him into his own orgasm, I'll never know. The man has more stamina than any human has a right to. But here he is, gorgeous, hard and ready to keep going. "What do you need, Alexander?"

"You know I want that ass, but I'll take that clever mouth of yours."

My hangups about touch aren't the only reason he and I have never had full intercourse. We're both natural 'tops'. While we both like sucking cock, neither of us has ever been on the receiving end of anal sex. Everyone has sexual preferences, his and mine are so similar that it's almost comical.

"Why can't you have his ass," Willa asks, curiously.

"Like me," Alexander says, running his hand along her leg as he speaks. "He only likes to fuck, not be fucked."

"Have either of you tried it?"

"No," we say simultaneously.

"Interesting," she says. "Please proceed." Her smile is wicked as if she can't wait to watch.

"You want to direct this scene, beautiful?"

"Can I?"

"Yeah, baby," Alexander says. "Tell him what you want him to do to me."

"You'll tell me if it's too much?"

"I'm okay. I want him to touch me," I tell her and fall a little more infatuated with her for asking.

"Then drop to your knees, Mr. March. Alexander really wants to fuck that mouth of yours." She grabs a pillow from the head of the bed and tosses it down at my feet. "Make yourself comfortable."

Alexander chuckles again, making his cock bounce from where it proudly stands between us. I kneel, placing one hand on his ridiculously large thigh. The other I move to his base, but Willa tsks.

"No. Let him fuck you," she says. *Damn.* How every man in Seattle doesn't worship at this woman's feet, I'll never understand.

"You heard her, Damian. Relax, I'll do all the work," Alexander says, bending over to kiss me first. It's not long, but it's deep. He still tastes like her, and I chase him as he pulls away, amusing him further. To pay him back, I lick the length of him, from base to tip. Hard. "Fuck."

He palms the back of my head, finding the angle he wants. As soon as I open my mouth for him, he pushes in until fully seated. I swallow, making him groan in pleasure. Possibly my favorite sound in the world.

"Fuck me, you look hot with your mouth full," Willa purrs from the bed. She dangles her porcelain legs over the edge to gain a better view. Wrapping my fingers around one of her ankles, I tether her to me. To us.

Alexander slides in and out, slow and shallow at first. A short moment is all it takes for his pace to quicken, primed from being inside Willa only a minute ago. I focus on relaxing, my eyes turned up to his remarkable body, her hand tentatively reaching out to feel as his abs ripple from his imminent release.

"Fuck," he curses. His thumbs frame my full mouth. "Fuck, Damian."

The first drop lands on my tongue and it's my turn to hum in appreciation as he explodes down my throat. I take every bit and feel the slight tremble of Willa's leg in my hand. Before I have a chance to check on her though, Alexander is again bending over to kiss me, licking the last of himself out of me.

Her small whimper echoing off the walls is what breaks us apart.

"Oh, baby," he coos. "You need to get off again, don't you?"

"It's not my fault. You two are insanely sexy." She pouts, flopping back on the bed dramatically. Alexander climbs up next to her, cradling her cheek in his hand.

"Can Damian fuck you?"

"Only if he wants to." They both look my way, gauging my state.

"How wet are you," I ask. Fucking her is all my dick wants to do right now, even if my nerves are firing high. The last few days have been an overload on my senses. It hasn't been bad, like I told Alexander, she settles me in a way nobody ever has. But my brain fights it, telling me it won't last, or it's not true. It takes effort for me to quiet the invisible voices in my brain.

Willa starts fucking herself with two fingers. She doesn't have to answer me, I can see and hear the evidence myself. Instead of any signs of being ashamed of herself, she looks as if she's just accomplished something magnificent.

Where has this woman been all my life?

"Do I need a condom?"

"No, Damian. I only need you and that cock."

Pulling her to the edge with my hands under her knees, I slide into her. It is as incredible as I expected. Her chest arches up, and Alexander takes a breast in his mouth.

"Oh, fuck," she cries. He moves his hand to her clit, working her up to a frenzy. She's so responsive, her hips working to fuck me back with the same force as I thrust into her. "I'm close."

"Right behind you, beautiful," I groan. We end up coming together, her clenching cunt pulling me right along with her. I don't leave her until the aftershocks have passed. Her chest heaves where Alexander's cheek now rests. His eyes are hooded with the sleepiness that comes after good sex. I slap his ass as I step away from the bed. "To the bathroom with you, Willa."

"What?"

"Go pee, baby," Alexander explains, knowing where I'm headed with this.

"You're not even going to give a gal a second to recover," she says, laughing.

"Nope. Need you healthy for all future play dates," I say, and she smiles.

"She blows my mind," Alexander says, when she leaves the room.

Fucking same.

13

WILLA

I take my time in the bathroom, staring at myself in the mirror. Surely something has changed in my appearance after such a momentous night. But I don't see any signs of age or wisdom, and there certainly isn't a stamp on my forehead reading 'dirty birdy'.

Nothing we did felt particularly dirty, though. It was hot as fuck; I've never been more ready and wet in my life. Nor have I ever come so easily. Not even close. Yet not once did it feel scandalous. Watching Damian swallow Zan down was beautiful, not lewd. And how he held me the whole time was sweet and inclusive. I wasn't on the outside looking in, I was there with them.

Something about Damian has leveled the awkwardness Zan and I have always had with each other. We're no longer carefully tiptoeing around one another in whatever weird dance we've been performing for years. Like he's keyed us into his rhythm and now we're all in sync.

I like it here with them. But I'm also weary about getting ahead of myself, or getting too attached to them both when this is all so new for them. It can lead down so many paths and far too many of them leave me heartbroken. Remembering how that was for Isla, I don't ever want to experience it. While I won't run from the possibilities this new relationship has, I need to be smart and not let my body, and those amazing fucking orgasms, take the lead.

Dampening two washcloths, I return to the men, handing one to each. They showed such concern for me, the least I can do is help them clean themselves up.

"I didn't know if you wanted showers, or if this will do."

"I'm too exhausted to move again," Zander says. "This is perfect, thank you."

When they're finished, I'm invited to crawl in between them on the bed, facing Zan with Damian spooning me from behind.

"Are you good," I ask him, craning my neck to see him.

"I'm great," he says, pressing a kiss to my lips.

"Good." I snuggle in a little more. "How about you, big guy? You still have a bruise on your hip, does it hurt?" I noticed it last night, but that's not unexpected with his career. Honestly, I'd expect more.

"It's fine, not anything new."

I yawn as sleep creeps in quickly. "You know you guys can fuck my ass instead of each other's. I know it's not the same. I'm just saying, the option is there."

I fall asleep to their soft laughter.

***

"Oh, that's beautiful on you," Kit says when I step out of the dressing room in the Marchesa gown.

"It fits you perfectly, too," Isla agrees.

A shopping trip was needed since I have nothing to wear to this charity gala with Zander. The theme is the Blade's colors, black, white, and silver. All the wives and girlfriends have decided to go in silver dresses. I'm not technically a WAG, but I'm playing along for Zan's sake. Finding a silver dress worthy of the occasion on such short notice is trying at best.

This dress is a dream with its simple silhouette and plunging neckline. I'm busty enough that though the dress itself is quite classy, my shape gives it a nice provocative edge. If I must get glammed up, I want to go all out, since it is a rare occasion for me.

"But the price is a big oof," I tell them. I'd have to dig into my savings or use the credit card Dad insists I keep for days like this. Neither option is my favorite choice.

"Say yes to the dress, Willa. It's on me."

"No, Isla. I don't want you to do that for me," I argue.

"You can pay it forward by helping thousands of people when you're a hotshot head of a women's center someday."

"My chosen career path is never going to pay me Marchesa gown type of money." It won't come anywhere close.

"It's not about the money, Willa," she says. "Let me spoil you for once."

Looking in the mirror, I take in how magnificent my ass looks in the dress and succumb.

"Once, and once only," I agree.

"If you find me sitting in your closet, staring up at it, and dreaming of the day I have a reason to wear such a divine garment... no, you didn't," Kit says.

"Well, I hope you find a reason to borrow it. Something this pretty should be shown off more than once."

"So, how serious is it with you and Zan," Isla asks after the dress is purchased and we cross the street to a small French bistro that isn't very crowded, thanks to it being a weekday evening.

"We're dating, I guess. Seeing if it has potential and where it may lead."

"And how does Damian fit in to that?"

"We're dating, seeing where it may lead."

"Like a polyamorous thing," she asks.

"There are three of us in the relationship," I clarify. "We spend time together and separately. I don't know what the best label is, but we haven't defined much."

"Much," Kit asks.

"We've agreed that we're exclusive to the three of us. That's about it. It's early days, really."

"Sure, but you've already spent two nights with them. Which isn't like you, at all," Kit says. "So, it must be serious."

"Two? Already? Didn't this just start up," Isla asks, her signature concern for me evident.

"That sort of happened on its own." I shrug. "Other than the gala this weekend, I have no plans with either of them."

I know as well as these two do that I need to be wading in, not diving. Falling for two men before we know if we have a sturdy enough foundation to build off is a recipe for disaster. They've been inviting me over and I've been conveniently very busy for the last several days.

Zan and Damian need their time together, anyway. I don't need to be present for everything. Besides, my workload can't handle too many sleepovers. Not if I want to be awake for classes and lectures, anyway.

"It's more than just sex though?"

"Of course it is, Isla."

"Hey, don't blame me for asking. I'm just being protective of my only sister."

"I know you are. But you know me, and you know Zander."

"But I don't know Damian much at all."

"You'd like him, I think. He's a lot like Zan, quiet and reserved. Unless he's being flirty, then he's much more like me."

"What does he want to do after school," Kit asks.

"He says he wants to write books, help develop documentaries, and aid activists in exposing cults," I answer her. His passion about it is just one of the many things I'm coming to admire about the man. "He's smart, has an intuitive sense about people, and has similar interests as me, professionally."

"Kind of the best of both worlds, then. You get the athlete and the intellectual," Kit says.

"I guess so," I agree. "For Damian, too. As for Zan, he gets me, plus the bonus of a male version."

"Are you bringing them both to the next family dinner," Isla asks with a shit-eating grin.

"Here I am, basking in my all new sexed up glow and you wanna go ruin it like that?"

"Dad will be surprised, but he'll be supportive."

"Probably. But maybe only after he clocks Zan a time or two."

"That's just hockey rules," she says.

I laugh, because yeah, hockey players are weird.

"Did you tell Coach you were coming with me?"

"No, I figured he'd hear from you or Isla," I answer on the drive from our building to the aquarium where the gala is being held. Zander nearly mauled me when I opened the door for him earlier. It's flattering, but it took hours to get my hair to stay in this updo, he's not allowed to ruin it yet, so he was relegated to only a sweet before-date kiss. As hard as that was, because damn, the man wears a suit well.

"I didn't say anything, so we might be blindsiding him."

"It's going to be fine. Dad loves it when I'm around. Besides, he won't punch you in public."

"Jesus," he mumbles. I turn to stare out the window so he can't see my smirk. No need to amp up his anxiety. As soon as we drove off, he reached to hold my hand over the center console. I circle my thumb on his hand to try to relieve some of his tension.

"I'd give you a BJ to help you loosen up, but this dress is too tight for all that."

"Oh my God, Willa." He laughs, squirming in his seat. "You cannot say that kind of shit to me right now. The last thing I need to do is show up with a hard-on and you on my arm. I'm already struggling with how amazing you look."

"Not as amazing as I look with your cock in my mouth."

"You fucking minx, I'll punish you for this later."

"Ooh! Yes please, sir." I have a hard time keeping a straight face when I say it, causing both of us to burst out in laughter. "All right, I'll stop now. How's Callie doing?"

"I think she's doing okay," he says. I've met his mother and sister once, when Zander was playing junior hockey here and living with a billet family. She was a sweet kid. Shy but wide-eyed, taking in the big city. "She hasn't answered my calls in the past couple of days, which is weird."

"Have you talked to your mom?"

"Yeah, but that rarely goes well these days."

"I'm sorry to hear that. Any chance you'll be able to get them to a game to see you play soon?"

"Maybe when we're in Minnesota next week. We'll see." He pulls into the lot and finds a spot. Before we get out, he turns to me and hands me an envelope. "Damian gave me this for you."

Inside is a note and a credit card.

> Beautiful,
> This is yours for the night. Alexander knows the limit, he'll let you know if you get close. Have fun, spend my money on a great cause, and make sure the big guy enjoys himself.
>
> Always,
> Damian

"This was unnecessary of him," I say quietly. Thoughtful but wholly unnecessary. "This is like a weird *Pretty Woman* moment or something."

"I think you'll find he spoils those he likes," he says, brushing a thumb under my chin. "He likes you a lot."

"The feeling is mutual." I kiss the tip as it brushes over my lower lip. "I quite like you a lot too."

"Same." He leans over and presses a careful kiss to my lips. "Now, let's go show off that dress."

He comes around to the passenger side, helping me out of the car, then ushers me to walk ahead of him. I turn to see him filming me with his phone.

"What are you doing," I ask, amused.

"Sending live footage to our friend."

I twirl once and blow a kiss at the camera, before he shuts it down and shoves it back in his pocket. Grasping my hand, we walk inside as a couple. The large room shines with a blue glow, the walls all lined with large tanks full of colorful fish. A server offers us champagne flutes; I take one while Zan declines.

"Such a good boy," I tease.

"Always."

"Sometimes," I correct with a wink.

"Shh, that's our little secret," he whispers in my ear, sending a shiver down my neck.

"Willa?" Turning, I see my mother stepping up to us, my dad following close behind. "I didn't know you'd be here."

"It was a bit last minute, and I've had a busy week. Sorry," I say, giving her a hug.

"Oh, no need to apologize. I'm thrilled, we hardly see you these days. How are you, Zander?"

"Doing pretty good, ma'am. Happy to be back in Seattle."

"Hi, Dad."

"Hey, baby girl," he says, also giving me a hug. "You look beautiful."

"Thank you. I think you may know my date."

"I may have heard of him a time or two," he says in his Coach tone, which makes it much harder to know what he's thinking.

"Hi, Coach," Zan says, to his credit he doesn't sound nervous in the least.

"Is this something we need to talk about?"

"No, Dad. I love you, but my personal life is mine."

"Good girl," he says, giving me another hug. "Treat her right or it becomes my business, Fane."

"Yes, sir."

"Go mingle, darlings," my mom says to us. "Isla and Cillian are here somewhere."

"We should go find them. She's excited to spend time with you," I tell Zander.

"Ah, she misses me."

"She does," I confirm. "She definitely misses working out with you. She's been going with Cill, but he's too distracting for her."

"Those two are like rabbits." Zander laughs. "We should take bets on how many more kids they pop out." Again, he takes my hand and leads me through the crowd.

"It's bound to be a lot." We say hello to a few players, some I know, some are new to me. That's the way of it in hockey life. You never know when you can be traded off or sent down. Some of these guys could be gone next week and replaced with new faces. Not the easiest life for even a single guy, but a lot of them are married with children. Zan could be sent down at any time. Even if he isn't, he could be placed on waivers, or his contract not extended. There isn't a guarantee that he'll be here long enough for me to finish school. It's maybe what I'm most apprehensive about when I think about us.

I could always transfer to another university, but his next stop wouldn't be a guaranteed a long-term stay either.

There you go counting chickens before they're hatched, Willa.

We find my sister in a swirl of blonde-topped silver dresses. I smile devilishly at her discomfort as I try to rescue her.

"Hi ladies," I greet the women. "Can I borrow my big sister for a few?"

"Thank you," she says discreetly after a few minutes of polite chatter and when we're out of earshot. Isla grew up hanging out with boys, she's useless in a henhouse.

"You got it," I say, taking her arm in mine and leading her to where I left Zan chatting with Cillian and Gavin Vaughn.

As expected, Isla monopolizes my date's attention for the next twenty minutes as I make friendly conversation with Vaughn. The poor man is dateless tonight. He and his wife of seventeen years divorced last year and he's struggling at adjusting to his new life as a single man.

"How is Tori," I ask, referring to his daughter.

"She's doing okay." He smiles. "She took a gap year, not wanting to make things more difficult with the divorce happening. She's been living with her mom in New York, but travels to about half of our games."

"It must be hard having her across the country."

"You have no idea. But I think she may move here for school next year." He holds up his hands, showing me his crossed fingers.

"Oh, that would be wonderful. What's she going to study?"

"Fashion Design."

"And she's choosing to move here instead of staying in New York?"

"Believe it or not, for how much she hated the initial move here, she fell in love with the Evergreen State."

"Oh, that I can believe," I tell him. After all, there are few other places I've traveled to that I could see loving as much as the Pacific Northwest.

Dinner is served before the silent auction is opened along with the dance floor. While we eat, a few people speak about the charity, the team and the arena back. Including my father, who shows a rare moment of the charming personality he always showed to his wife and daughters. It's probably good for his players to see, it makes him relatable.

The items up for auction are luxurious. Quite a few are extravagant vacations, but only for two people. Not three. So, I skip over those, as well as items I don't think any of us will find much use in. The first item that catches my attention is a Cartier Trinity bracelet. Dainty and sparkling with a gold band, a rose gold band, and one encrusted with tiny diamonds. I run my finger along the dainty chain.

"How much do you think it's worth," Zander asks, tickling the shell of my ear.

"About three thousand," I guess, trying to remember prices when I was helping Dad pick out a piece for my mother on their last wedding anniversary.

"You should place a bid. It's the right piece."

"I don't know, it's so expensive," I say. The starting bid is set twenty-five hundred and it's been upped twice. Currently, it sits at six thousand.

"Not for him, and he'd love to see that on your wrist." When I hesitate, Zander takes the decision from me. Writing down a ridiculously high number.

"Zander," I hiss.

"Trust me, Willa. You're still nowhere close to the number he gave me. Keep looking."

"You're joking," I say in disbelief.

"Not even a little, gorgeous," Zander answers, wrapping his fingers around my waist to lead us to the next item. "He has more money than he knows what to do with."

We place bids on a few other items, at much smaller amounts, because it still feels wrong spending his money when he's not here. When we reach the end of the line, I excuse myself to use the ladies' room. When I get back, he's talking to a couple of people I'm not familiar with. He sees me and waves me over.

"Michael is going to take some pictures of us," he tells me, leading me to the dance floor.

"Okay, does he want us to pose?"

"No, just dance with me. He's going to take candid shots." Zander wraps me up in his arms and begins swaying us to the music. Though it isn't supposed to look like a photo opportunity, it feels like one in subtle ways. He feels stiff around me, uncomfortable.

"Hey," I say, placing my palm on his jaw. "Relax, it's just me."

He drops his forehead to mine and slides his hand lower down my back, nearly to my ass. Yet he doesn't relax even as the song plays on. As it ends and we walk off, I see Isla looking on, a concerned ruffle on her brow.

Did I miss something?

14
ZANDER

It's taken days but my mother finally agreed to drive down to St. Paul for my game. The first she'll have attended since I was called up. The first she'll have attended in almost two years. I lied when I told her I could only manage two tickets when she wanted three. My father only wants to be there for some misplaced bragging rights. Fuck that. If he had any role in my success, it's because I worked harder to ensure I could escape him.

No doubt he'll make her feel guilty about going without him, but she, and especially Callie, deserve the night away from his drunk ass.

"If you lot are going to forecheck as well as you did last game, the least you could do is come down to my net and say hi occasionally. I got lonely the other night." Blom pouts in the locker room as we go through our pre-game habits.

"Ah, Bloomy, you need a friend with you in the net," Lehtinen teases.

"Yes, damnit. All I have is my posts to talk to and they're boring company," he says. "It's lonelier than my bed down there."

The guys laugh, but we know he hooks up with random fans enough for his bed to stay warm. Some of the guys in the league call them puck bunnies, which has always sounded too derogatory for my liking. Maybe I'm more sensitive to that because I'm queer. But some of the guys have married women that started out as a random fan hookup. Those guys are far more careful about what they call female fans now.

"We'll try and do better," Cillian says.

"You better fucking not," Coach chides to another round of laughter. "It's not going to be an easy match tonight, fellas. Be aggressive, get your shots on the net, and let's keep it as clean as we can. This team capitalizes on those power plays, don't give them the extra opportunity."

"Yes, Coach," I say in unison with the other players.

First period ends up being a grind with no goal on either end of the ice. We're all exhausted and happy to head back to the locker room for the first intermission. Though I never check my phone during games, I make an exception this time, hoping Callie or my mom sent confirmation that they arrived all right.

CALLIE:

These seats are great, Z! Lily is
going to be so jealous!!

"Who the hell is Lily," I mumble.

"I don't know, who," Vaughn answers from the stall next to me.

"My kid sister is here," I explain. "Says Lily is going to be jealous of their seats."

"How old?"

"Fourteen."

"Tough age for a girl. Tori was a beast between twelve and sixteen."

"That's encouraging," I say, making him chuckle.

"Eh, it'll pass. They're formidable years for girls, it's when they figure out who they are. Us shitheads trail way behind."

"Some of us still don't have it figured out," says Wallin from my other side.

"You don't, that's for fucking sure," Cillian snarks.

"Fuck you, Wylder. Let's ask that pretty wife of yours when you got your shit together."

"Yeah, let's not," Cillian answers, making Wallin laugh. "They live up North?"

"Mhm, a few hours away. Right near the border," I answer.

"She's gonna be dating smelly hockey boys," Letty says.

"Not if I can fucking stop it," I gripe. Which I can't, of course. Not from Seattle anyhow.

"I bet Coach used to say the same thing about his daughters, and now look at them," Wallin chimes in.

"In what world did you think it was okay to bring my daughters up in the locker room," Coach hollers from the other side of the room.

"Sorry, Coach!"

We all get our heads back in the game and talk through any adjustments the lines need to make. I rehydrate with my favorite sports drink and try to ignore my sister almost being old enough to date.

The rest of the game is just as rough as the first period, but we manage to win with two goals in the third. Wasn't the prettiest game, but a win is a win. Though I try to shower and clean up as quickly as possible, I have a few new cuts and bruises that take some additional attention. Tonight was brutal, and I took the end of the stick to my jaw as proof. It looks worse than it feels, thankfully. Still, it's bad timing. Callie always hated seeing me beat up when she was younger.

She doesn't notice when she launches herself at me as soon as she sees me exit the locker room area.

"It's good to see you, baby sis," I say into the knit cap that's containing her mass of hair. "Did you have fun?"

"Yes! Mom cried." I set her down and give my mom a hug next.

"How was I supposed to help that," she asks, a few new tears leaking out of one eye. "I'm so proud of you, Zander."

"Thank you, Mom. And thanks for driving down."

"Oh, you know I'd be at all of your games if I could," she says. We both know what stops her from coming to more, of course. My father. My manipulative, volatile, and needy father. He hates it when she's not there to tend to his every need and continue to fill his cup with vodka. It's been the way of things for as long as I can remember.

"You got two assists tonight, Z! It was amazing," Callie squeals, throwing her hands in the air. The sleeves of the jersey she wears, the one I sent her only a couple of weeks ago, slide down her arms, chilling me to the bone.

Around one of her small, pale arms is a dark and ugly bruise. Gently, I reach for her as she hurriedly tries to cover the slipup.

"Callie, let me see." Something in the way I say the words stills her and I fear I'm scaring her. But I have to see. When I pull her sleeve up, it reveals exactly what I expected. A clear imprint of fingertips that held on far too tight. "When?"

"It happened when I was playing volleyball," Callie starts to say, her voice trembling.

"No, it didn't. When," I ask my mother again.

"Last week. Callie accidentally knocked over a cup," she says, sensing I won't let another lie pass.

"Are there more," I ask Callie, and she shakes her head vigorously. "Have there been other times?"

Now, her eyes fill with unshed tears. If you could feel your heart break, surely, I'd be on my knees in pain right now. I pull her into my arms and glare at my mother. How can she continue to let this happen? It was bad enough he treated me horribly, but Callie is small and sweet. She doesn't fight back like I always did, and she can't stand on her own.

I can't remember a time when I liked my father. Now, all I have for him is vitriol. Her small body shakes in my arms. Red colors my vision as I focus it on my mother.

"It hasn't been often," she says apprehensively.

"Once is too often," I grind out through a tight jaw. "What did I tell you?"

"Zander," she hisses because my voice is rising and there are so many people still lingering.

"What did I tell you," I ask again.

"Hey, is this the little sister I keep hearing about?" Cillian says, stepping up beside me and placing his hand on my shoulder. Callie's eyes widen.

"It's Cillian Wylder, Z," she whispers.

"Yeah, Callie, it is. Maybe we can get him to sign your sweater." I look at him for a little help, and he nods in understanding.

"I'd be happy to," he says. "Come with me. We'll find a few of the other guys, too."

"Thanks, Cill. Go have fun, Callie, I'll find you in a few minutes." I wait for them to walk away before I pull my mother to a secluded corner. "She comes to live with me."

"How would that even work, Zander? You're on the road as much as you are at home," she whines, and it frays every one of my nerve endings.

"That's not anything I can't figure out. Besides, I'd quit the game if that's what I had to do to keep her safe."

"Zander," she begins to argue.

"It's more than you can say, though. Isn't it? You wouldn't leave him to keep either of us safe." Tears well instantly in her eyes. Maybe I should feel bad, but I'm done sparing her feelings. "You either leave him together, or I hire an attorney and fight like hell for her. He doesn't lay a single finger on her ever again. Do you understand me?"

"I don't know if I can leave, Zan," she says through soft sobs. This is always what she says. Sometimes she'll add that she still loves him, sometimes it's because the church would frown upon a divorce. Other times, it's the adage of what people would think.

She should be more concerned about what her children think. Or what her community thinks of her being a punching bag and how she allows that to transfer over to her daughter. I love my mother, but she makes it hard to respect her.

"Then don't." I give a shrug, pretending I don't care. It's a lie. I want her safe and away from him, too. That decision is solely hers to make, however. "Stay in the hellscape you've made together. But don't damn her to it."

When I find Callie, she's surrounded by a handful of other players, all of them signing her jersey.

"Everything okay," Cillian asks me.

"No. I need to find a way to gain custody of her. Soon."

"I can email my attorney tonight, have him get in touch with you tomorrow."

"You don't have to do that," I protest.

"I saw the bruise, so I'll have to disagree with you on that one."

"Thank you, Cillian. I owe you one."

"You sure as fuck do not. Isla loves you like family, that means she"—he points to Callie—"is family too."

"Isla isn't too happy with me just now." She had a lot of questions for me after the gala. I tried explaining but she doesn't agree with how I've handled it all.

"She isn't, but I trust you'll fi x that when we get home," he agrees. "Regardless of that, she'd still want to help you. And so do I. We take care of family. Whatever you need, Zander. Understand?"

Nodding at him, I try to hide my emotions. It means more than maybe he knows. Growing up with a large family means nothing when they don't support you. Acceptance is what Isla has always off ered. I guess it's true when people talk about 'found family'. What does it say that Cillian will do whatever he can for Callie, a stranger, when my mother will do next to nothing?

I rub my temples, pressure growing so quickly, it's bound to be a migraine before I make it out of the arena and back to the hotel. As soon as Callie has all the signatures she can get, she hops back into my arms.

"You're the coolest brother ever," she says.

"And you're the most important person in my life," I tell her. "Keep your head down as much as you can. I'm trying to get you out of there."

"Okay," she says, but she sounds defeated. She doesn't believe I can do anything.

I aim to prove her very wrong.

"Everything okay," I ask through the screen of my phone.

We're on the longest road trip of the season and the only thing helping me keep my shit together are video chats with Willa and Damian. Our schedules have all made that more difficult than I like. Tonight is the first time I've gotten them both in the same place.

Only they are both acting weird.

Neither answers me.

"What happened? You both went to the capitol today, right?" Damian got in touch with one of the state representatives to talk to them about the legal age of marriage. He was taking Willa to meet them. "Did it go okay?"

"It went great," Damian says, a smirk playing on his lips. Willa sighs and looks down at her lap.

"Willa?"

"We had sex," she blurts. "It's my fault, probably. But he looked really good in his suit, like *really* good, and he was so eloquent in the meeting. It was all I could do to keep it together until we got back here. It turned me on in the same way it does when you get into a fight on the ice. But, anyway, I'm sorry."

Her outburst stuns me into silence for a few seconds.

"Sorry for what, exactly," I question, trying to keep from laughing. Her eyes snap to mine.

"We never discussed the possibility of two of us being with each other when the third isn't there. After the glow faded, I was instantly upset. Because here we are, fucking against the wall while you're away in Chicago with a bunch of smelly teammates."

"Against the wall, huh?"

"Yeah," says Damian. "She was wearing this tight skirt, with nothing on underneath, I might add."

"I didn't want panty lines," she explains.

"The little tank top she had on under her blazer is ruined though."

"You ripped it?" I ask.

"There wasn't time to remove it properly." His smirk has grown, and Willa follows our conversation with her eyes.

"You're really not bothered," she asks.

"I'm only sad I missed it, baby." The tension in her jaw eases and her eyes gain a little of their normal sparkle. This woman is too kind for her own good.

"I told you he wouldn't be upset," Damian says.

"I told you, I needed to hear that for myself."

"Well, now you have," I tell her. "Maybe you two want to tell me what happened in more detail, so I have something to satisfy myself with before I fall asleep.

Now, she blushes.

"First, tell us what's going on with Callie," Damian says. I've filled them in on what happened in Minnesota. Cillian got me in touch with his attorney, Mark, the next day, but legally, I don't have many options.

"Mark's drafting some documents, but right now, if I can't get my parents to willingly give me guardianship, there's no quick way to get her out of there." Without documented abuses, there isn't a lot we can do. It's not like I can just kidnap her.

"What if we pay him off?"

"Would that work," Willa asks.

"Maybe," I admit. My mother has said he misses more and more work since his drinking habit has increased. Many times, I've offered to send her money, but so far, she's refused. That doesn't mean he would. But in exchange for custody of my sister, he'd want a lot. "It would probably take more than I have."

"Not more than I have, though."

"I don't want you to do that."

"More than you want to get Callie out of there?"

"Of course not," I relent.

"Then make him an offer he can't refuse, and let's bring her home."

How much would it take for him to give up his daughter? She's an easy target, timid and kind. He won't want to let that go easily unless it's for a very attractive price. My stomach turns at giving him anything he doesn't deserve.

But for Callie, I might have to set principles aside.

"We can talk about it more when I get home. For now, can we circle back to how hot and bothered Willa gets when I fight."

15

WILLA

Spring is coming early this year. It's still early in the year, but with all the sun we've been getting, the plant life is confused. The cherry trees are starting to sprout their buds. I'm finished with classes today and meeting Isla and Sadie for an early dinner. The team isn't back until tomorrow so we're getting a girls evening in. I've been so occupied with school, and Isla with work, that we haven't seen one another since the gala. It's been longer since seeing Sadie.

I used to live with them both, before Cillian came back to Seattle. It was a hard adjustment for me to not see Sadie every day. They don't know this, but I cried myself to sleep the first few nights. She's where she needs to be though, with a daddy who loves her.

It's not lost on me that I was lucky in that department. My dad was gone a lot, but I never questioned his love and commitment to our family. Callie's situation makes it more evident. Zander has said he had it easier in some ways because he was gone for hockey so often. Callie is stuck there in that house with a volatile man.

There isn't much I can offer in ways to get Callie removed from her father, but I have promised to help however I can once she's here. If that happens. Zander doesn't believe his mother will come along, which would make him a single dad of sorts, who happens to spend as much time on the road as he does at home.

As soon as I walk into the café, I see Sadie waving from a window overlooking the lake. She jumps up and down, making sure she has my attention.

"I lost a tooth," she exclaims when I get to her.

"No way, let me see?" She smiles wide, showing a new gap. "Goodness, that's a big hole!"

"I know! It looks so cool."

"Because *you* are so cool," I tell her. "Hey, sis."

"Hi," Isla says. "I ordered margaritas."

"Thank fuck."

"Ooh, Auntie, you can't say that."

"Sorry, squirt. I'll do better."

"Good girl," she tells me, making me giggle. "Mom, do they have potato tacos here?"

"Yes, that's what you got last time. Remember?"

"No, but that's what I want. And beans! And chips with green salsa, not the red."

"Got it," Isla tells her.

Our drinks arrive and we order food. Sadie occupies herself watching boats on the water and making up stories of mermaids who have fish friends.

"How are things with Zander?"

"Good, I think. I've missed him since they left on this road trip. Which is new, I guess."

"Did he tell you we spoke the day after the gala?"

"No," I say, wondering what she's getting at. "He's your best friend, I imagine you talk often."

"This was specific. It was about you and your relationship."

"Why?" It's not weird that they'd talk about it. I talk to Kit about my relationships, it's what friends do. But Isla sounds far too concerned for it to have been a normal friendly discussion.

"I overheard something at the gala that made me uncomfortable," she hedges.

"I'm a big girl, Isla. Spit it out."

"Don't spit," Sadie says. "That's what Daddy does when he plays hockey. It's so gross."

Her esses hiss through her holey mouth. Isla waits for Sadie to start talking to her imaginary water creatures before she turns back to me.

"Audrey was there. She works in the PR department. Zan was talking to her and the photographer about the benefit of having pictures of the two of you."

Oh. That's not what I expected. I'm not sure what I expected, but not that.

"I can see how it would benefit him right now," I start. "Why not include me in that conversation?"

"That's what I wanted to know," Isla says. "When it didn't seem like you were in on the plan, I asked him about it. We argued."

"You never argue with him," I say, genuinely shocked. In all the years they've been friends, there's never been a ripple of drama between them.

"He's never dated my sister before."

"What did he say that made you argue?"

"That he didn't want to tell you he suggested being seen publicly with a woman would help kill the rumors floating around the league." I slump back in my chair. We've discussed the importance of honesty and yet he didn't want to talk to me about this. I'm not sure how I'm supposed to take that. "I told him he needed to talk to you about it, or I would."

"You threw him a line and he didn't grab it," I say.

"He does care about you; I don't question that."

"But not enough to fill me in," I argue.

"Maybe he's waiting until they're back, Willa. He's been preoccupied with Callie. And we both know he's a good man."

"We do. Doesn't mean I don't feel used, though."

"That's what I was afraid of."

The food is dropped off, and I eagerly divert conversation to other topics. Obviously, I have a big one ahead of me with Zander, but I don't need to drag our night down by hashing it out with my sister. Especially, when I hardly see my niece these days.

Sadie rambles on about school and how her teacher, Miss Ly, shows her how to write names. I dig out a small notebook and pen from my handbag and let her show me. She painstakingly writes her own with her pink tongue sticking out the corner of her mouth.

I've never had baby fever before. Maybe that's because I lived with Isla for the first few years of Sadie's life. But she's at a fun age right now and something inside me wonders what it would be like to have one of my own someday. And then I wonder if I'm in too complicated of a situation for that. I don't know if either Damian or Zander want children. It would only take one to say no.

So far, there hasn't been any sense of jealousy between the three of us, but would that change if I had a baby with one of them? My mind begins to spiral with all the subjects we've yet to discuss, and again, I'm struck with the idea that maybe I'm invested more than I should be. We just started dating, after all.

"Do you want to try my name next," I ask.

"Yes! It starts with this," she says, drawing a big W.

"You're so smart."

"That's what Daddy says, too. I'm smart like my mom."

"Your dad is no dummy."

"Nope, and he still has his teeth," Sadie says, as if her father's dental situation is somehow a credit to his wisdom.

For the past few days, I've largely ignored the guys. Besides responding in our group text, I haven't spoken or seen either of them. The time was needed, for myself, to clear my mind. Zander hasn't alluded to needing to discuss anything with me, which concerns me.

The time has come, however. I've sat with the subject as much as I can, and now, it's time to talk. They both threatened to knock down my door if I didn't poke my head out for proof of life soon, anyhow.

Truthfully, their threats were kind of hot.

I guess I'm 'that girl'. At least I know it.

Kit wants to go bowling tonight, and I invited the guys to go along. Maybe I can get out my excess emotion by kicking their asses with a ball and pins. Then we can have another discussion about the importance of honesty.

I have dinner with Kit before we head to the bowling alley. Dinner included a few rounds of drinks, and by the time we trek the two blocks to meet the guys, I'm tipsy from saki and full-on sushi. We still beat them there and have reserved a lane before they arrive.

"That might be the best bowling outfit I've ever seen," Damian says, giving me a once-over. I'm wearing a classic bowling shirt, black with pink accents, except it's not just a shirt, it's a boy-short body suit. I found it about a year ago at a vintage shop and fell in love with its quirkiness. This is the first time I've worn it though. It's fun, but I don't normally show so much skin in public.

"Thank you, sir," I tell him with a curtsey. "Find your balls, boys. You're gonna need them."

"You look good," Zander says, stepping up to me. "Missed you."

"Hi, big guy. Hope you're ready to have your ass handed to you."

"Is that how it is," he asks with a raised brow.

"Honesty, remember? I'm not fucking around. Tonight, you lose," I say, pointing my finger at him.

"Bring it on, Cole."

"Oh, it's already been broughten," I snark back.

"Fuck, girl. No more drinks for you." Kit laughs before handing me yet another drink.

"How many have you had," Damian asks.

"A few," I say, shrugging. "I'm good though. For real, grab your balls."

They both wander off, while Kit and I set up the names on the screen.

Big Guy for Zan, Richie Rich for Damian, Willard for me, and somehow, we go from Kit to Kitty Kat and then finally landing on Pussy for my best friend. Thankfully, this bowling alley is twenty-one and up, so I don't expect much backlash for that last one.

"Richie Rich? Seriously?"

"Best I could do, Mr. Money Bags," I tell him.

"You'll pay for that," he says darkly, waking up my lower regions.

"I sure fucking hope so."

They all bowl before me, each of them taking out some pins. Kit and Zan both grab spares, but Damian leaves two pins behind. I stride to the end of the lane and roll a strike. It's the beginning of a streak for me. After six frames, I'm ahead by more points than any of them can hope to overcome. By the end of it all, I win by nearly a hundred points.

"Holy fuck," Zan says. "I knew you held back, but damn, Willa."

"Too many summers in North Dakota with nothing to do but either watch hockey camp or go bowling next door. I chose bowling more often than not."

"I'll take a loss every time if you wear this outfit," Damian says.

"You'll take a loss every time no matter what I wear, Mr. March."

"Yes, ma'am," he says, holding up his palms as if surrendering. "You coming with us?"

I nod and we walk Kit outside and get her in a ride share before we jump into Damian's sleek sedan. He and Zander go on about my bowling skills during the ride, but I'm mostly quiet and contemplative. I have the tendency to be nonconfrontational with those in my personal life. With people I love and admire. Strangers are different. But I've never liked to make waves with family or friends. I'm like my mom that way, whereas my dad and Isla are hotheads. You can set my sister off at the drop of a dime and for the dumbest reason. While I slowly simmer and hardly ever boil over.

"You've been quiet," Zander says when we step out of the car.

"I've been thinking about a conversation we need to have."

He swallows hard, so I know he knows what I'm getting at. Nodding, he follows a few steps behind me into the house.

"Sit down and have it out," Damian orders us both.

"Will you let me explain?"

"I'm not stopping you," I tell Zander.

"Not once since we started this have I thought about being seen with you for the benefit of my career. Not a single time. When Audrey mentioned it at the gala, I was annoyed that she was probably making assumptions based off what I had said in our initial meeting. But that isn't why I invited you to go with me."

"Then why not be up front with me about it that night? Or even explain afterward?"

"I thought if you never knew, you'd never feel like I was using you."

"But you knew Isla would tell me," I argue.

"I did, and I thought we'd talk about it when I got back from the road. Discussing it with her made me see I was being thickheaded about it. But you've practically ghosted me since I've been home."

"Because I *did* feel used. Not because you let them take pictures of us, but because you weren't up-front with me," I say. "Did you know about this?"

"Not until today when he finally told me," Damian says.

"Honesty, Zander. Remember? We all promised that."

"I know we did, and I meant it. I've never had a relationship before," he reminds me. "I'm going to flub it from time to time, but I am trying."

I study him for a few moments. This isn't only new for him, it's not as if I've spent much time in serious relationships, either. The men I've dated never felt long term to me. They never caused me to think about futures or families. Not the way Zander and Damian do. Maybe that's why this entire thing was hurtful at all. Because I care about Zander enough that it gives him the power to hurt me. That is very new for me.

"You're shaking," he says, clasping my fingers in his and rubbing them between his palms. "I'm sorry, Willa."

"I don't have the experience either, but this only works if we're in it together."

"We are," he reassures me.

"The two of you need more time together," Damian suggests.

"I agree," I say, knowing he's right. There's something missing between Zander and me. "Maybe we don't know each other as well as we think."

"You don't think I know you?" Hurt flashes across his face, and I instantly feel bad.

"We're not as in tune with each other. It's why I thought you'd be upset that Damian and I had sex. He knew better, but I couldn't believe it. Our history has been buffered by Isla, and now him."

"Okay, I can see that," he says, rubbing a hand through his hair, making it deliciously messy. The physical aspect isn't what's missing, obviously. I heat up just by looking at the man. "So, we spend a little more time together. Just the two of us."

"Until you and I feel as strong as you and Damian do. Or Damian and I do," I say.

"I hate that we're the weak link here," he says, his brow crinkling with discomfort. He pulls me on his lap and wraps his arms around me. "I'm sorry."

"You're forgiven. We'll fix it, big guy."

"Can I kiss you?"

"Yes, please."

His warm palm lands on my cheek. It's a comforting and protective action that I love. If they always kissed me this way, I'd never complain. Zander's mouth starts slowly and tentatively. It's not until I wrap my own hand around his neck that he allows the kiss to deepen. When I open a bit more, he tastes me with his tongue and a pleasurable sigh escapes me.

"I know sex doesn't fix anything," he says when he pulls away. "But I'd be happy to help make it up to you in orgasms."

"How many do you think it will take?"

"As many as it takes for my mouth and cock to shine from you."

Oh. Yes, please.

16

ZANDER

Willa drives me mad. The attraction was always there, sure. It's more now, though. How she opens up and softens for me sets me to a new high.

I don't know if I can ever get enough.

They're both right, though. She shouldn't have doubts about me. That's my fault. I've kept her at a distance for so long. Willa's only asking that I be as willing with her as she's been with us. She should feel cherished and protected, especially since she came into an already, somewhat established relationship. I've already failed her, and it guts me to know it.

Kissing her again, I start to unbutton her sexy bowling romper. Her ass cheeks practically fell out of it each time she threw a strike. Teasing me all night long with both how hot she looked in the outfit and how hot it was to be schooled by her at bowling.

I'm as competitive as they come, but I find that same quality equally attractive.

Being better at things than her doesn't do shit for my ego, and fuck any guy who thinks that way. I want her on my level. Or higher.

Right now, I want to make her fly.

I stand and haul her over my shoulder. We need a big bed for the things I have planned. Setting her on her feet in Damian's room, I take note of the heat on her cheeks as she watches Damian take a seat in his favorite viewing spot. I strip off my clothes and toss them aside before helping her out of hers.

Then I lie down.

"Ride my mouth, Willa. Watch Damian while you do it."

She climbs up slowly, prowling up my body like a hungry lioness, her hair falling in soft waves to frame her heart-shaped face. Even though her cheeks still wear a bashful stain, she doesn't hesitate to run her fingers along my side and chest. Feeling every ridge of muscle with her soft fingertips. When she reaches my neck, she pauses, placing her hands around it and rubbing her thumbs in circles.

Damian chuckles in the corner.

"What is it," I ask.

"Willa likes your thick neck even more than your hockey thighs," he answers.

"Traitor," she hisses at him.

"Is that so?"

"It's a nice neck." She shrugs.

"My mouth is better, baby. Get up here, and while you fuck my mouth, you tell me everything Damian is doing," I tell her. "Don't be shy, fuck it like it's his cock."

Her eyelashes fl utter and I know I if fi ngered her pussy she'd be soaked. Willa loves to hear dirty talk as much as we like to speak about it. As soon as her knees are on either side of my chest, I grab her ass and pull her up the rest of the way.

My tongue hits her clit, and she grabs on with force. One hand in my hair, the other reaching behind her to land on my chest.

"Oh fuck," she cries. I hum my appreciation into her.

With my hands still on her perfect ass, I encourage her to grind all while I lick, suck, and thrust. It's only seconds before she's writhing all on her own.

"Don't let him down, beautiful," Damian reminds her.

"He's unbuckling his belt," she says, practically gasping out the words. Damian's belt snaps in the air—*I assume he yanked it off quickly*—and Willa gushes. "Fuck, that was hot."

"Mmm," I sound, hoping she keeps going.

"He's unzipping. Slowly, like the fucking tease he is," she says, and I can picture him, eyes laughing with a dangerous glint. "His cock is so hard already, Zander. He likes your tongue inside me."

"How do you like his tongue inside you," Damain asks her.

"It's amazing. Fucking fantastic," she stutters as I dive in deeper. "Damian's fisting his cock now. Do you think he's imagining it in your mouth? Or my ass?"

Fucking hell, this woman. I dream about fucking her ass, with Damian in her pussy. I can almost imagine how it will feel, the two of us moving inside her and against each other. That's not where we're headed tonight, but soon, I hope.

"Definitely your sweet ass, Willa," he says. His voice tells me he is just as affected by that mouth of hers as I am. I gaze up her body and watch as her fingers find her own mouth, and she moans around them as she wets them, not skipping a beat on the music her hips make on my face. When they're nearly dripping, she reaches behind her.

"This ass," she asks. Her hand brushes my fingertips that pull her cheeks apart as she starts to rub a finger against her other hole.

"Who's the fucking tease now, Cole?" His voice is dark, as he's struggling with the need to come. And possibly battling the need to touch her.

I move back to her clit, focusing my effort there. My dick really wants her to finish and get some play time of its own.

"Your damned mouth is pure magic," she whispers. "Pre-cum is dripping down his cock, Zander. It's so fucking pretty. Oh, God!"

She cries as she starts to fall over the edge she's been teetering on. Again, I help move her hips, letting her ride through it until she's heaving for air and I'm drowning in her. When she starts to mellow, I sit up, bracing her until I have her on her back between my legs.

"You have a dirty mouth, Willa."

"Not as dirty as yours," she says with a sly smile.

"Damian? Want a taste?"

"No," he says. "I want to watch you take that ass she's been teasing you with for the last few hours."

"Hours," she protests, and I answer it with a small swat to the flesh in question.

"You knew exactly what you were doing in that outfit."

"Maybe." She laughs.

I slide my hands up her legs, pushing behind her knees until her ass is up in the air.

"Hold it," I tell her, helping her with one hand. The other I use to transfer some of her own wetness from her pussy. "She's tight, Damian."

He stands, digs in a nightstand drawer, and finds me lubricant. While I prepare her, he takes his belt to the other end of the bed.

"Will you be okay if I bind your wrists?"

"Fuck yes," she answers him, eagerly. I'm not sure she's afraid of anything sexually. Damian wraps the belt around her wrists and makes sure she's comfortable with it before he returns to his position on the chair.

"Have you ever done this before," I ask her.

"Only a couple of times."

"Did you not like it?"

"I liked anal sex. I just didn't like the men attached to the dicks," she says as I slide my index finger in just a tiny bit. "Fuck me."

"In a minute. I want to be sure it doesn't hurt."

"It can hurt a little."

"Where the hell have you been my whole life," Damian asks as in awe as I am.

"Here, just waiting to be found." She wiggles and sighs. Obviously, she's ready. I let her legs down and roll her over. She immediately pulls her knees under herself and raises that pretty ass in the air for me.

"You tell me if it's too much, understand?"

"Yes, Zander." Her wrapped hands stretch out in front of her. She rests her chin on her arm and stares Damain down. I stare down at her and all the flawless, soft skin before me. Such a contrast to my hard ridges covered with bruises and cuts. I move to hover over her my cock nestling in the crack of her ass.

"I mean it, Willa. Be vocal. Damian wants to hear you as much as I do," I whisper in her ear before kneeling back. Spreading her again, I maneuver the tip of my dick to her entrance and push in just slightly. She relaxes and lets me slide in further. Once I'm in far enough, she clenches like a fucking pro and pulls me in. "That's beautiful, baby. Fucking perfect. You okay?"

"I will be when you and Damian start moving. I'll be even better when you both come."

"Fuck her, Alexander. She's ready, she can take it."

Still, I take my time with small movements, making sure she's not in pain or discomfort. It's difficult, my body wants to rut her like a mother-fucking animal. Luckily, I'm lucid enough to take it easy on her. This time, anyway. Until she starts to push back when I move forward. *The little minx.*

"Fuck your hand harder, Damian. Fuck it like you want Zan to fuck me."

My eyes snap to him and find him staring back at me. He thumbs the fluid leaking from his dick and sucks it into his mouth. I thrust hard, and both Willa and I moan. Now, Damian picks up the pace, his hand keeping perfect time with me.

"You watching him?" I stretch over Willa and grab her hair, pulling her chin up.

"Can't look away," she says, gasping again. "You feel so good, but I need more."

"What do you want?"

"Damian's cum in my mouth."

Jesus fuck. I can't help it now as I fuck her with abandon, while circling my free fingers on her clit, working her up again. She keeps up. So does he. The louder she gets, the more blood rushes to his neck, his face. I know he's close. I *hope* he's close, because she keeps clenching around my cock, and I can't keep it together much longer. It's too good, she's too damn good.

Finally, Damian stands, coming to the edge of the bed and winding the fingers of his spare hand in her hair with my own. The first spurt hits her tongue and I lose it. As soon as I start to fall over the cliff, so does she. Within seconds, we're all sticky, spent messes.

Damian picks her up and carries her to the bathroom. I follow and run the bathwater. It's a large tub, we can all fit, but it will be cozy. Damian seems over whatever was going on that kept him from participating. He wets a washcloth and starts to clean Willa.

"I can do that," she tells him, a little aghast.

"So can I," he says. "Don't get bashful on me now, Ms. Cole."

She starts a rebuttal, but he seals his mouth to hers for a long kiss. When the tub is half full, Damian and I climb in, one on each end while we help Willa to step in between us.

"Can I lean on you," she asks him before sitting.

"Please," he tells her.

The way she's so careful with him warms me up. She understands him. More importantly, she accepts him. Quirks and all. Like me, she doesn't take it personally when he wants or needs his space. It reinforces what we talked about earlier, she and Damian are in a good place. Her and I need to catch up. Obviously, physically, we're fine. But I need her to be as comfortable with me as she is with him.

"I don't have a game on Tuesday," I say. "Will you go on a date with me?"

"I'd love to," she answers, swirling her arm up and around Damian's neck while he lathers soap over it. My legs tangle with his, and I pull one of her feet into my hand, massaging it. "You guys spoil me."

"Other way around, I think," Damian mumbles.

"I agree with him."

We keep tending to her until the water turns tepid. While drying off, I hold Damian by the neck and kiss him. He mirrors my hold and steps closer at the same time Willa tries to step away. I stop her with a hand on her arm and pull her closer to us.

We end up falling asleep with Willa curled atop me, Damian's head on my outstretched arm and his inked-up hand palming her ass.

It's the best night of sleep I've ever had.

"Whatever it takes," Damian says. We've been discussing my father. More specifically, how much money to offer the asshole for him to give up paternal rights.

"I don't know what that means," I say. I know Damian is wealthy, but his version of wealth and mine may differ.

"Hundreds of thousands. Millions. Whatever it takes to give your sister a safer life."

Millions.

I can't fathom giving up that much money so easily.

"This is a lot to ask, Damian. You can say no." I pour myself a cup of coffee. Willa is still sleeping. She groaned in protest when we got out of bed and yanked the covers over her head. Her schedule today allows for a good sleep in, though.

"You're not asking. I'm offering," he says. "Is the attorney drawing up papers?"

"Yes, they should be ready in a few days. Before the All-Star break, anyway. I think I'll fly home and try to deal with it then."

"Do you want company? If he wants money, it's easier if I'm there."

"You're probably right," I say. "I still hope it doesn't come to that."

"I know," he says, taking a sip of his own coffee. "But better to be prepared for anything."

"True. With any luck, Callie will be here within two weeks."

"Do you have a plan for that, Big Guy," Willa asks, coming into the kitchen, wearing one of Damian's tees and a big yawn. "Teenage girls like space, their own rooms, a bed."

"If I get her and my mom doesn't come along, I'll take the couch until I can figure something else out." My options are limited. The lease I signed on the condo is for a year, I'm stuck with it regardless. But Willa's right, I'll have to find a larger apartment either for me and my sister, or my mother and Callie.

"Coffee," Damian offers Willa.

"Yes, please." She steps past me, but I grab her hand, giving it a gentle squeeze.

"Did you sleep okay?"

"Mhm, you two make great pillows." She bends down and kisses me. "Good morning."

"Morning."

Damian places a fresh mug on the table, before he, too, gets a hello kiss from her. She doesn't take her own seat, opting instead to let me pull her into my lap. Her hair still smells of the shampoo he used to wash her with last night. She smells like him. I like that.

A lot.

"I'm making avocado toast and a potato spinach hash," Damian says.

"With bacon," I ask.

"No. If you want to keep fucking like last night, we're taking Willa's advice and going plant-based."

"This is your fault," I whisper in her ear and tickle her side, making her squirm.

"I didn't know he'd run with it," she says, laughing. "We were just having conversation."

"About sex drives?"

"About diet," she argues, still wiggling on my lap.

"Stop that, I need to make it to morning skate soon."

"See, the plant-based diet is already working," Damian teases.

"Fuck that," I groan. "It's all Willa."

"Ah, thanks, big guy."

"What do you have planned for your birthday," I ask her.

"What? When's your birthday?"

"In a few weeks," she answers him. "No plans yet, but the family will probably want a dinner. So, I guess you should both prepare for that."

"All three of us," I ask. "With Coach?" She nods, and my relaxed, happy mood changes into something a lot more like fear.

17

WILLA

"Does this look okay?"

"Since when are you self-conscious," Kit asks from her spot lounging on my bed, as I stare at myself in the mirror checking every angle. It's a new dress that covers everything, but it is short. Not bowling outfit short, but close. Snug in all the right places in a metallic teal and fuchsia floral print that keeps it cute but still elevated. Zan told me to dress up.

"Since I have places to go that require more than yoga pants and over-sized hoodies, I guess."

"Well, you look amazing. So, quit it."

"Yes, ma'am," I say. "I don't know why I'm nervous." Butterflies have been dancing in my stomach all afternoon.

"Because it's Zander and this is your first official date."

"We went to the gala together," I remind Kit.

"Right. With your parents and your sister and like three hundred other people."

"Good point," I concede. I shake my arms and ease my nerves. It's stupid. This man's penis has been in… well, all my places and not made me anxious. Why should a simple date?

"Feel better?"

"Less nervous, more stupid maybe."

"You're not stupid, you're just human. Allow the emotions," she says, getting up. She swats my ass on her way out of my room. "This ass looks great in it, by the way."

"Thank you." I laugh.

A few minutes later, Zander is knocking on the door. I open it and all my frayed edges vanish when I take him in. He's wearing a black suit that fits him gloriously, highlighting his thick thighs and broad shoulders.

"Damn, you hockey guys clean up nicely," I say.

"You PhD students do, too," he says, leaning in for a kiss. "You look fucking delectable."

"Well, maybe after you feed my empty stomach, I'll let you have a taste."

"Deal. You ready?"

"Sure," I say and grab my clutch before waving goodbye to Kit.

"Have you ever dined here," he asks when we reach our destination.

"No, surprisingly. Lived here my whole life and though I've been up in it, we never ate here." Zan is taking me to the Loupe Lounge atop the Space Needle. It's the level that's all windows and revolves very slowly, offering three-hundred-and sixty-degree views of the city.

I've heard stories of how posh the place was back in the days when it was so new. Now the lounge offers a limited menu paired with upscale artisan drink pairings. Perhaps a little fancy for Zander's normal taste, but I appreciate that he's trying to make it a special experience for me.

The host seats us and we immediately start pointing out places we recognize below us.

"The regular menu is very mushroom heavy, so they're giving us a special menu."

"You didn't have to do that," I say, but he shrugs it off as if it isn't a big deal. They serve me my first drink that honestly sounds disgusting. Something with tomato and peach that we both eye with curious disdain, but once tasted, we decide it's not too bad. When the food and the next round of drinks come, I can't help giggling. "This looks obscene."

"I think it's supposed to be a mushroom cloud," he says through his own laughter. It's contagious and only makes me laugh harder. The drink is purple and served in an extremely phallic glass.

"Oh my god, this is the best drink ever."

"You haven't even tasted it, yet."

"Doesn't matter," I say with a huge smile. When I take a sip, I moan, and he laughs harder.

"I can't take you anywhere."

"You can take me *everywhere*." He winks at me, and the jitters start up again. Zander is a very good-looking man always, but happy and dressed up, he's a fucking walking panty soaker. "Speaking of, when are you flying to Minnesota?"

"Last game before break is Friday," he says. "I booked the first flight out on Saturday."

"Damian is going to meet you there?" He's leaving tomorrow for New Orleans, so I assume he'll be heading from there to Zander's hometown.

"Yeah, you'll be on your own for a little bit," he tells me since his Friday game is in Michigan.

"I'm proficient at taking care of myself."

"Still, I like it better when you have Damian while I'm gone."

"That's sweet of you," I tell him then take another bite of the tiny toast with fig jam. It does pair surprisingly well with my purple bulbous peen drink. "But I'll be fine, and you'll have enough to worry about trying to get Callie and your mom out of there."

"Speaking of, I had a favor I wanted to ask you."

"Okay."

"If things look promising at home, meaning if it looks like I'm going to be bringing her home, could I get you to run and grab some girly things for her? Set up my apartment for a teenage girl?"

"Absolutely, I'd love to help."

"Thanks, Willa. I really appreciate the support."

"No worries, big guy."

"What are your plans after school?"

"You know, hardly anyone asks me that," I say, and he looks surprised. "Ultimately, I'd like to run a women's center. There's a program down in Pierce County that works with homeless youth. They have their own coffee shop and roaster. It's a place where the teens can learn the skills needed to work and run the place. When they're ready they can take them into the workforce outside of the charity. I really love that idea and would like to duplicate it in some way. Maybe even try to find investors that would help women with the capital needed to start their own ventures where they could then help more women."

"That's a great idea," he says.

"I have a million of those. But this is the one that I've thought about the most. I want built-in childcare and counselors. Even an outreach for girls who are about to age out of foster care," I say. "What about you? Have you thought of post NHL plans?"

"I've had to. We don't usually have long careers," he says, and I nod. It's something I understand well. "I'd like to coach. Not in The Show or anything. But maybe peewee leagues where I can help kids develop."

"You miss being around kids?"

"I do. Some days more than others, but yeah. I'm one of the oldest of all my cousins, it's weird not having a bunch of munchkins running around."

Which explains why he never minded hanging out with my sister and my niece so much. My childhood was full of family, too, but on a much smaller scale since both my parents are only children.

"Do you want children of your own?"

He leans back in his chair and drags his gaze over me.

"Willa, I have dreams of getting a baby inside you."

Oh.

Flushing, I let him appreciate the reaction he gets out of me. We finish dinner and get a tower of macarons for dessert, along with another deca-dent drink.

If the path of this relationship continues, it's something we'd need to discuss further. I've never put a lot of thought into having children, fig-uring it would happen when it was supposed to. If ever. But if the three of us stick, and they both want children, how do we do that? Does anyone marry? Do the children take each of their father's names?

It's complicated, but it's also exciting to see the possibilities of families existing in non-traditional ways. And working.

By the time we leave, I'm full, toasty from liquor, and full of dreams of the future.

Once in Zander's car, his phone buzzes before we can pull out of the parking lot.

"Shit, it's Callie," he says to me, then answers, "Whoa, slow down. What happened?"

I can hear her rapidly giving information on the other end, I don't catch all the words, but I get the gist. Their father touched her again, and she's in hysterics over it. Rightfully. Zander loses it and starts rattling off every foul word in his vocabulary while she cries.

"Zan," I say, crawling over the center console and onto his lap. "Let me talk to her."

"I've got to figure something out. Fuck!"

"Zan," I say again, grabbing the phone. He relents, and I put it to my own ear, my heart breaking at her wails. "Hey, Callie. It's Willa. Can you tell me where you are?"

"I ran," she says, hiccupping. "I'm in the park."

"How close is the park to your house?" Zander wraps his arms around me but only so he can grab the steering wheel so tight, his knuckles turn white.

"A few blocks."

"Okay, do you have a safe place that you can get to?"

"Um, I can probably go to Katie's."

"Who's Katie, honey," I ask.

"She's my friend. Her mom is really nice."

"Okay, good. Does she live far?"

"No, her house is over by the ice rink." I don't know what that means, but I'll take her at her word that it's close and she can get there.

"Can you start walking there now? I'm going to stay on the phone with you until you get there. Okay?"

"Okay," she says. I check the time and realize how late it must be there.

"Where's your mom at, Callie?"

"She's at work, she took a second job at the hospital. She works in the laundry room."

"Oh, I didn't know that." Zan must have heard it, too, because he frowns.

"Is Zander still with you?"

"Yeah, honey. He's right here. Do you want to talk to him?"

"Yes, please. But thank you, Willa."

"Anytime, Callie."

I hand the phone back to him and he talks to her while she finishes the walk to her friend's house. Once she's there, he talks to Katie's mom and asks her to try and keep Callie there until he gets to town. She agrees to do her best, but we all know that if her parents show up, all bets are off. However, Katie's uncle is one of the town's deputies and her mom promises to call him and see if he can get involved.

It's the best we can do right now.

"He punched her, Willa," he says when he's finally hung up.

"I know. I'm sorry."

"Thank you for talking to her. I couldn't focus on anything but wanting to kill him," he says, dropping his head onto my chest.

"Of course, Zan. Do you want to call my dad, see if there's a way to get you out of the Detroit game and get you home earlier?"

"I doubt much can be done, but it's worth a shot."

We drive back to our building, and he proceeds to call my dad and the general manager. It's not my father's call, but Zan trusts his opinion over most other people's. His expression tells me it isn't going well.

"The only option would be to put me up on waivers," he says, ending his call. "It's too risky, I can't take that option."

Understandably, because if another team picked him up, he'd have to make another move. It could be anywhere, and he'd lose the support system he has built in here. And he would most definitely be picked up; he's been playing so well.

Someone needs to get to her as soon as possible, though.

"I can go."

"No, Willa."

"I can fly out tomorrow, check in with Callie, maybe your mom. I'll stay there until you can get there."

"No," he starts to say again.

"It's the best option, really. I'll be there if anything happens. It's only a few days."

"Willa, I don't want you anywhere near my father."

"I appreciate that, but the odds of him doing anything to me are very low. So, I'll go until you can get there. You can't talk me out of it."

His hard stare narrows, then softens after a moment.

"I love how much you care," he says. I try not to be affected by that particular four-letter word. "But I don't love this idea."

"You don't have to love it to see that it's the best move. It's the only one that doesn't impact your career."

"Damian can go."

"Are you saying it's a man's job? That better not be what you're implying, Fane."

"I wouldn't dare," he says, a smirk blooming on his mouth.

"Good. Then it's settled." I pull my phone out of my pocket and click on the airline app I like most. It only takes a minute then to find a seat on an early morning flight. "I can fly out at seven in the morning."

I'll miss a couple of classes, but I can email my professor and login to most lectures online. The assignment I have due can be done on the plane and turned in once I get to a hotel.

"To Duluth," he asks, and I nod. "Promise me you'll keep yourself as safe as you keep my sister?"

"Of course, Zander. I'm not going to do anything stupid. Just be a presence, is all. Besides, I'm family of hockey royalty, who's going to fuck with Coach Cole's daughter and Wylder's sister-in-law?" Cillian is as famous as it gets in the NHL, my dad isn't long behind him, and I'm going to the hockey heartland. I'm not worried.

"Shit, that's true. If you name drop, the whole town will pull out the red carpet for you," he smiles, and I'm relieved to see it. He's been so tense since Callie called. Not that I blame him.

"Where should I book a room?"

"I have one at the lodge, I'll call and extend it and add your name. You'll need a rental car, it's about two hours from the airport and the lodge isn't downtown."

"No problem," I say. "Try calling your mom again, I'm going to go pack a bag."

"Then come back here?"

"I can do that, big guy." I run my hand down his arm and give him a reassuring smile before I leave. It doesn't take long to pack a carry-on and my laptop. Then I send a message in our family group text, letting them know where I'm headed. Dad gives me similar warnings as Zander did. Be safe, drive carefully, etcetera. He has a friend in Eveleth, Minnesota, who I'm supposed to call if I run into any trouble. I'm not sure what everyone thinks could happen, but I shrug it off as just their protective sides coming out. I won't complain that I have people who care about me.

By the time I get back down to Zan's apartment, he's wiped out. Lounging on the couch, his fingers furiously texting on his phone with his eyelids only half open.

"Hey," he says, sleepily. "I'm letting Damian know the plan. My mother finally answered. She cried when I wouldn't tell her where Callie is."

"I'm sorry," I tell him, leaning over the back of the couch to wrap his arms around his shoulders. His hair is growing out, the waves soft against my cheek. "Let's get you to bed. We have some long days ahead."

Both of us strip down to nothing, but neither of us are in the mood for anything other than comfort and sleep. What started out as a perfect date night ended in far too much stress. After climbing under the covers, Zan pulls my back to his chest and cocoons me.

"Thank you, Willa," he says softly. "You're like a soothing balm all my frayed nerves. I don't know how you instinctively know what I need and when I need it. But you do, and I couldn't have gotten through tonight very well without you."

Ah. Be still my beating heart. If he keeps saying sweet shit like that to me, I'm never letting him go. Who am I kidding? I can't see ever letting either of them go. His words remind me of what Damian said about him, how he warms his heart. Funny how they are each so soft-hearted. You'd never expect it to look at them. Not with Damian's dark, tattooed looks and Zan's hockey build that always comes with a few bruises.

Even during sex, they talk dirty and fuck me good, but it's always with an element of tenderness and care. A constant pattern of checking on me to make sure I'm comfortable and finding as much, or more, pleasure as them. If luck or fate plays a part in any of this, I've been dealt the winning hand. A royal flush.

In love isn't something I've ever been. It seems it's true what they say, though. When you know, you know.

I *know* that I'm falling in love with two men.

18

DAMIAN

E ven in late winter, the heat and humidity in New Orleans can be impressive. Especially, when you've been living in the Pacific Northwest for so many years. I take in all the familiar buildings as I walk to the café where I'm meeting my oldest friend, Fig. I arrived in my home city yesterday and spent the afternoon with my financial guy moving around some things, setting up some new accounts and trusts. My priorities aren't what they were the last time we met. It was time for adjustments.

After that, like a proper dutiful son, I had dinner with my parents. It's mostly a farse, but I like to put my eyes on them from time to time. If for no other reason than to give my father the peace of mind that I'm alive and well and he doesn't have to produce another spawn to carry on the family pretention.

Wealth is great, I'm not complaining about it. But it's often a lonely life. Being here reminds me of that. Makes me even more appreciative of the family I've found, the one I've chosen and that has chosen me. The feeling is worth its weight in gold.

I get to the café before Fig and order from the server who looks like she hardly got any sleep but still places my cup of chicory with a pleasant smile.

"Thank you," I tell her. "Can you bring out an assortment of your fanciest pastries? You choose. My friend has a sweet tooth."

"Sure thing, hon."

"You're looking like a pasty ghost, Damian. What's Seattle doing to you," Fig asks, taking the chair across from me.

"Not drenching me in sweat every time I walk out the door."

"It's good to see you. Pale skin and all," he says.

"Good to see you, too, asshole." Fig looks no different than he always does, dressed in bright colors and prints that lend to his Creole heritage. His family has deep roots in New Orleans, everyone knows the Parnells for one thing or another. Either from business, their ties to the city's historical preservation, or for the fact that Fig's parents are the most notorious swingers in the state. His mother is part owner of a small and very exclusive chain of sex clubs. I used to be a member, once upon a time. Mostly because it was the best place to watch, as I like to do.

All of them, including his sister, Cookie, are eclectic, artistic, and classy with a side of geekiness. They're the best people I've ever known. I miss Fig, and New Orleans, but I don't miss the life I had here.

"How's school?"

"Nearly done, so great. It will be nice to be done," I tell him as the waitress comes by with a plate of pastries that make Fig light up with childish excitement. "How's Bree?"

"Great, five months pregnant."

"What the hell? Why didn't you tell me?" He met her a few months before I moved away. A sweet girl who flipped this man on his head so quickly it was almost comical.

"I don't know, she has some superstition about the first trimester or something. She swore me to secrecy until just recently, but by then, you had made plans to visit." He shrugs and takes a bite of something that's covered in glazed almonds. "What about you? Still talking to that guy?"

That guy.

Even with my best friend, I was always vague about my relationship with Alexander.

"Yes. Alexander's back in Seattle now."

"He played hockey, right?"

"Still does, he's playing for the Blades."

"You're dating a professional athlete?"

"Listen, I'm a motherfucking catch. Okay?"

"I know you are." He laughs. "Is it serious with him?"

"With them," I correct.

"Oh. Is he non-binary?"

I shake my head. "It's serious with Alexander and a woman named Willa."

"Do they know about each other?"

"Of course," I say. "It's something of a menage."

"You always could find yourself in the most deliciously complicated situations."

Isn't that the truth?

"What can I say? I'm in love for the first time in my life, it just happens to be with two people."

"Only you." He laughs again. "I bet that helps with your... proclivities."

"It doesn't hurt," I agree. "How's Cookie?"

"You know her, she's like a cat. Whatever happens, she lands on her feet and keeps going. She's been painting a lot, sold some even."

"Good for her."

"You going to see Delilah while you're here?"

"Probably not. I'd planned on a longer stay, but something has come up and I need to fly out tomorrow. Only here long enough to sign some papers."

Getting to Minnesota is imperative. The quicker we deal with Alexander's father, the better we'll all feel. "Next time, I'll bring Willa. You'll love her, she's smart, funny, and just has a way of making you feel comfortable."

"Can't wait to meet them both. I'd say we'd come visit you, but with the baby on the way… you know how it is."

"No worries, I'll try to get back soon. Maybe when the newest Parnell arrives."

"Bree would love that," he says. "Everyone was hoping you'd move back after school. I'm guessing that isn't happening."

"Not unless life fucks me over somehow. Willa's family is all there. Her dad is Alexander's coach. It just makes sense to stay put."

Zander getting traded will always be a concern, but I'm lucky enough to be able to follow anywhere he lands. It's something I never considered before I started feeling actual affection toward him. Alexander made me less selfish, and Willa even more so.

"You're in that deep?"

"I am," I admit. "Alexander is the perfect combination of hard and soft. Willa is passionate and dirty as sin. There's no judgment between the three of us. Honestly, Fig, it's been easy with them."

"You mean your anxiety? You let them touch you?"

"I *want* them to touch me," I clarify. Fig and I grew up together, and he noticed early-on that I was different than the other boys. When girls became the major focus of most of our friends, I took an even greater step away from the crowd. Girls wanted to hold hands, to hug, and kiss. I wanted no part in any of it. There was a party when we were maybe thirteen and a girl had pushed me into the closet with her, hoping for a make-out session. Fig saw and intervened, but I had a full panic attack from it. He made me fill him and became a constant buffer for me after that. His mother was the one who found me a therapist and helped me work through ways to handle my 'issues'. "I want to touch them, too."

"That's good, Damian. That's really good to hear," he says. Fig has always worried I'd end up alone. While he used to encourage me to go along with him and his dates, we both knew that would die off when he found someone he loved. "It's the death of the Voyeur Extraordinaire."

"He's not in full retirement just yet," I say.

"Still. You look happy, my friend."

"I am."

I really am.

It's early evening by the time the driver gets me to Ely, Alexander's hometown. The sun is just beginning to go down. He described it as small. I thought that was an exaggeration, but I can see that it's not. Not quite a one-street town. Close, though. When we turn on the road that leads to the hotel, I take in the beauty of the place. Even covered in snow, nature shows through.

It's cold as fuck, though. I have to pull my collar around my neck when the driver drops me off. As soon as I step inside the lobby, my body starts to thaw from a raging fire in the stone fireplace. A few people stand close to it, warming up themselves. The front desk employee smiles at me and I nod before taking in the rest of the room. It's a cozy place but dated and cliché with all the peeled log beams and furniture trimmed in buffalo plaid.

"Hey," Willa greets me. I'd texted her on my way, so she'd know when to expect me.

"Hi, beautiful." I pull her in for a hug and a kiss. It's longer than I planned, but she's warm and I don't want to let go too quickly. "There are dead animals watching us."

"They're everywhere," she whispers.

"Please tell me not in the room."

"Not in the room."

"Thank fuck for that," I say. "They're creepy as hell."

"Don't get too excited," she warns with humor.

"It's that bad?"

"It's more of this." She gestures to the décor. "But it's clean."

"Good enough," I say. "Are we still meeting Callie for dinner?"

"Yeah, let's drop your stuff in the room, then we'll go pick her up."

The room is straight out of a *Field and Stream* magazine. It's a spacious two-room suite, though, and she's right about how clean it is.

"How's Callie doing?"

"Better. Maybe too excited about the idea of moving to Seattle. I'm afraid of what happens if we can't get the go ahead."

"He'll sign," I tell her. I've never been more confident. Or more prepared. Whatever it takes is what I said to Alexander and I plan on following through.

"She has a bruise, Damian," she tells me, emotion choking her words. "He hit her on the face. She's lucky he didn't break a bone."

"Fuck." I tug her in for another hug. "Alexander is going to go ballistic when he sees that."

"I know," she mumbles into my chest. "She's very self-conscious about it, too."

She's probably feeling embarrassed atop feeling ashamed of her father. In such a small town, gossip must be spreading like wildfire.

"Tell me anything I've missed in the car. Let's go get our girl."

This will be my first time meeting her, or any member of Alexander's family. She won't know who I am, or who I am to her brother. It's good that she already knows Willa, I don't want to cause her any more discomfort.

"I talked to Ellen yesterday after I met with Callie. She said Steve's drinking has increased in the last few months. He lost his job and that only made things worse. Because she had to take on an extra job to make ends meet, she's gone a few evenings a week. Callie tries to keep out of sight as much as she can."

"She shouldn't have to hide in her own house," I say, instantly irate. Even in my own childhood, where I spent plenty of time avoiding my parents,

I never felt unsafe at home. Alexander has said, that though there were a few times when his father was physical with him, it wasn't an occurrence that happened often. And only when Alexander pushed the limits, itching for a fight as much as Steve was. It surprised him when Callie called him the other night. Not because she'd had an altercation with their father, but because it had been as violent as it was.

Unfortunately, it has soured his feelings for his mother even further as well. She's not a victim in the same way as Callie, but a victim, nonetheless.

"No. It's a horrible way to live," Willa agrees. "I think Ellen is inching closer to leaving him, but she's not there yet."

"Foolish. Though, I know it's not easy to leave abusive relationships."

"I'm sure it's not. Nor will it be easy to send her daughter away." Regardless, we're going to make the offer a tempting one. Willa pulls down a residential street lined with quaint, cookie cutter houses. All the driveways are perfectly shoveled of the fresh snow that blankets the rest of the ground. There was nowhere to hide Callie in this small town, but at least here, at her friend's house, any altercation would be noticed by the neighbors. It's as protected as she can be here. "She expressed an interest in going to a pizza place tonight. I guess they play all Zan's games on the televisions."

"Whatever she wants to do," I say. Callie exits the house as we park. She must have been anxiously waiting with her nose pressed against the window.

"Hey, Callie," Willa greets as we step out of the car.

"Hi," Callie says, her eyes darting to me shyly. She resembles Alexander quite a lot. The same round eyes, so dark they're almost black. The same flat tip of the nose. Only this girl comes with long waves of hair trailing below her knit cap. And a purpling bruise she tries to hide behind that curtain of hair.

"Hi, I'm Damian."

"I'm Callie," she blurts. "I mean, hi."

"Hop in," I say, opening the door for her. "I hear we're going for pizza and hockey."

She and Willa chat for the short time it takes to drive to the other end of town, Callie giving directions on where to go. She laughs easily, smiles genuinely, and has that same homegrown politeness as her brother.

Like Willa, she's impossible not to be enamored with. I've little experience with children, but within minutes, Callie has passed her infectious lightheartedness to me.

The restaurant is a hive of noise, the game is about to start on at least four screens that I can see from the entryway. It's crowded but not full.

"Hey, Callie," the young woman at the hostess station greets her. The expression she wears changes when she catches sight of the bruise.

"Hi, Claire. Can we get a table for three, please?"

"For sure," she says, glancing at both Willa and I. We offer soft smiles, hoping she won't make spectacle of the poor girl. She leads us to a table in prime position to two large screens just as the starting lineups are announced. Callie cheers gleefully for her brother, along with the rest of the patrons.

"Can we order pepperoni? Would that be okay?"

"Anything you want Callie," I tell her.

"Poutine?"

"Oh, man. Poutine sounds good," Willa agrees. "With Seattle being so close to British Columbia you'd think poutine would be easier to find on menus."

"I don't even know what it is," I say.

"Gosh, it's so good," Callie says dramatically. "French fries with gravy and cheese curds. It sounds disgusting but you have to try it!"

"I'll try anything once," I tell her. She resembles Zander. Same nose, same hair color, same shaped eyes. I haven't seen pictures of him as a kid, but I bet he looked a lot like she does.

They order the pizza, poutine, and a couple other appetizers when the server comes by. When it arrives at the table, the first period is nearly over. Alexander has already earned an assist in the two-to-nothing match.

Intermission comes and it gives the opportunity to get to know the girl better.

"What's your favorite subject at school, Callie?"

"Math," she says, brightly. An unexpected answer.

"That's great," I tell her. "I was never a fan."

"It comes easy to me," she says. "What was your favorite?"

"History."

"English is great. I love art, but we don't have that as a class. Oh, I do love history, too. Not as much as math and English, but almost. I really like Tudor history, especially."

Again, an unexpected answer.

"How'd you get into that?"

"Last year, we had to do a report on a historical European figure. We didn't get to choose; our teacher had a bunch of names written on pieces of paper in a hat. Anyway, I got Anne of Cleves, who was Henry the Eighth's fourth wife. Henry didn't like her because she wasn't pretty. But I've seen portraits of all six of his wives, and I think she was prettier than most," she rambles on. "But whatever, boys are stupid that way. And she came out of it all right. I mean, he didn't chop off her head anyway."

"Definitely better than the rest of the wives," Willa concurs.

"Did you know they had to have a crane to set him on his horse in the last years of his life?" I ask her.

"Yes." Callie laughs. "He'd gotten so big. He could have just not ridden, I mean, that poor horse."

"Right," I concur.

"Did you know he had servants that helped him go the bathroom? The Groom of the Stool." She giggles.

"So powerful he ruled countries and started his own church, but couldn't wipe his own ass," I say with a wink. She cracks up, a happy tear trailing out of one eye.

"Ewww, can you imagine?"

We banter back and forth with random quirky facts of the time period while we eat and wait for the game to start back up. Shortly after it does, Alexander scores a goal, and the place erupts with whooping. Several people nearby high-five Callie, who eats it up as her brother's biggest fan.

"All he needs now is a fight and Zan will have a Gordie Howe hat trick," Callie says, bouncing in her seat.

"What does that mean," I ask Willa.

"A goal, an assist, and a fight," she says. "All in the same game."

"Why is it called that?"

"Honestly? No idea. He was a famous player, but beyond that, no clue," she says.

"Hockey is a little on the weird side."

"That's what is so great about it," Callie says, turning over her shoulder to smile at me. Something behind her catches her attention and she pales. "No."

"What is it?" I follow her gaze to find a man having only just entered the restaurant. His face gaunt, but eyes full of anger as they lock onto Callie. "Is that your father?"

"What?" Willa turns now, too.

"Yes," Callie says quietly, watching the man make his way over.

"It's okay," I tell her, placing a hand on her arm. "Watch the game, sweetheart. Willa, stay here with her."

Standing, I meet the man a dozen feet away from our table. He tries to sidestep me, but I move into his way again.

"Turn around and leave, Steve," I say.

"Who are you? Get out of my way," he slurs.

"No. Leave now. There's no need to cause a scene in front of all your son's fans."

"My daughter," he stammers. "I need to take my daughter home."

"Callie will not be going home with you," I tell him, placing a hand on his chest. "Again, I'll ask you to leave. Alexander will talk to you tomorrow."

"Tomorrow," he asks, loudly and garnering more attention from those around us. "He's not home."

He tries to push past me again, but I don't budge, my fist now balling in his shirt.

"Leave," I hiss in his ear. "Right now before I fucking beat you until you can't even recognize yourself in the mirror. It's the least you deserve for what you've done to that little girl."

Steve blinks at me a few times, dazed for a moment. Right when I think he's found something to say, another man steps in. He's large, larger than me and certainly bigger than Steve.

"Come on, Steve. Time to call it a night," he says. Ignoring the drunk man's protest, the stranger turns to me and tips his chin up. I don't move until they're out the door.

Callie stares at me in awe as Willa rubs a hand up and down the poor girl's arms.

"Thank you," she says, starry-eyed, when I get back to the table.

"You're welcome, sweetheart. We'll make sure he doesn't hurt you again," I promise.

I've never meant anything more in my life.

19

ZANDER

Fucking Ely, Minnesota. It never changes. Absolutely nothing about the drive between the airport and my hometown has changed. The snow-covered tree lined streets are all so familiar, the route one I took often growing up, usually in a team van.

There were a lot of things I loved about growing up here. Like the rare occasion the lakes froze over before we would get heavy snow and we were able to skate on it. Or Miss Taylor who owned the burger joint giving us extra fries if we stopped in after practice because she believed we burned too many calories.

Then there were things I didn't love, like everyone knowing everyone else's business. I'm sure the whole town knows that my dad hit Callie. Especially, after he was trying to talk to her in a busy place last night. Willa sent me a text to fill me in on what happened. And that my little sister now has a burgeoning crush on our boyfriend.

Can't really blame her, he's great. He and Willa have both been so supportive throughout this ordeal, offering so much and asking for nothing in return.

It does bother me that Callie hasn't had anyone here in recent years to defend her. Of course, she's hero worshiping the first person who has. My heart aches so much. I should have done something sooner. It should have been me protecting her.

I'll never forgive myself for that. Or my mother.

Damian and Willa saw her safely back at her friend's house last night. Today I will talk to my parents, and with any luck, we'll be on a flight tomorrow back to Seattle, with Callie in tow.

However it happens, I'm not leaving without my sister. She'll never spend another night at the house we called home. If she chooses, Callie will never have to see this place, or him, again. She has friends here, people who care about her. But do they care enough to step in when they know my father is physically accosting her?

Doubtful. This town has too many of my extended family members in it and there's a long history of them covering up my dad's shitty behavior.

"Zander." I hear my name as soon as I step into the lobby of the hotel. My mother's sitting near the roaring fireplace.

"How did you know how to find me?"

"Owen overheard your friend saying you'd be in town today."

When Willa described the man that stepped in last night at the restaurant, I assumed it was my cousin Owen. Maybe one of the more reasonable of my family members, he's not one for confrontations or spectacles. He likes the family secrets to be just that.

"You should go home." I'm not ready to see her, or hear whatever her current round of excuses will be. She let it get to the point of my sister being physically harmed. More than once. The emotional toll it's probably taken on her is unimaginable as well.

If I ever become a father, I'll know how to put my child before my own selfish needs and wants. Because I've learned from the best of what not to fucking do.

"Zander, please. I haven't seen her in days." She stands, tries to reach out to me, but I step back.

"You should have been this concerned about her before you left her at home with him," I accuse, pointing a finger at her.

"I have to work, Zander. We have bills to pay," she pleads.

"You should have called me," I bite out. "I would have helped you both to get out of here."

"I can't just leave him," she says, and I scoff. Always the same story. My mother acts like my father is just as much a victim as she and Callie are. He's not. He has a disease, sure, but it's not an excuse for how he treats the people he's supposed to love and protect.

"Go home. I'll be there soon and we're going to have a long discussion." I glare at her, and she halts her attempt to stop me from walking away. "Go. You'll see me within the hour."

Maybe I shouldn't be so hard on her but fuck that noise. I love my mother, I do. That doesn't mean I can let that get in my way of giving Callie a better life. That's what she does, constantly putting my father before everyone else.

I recognize the woman at the front desk as someone I grew up with. Shelby. She once asked me to a school dance. I declined. She never spoke to me again. When I smile at her now, she barely reciprocates, so I'm guessing she's still not a fan.

Getting to the suite, I knock lightly. It's still early and I know Willa likes to wake up slowly. She's not the morning person I am. As expected, it's Damian who answers the door.

"Hey," I say.

"You sound exhausted," he tells me, taking my bag from me.

"Mentally more than physically," I say. "Where's Willa?"

"Shower. Do you want some coffee?"

"Yes, but I'm going to join her first." Showering after a flight always puts me in a better headspace because airports are disgusting.

"Go on, I'll have the pot ready when you're done."

She's humming some tune when I close the bathroom door behind me. Steam billows softly around the small room. I disrobe and step into the heat with her.

"Hi, big guy."

"Hi."

"Come here." She reaches out to me, swapping positions. Her hands direct my head under the stream. I let the water wash away some of the anger I carry toward my mother while Willa washes my hair and then my body. She refuses to let me help, saying it's her turn to spoil me, that I deserve it. But I'm not sure how. I don't feel deserving of anything; not my life, not her, or Damian.

Not Callie.

I'm going to change all that though. No matter how long it takes, I'm going to be as generous as Damian, as caring as Willa, a reliable role model to others like Coach. A life of just skating by on my talent isn't enough. Not anymore. Now it's time to be the man Coach taught me I could be.

"Thank you," I tell her when she's finished her ministrations. "You're one of my favorite people."

"One of," she asks, curling her upper lip in distress.

"Top five, for sure."

"Five?"

"Only because you missed a spot," I tell her, peering down at my cock.

"Only because I don't think getting you hard before we head to your parents is the best idea."

"You're right," I agree with a sigh. "It was a stall tactic."

"Are you nervous?"

"Not nervous, no. More afraid I'm going to kill him and end up in prison," I admit.

"That would defeat the whole purpose, Zan."

True enough. I'll be sure to remind myself of that throughout the day.

"Top three."

"That's more like it," she says, wrapping her arms around my waist and resting her cheek on my chest.

"Give me a kiss." She looks up at my command and meets my lips. It's comforting and encouraging. It's everything I need. More proof that she *does* know me, despite what she thinks. She always knows what I need.

From here on out, I need to focus on what she needs. And Damian, and Callie.

"Are we ready," Damian asks sometime later after Willa has dressed up and I've had enough coffee to wake up fully.

"I think so," I answer. "I have the paperwork for them to sign."

"I have the money." He smiles, but it's the dangerous one normally reserved for others. I know it's for my father's benefit.

"Let's get this shit done," Willa says. "I always wanted a little sister. I can't wait to get back to Seattle and spoil her fucking rotten."

The drive to my parents' home, the house I grew up in, doesn't take long. They live on the edge of town. The first thing I notice upon parking is that it hasn't been kept up. When I was a child, the lawn was always mowed, the gutters always clear of debris. Now the grass is long enough that the snow hasn't covered it in areas, the paint is chipping, and judging by the slight sag in the roof, I won't be surprised if my mother has a bucket set up somewhere inside to catch a leak.

It's another reminder that I should have come back sooner. I've been off living my dreams while they've been living like this.

"Fuck me," I mumble, stepping out of the rental SUV. The driveway is barely shoveled, the walkway not at all. "Be careful, Willa."

I hold a hand out to help steady her as she follows behind me. The knock I make on the front door is unnecessary, I see my mother peeking around the curtains of the front window. She takes a few moments to answer, I imagine her nerves are firing high. There's a small twinge of guilt in my gut about that, but then I remember Willa's description of the bruise my sister wears on her cheek.

"Hello, Zander. Willa, it's good to see you again," she greets with as much fake pleasantry as she can muster.

"This is Damian," I introduce.

"It's nice to meet another of Zander's friends."

"He's more than that. They both are," I say, and she pales. "Where is he?"

"In the back room, but Zander," she starts. I ignore it, stepping past her.

"Will you sit with me, Ellen," Willa asks, playing interference while Damian and I search for my father. "Maybe we can have a cup of tea."

Willa ushers her toward the kitchen just as I turn the corner to the back room. My father's favorite spot to sit and get drunk while he watches whatever sport is in season. The chair he's perched in is the same as from when I still lived here so many years ago.

"Father."

"The hotshot returns," he mumbles, his words slurred but not to the point where I don't think he'll understand the conversation we're about to have. Even if he does black out halfway through, I don't give a fuck, as long as he signs guardianship over to me.

"I have." I pick up the remote and shut off the television.

"What the hell, Zander?"

"We have something to talk about, no distractions."

"Is this about that brat of a sister," he asks, standing from his chair. He nearly falls over trying to go toe to toe with me.

"It is about my sister," I say, furious now. "My perfect, sweet sister. The one you put hands on."

"That was her fault," he begins to say. Before he finishes, I land my balled fist on his cheek. Let him feel what she felt. He falls back into his chair, dazed.

"It wasn't her fault, and if you say it again, I'll break your fucking jaw."

"You listen to me, you little fuck," he says.

This time, I grip my hand around his throat. Squeezing enough to get his full attention, but not enough to kill him. Though, goddamn it, is it tempting. My mother would hate me for it, but at least she'd be free of his fucking weight pulling her down.

"No, you listen to me now. I'm taking Callie to Seattle with me. I've brought papers that you're going to sign."

"You can't make me do shit," he spits. "I don't care who you play for, you ungrateful prick."

"You're right, I have been ungrateful. I wouldn't be where I am if it wasn't for the support you and Mom gave me. So, I'm going to repay all that," I say. It gets the reaction I expected; his face perks up with interest. "In return, you're going to sign papers, making me Callie's legal guardian."

"You can't afford to buy your sister away from us." He sneers. His eyes narrow and bounce between me and Damian a few times. "How much?"

"Piece of shit," Damian mutters from behind me.

"Who the fuck are you?" He tries to stand back up, but I shove him down. "Get your hands off me, Zander. I swear to Christ, kid."

"Fuck off, old man. The only reason you aren't already a pool of blood on the floor is because I don't want Mom to have to clean that shit up. You can't push me around anymore."

The truth settles on us both. He's frail, weak from the lack of nourishment he's been getting. The stench of vodka wafts out of his every pore. Even if I let him try to take a swing, which I have no intention of, it wouldn't hurt nearly as bad as what my body is put through in every game.

I know it, he knows it, too. He has no hold on me, no power over me. I'm not a vulnerable, easy target. The poor bastard stares at me as if he can see my disdain for him floating in the air like some tangible thing.

"Name your price, sign the papers, and we'll leave," Damian adds after the pregnant pause. My father turns his bloodshot eyes to him. "How much, Steve?"

"I already said he can't afford it."

"What's your price," I ask. "We all know you need it. Just say the amount."

His eyes focus on me, as he contemplates the insult I just threw at him. It's not that, it's only a fact. He's blown through so much on booze, and now with no job, he's broke. He grabs the bottle off the end table beside him, taking a huge swig from it.

"Five hundred thousand," he says, and I want to punch him again. And again. It's the same feeling I get when another player has landed a dirty hit on me or a teammate. When blood curtains your vision and you tunnel in on causing pain and chaos for a brief moment. But hitting him won't just land me in the penalty box for a few minutes. It won't do any good, even if it feels amazing.

Damian laughs, startling my father out of his stupor.

"You're more pathetic than I thought," he says.

"I said you couldn't afford it," my father replies, and Damian laughs harder.

"I've known Callie for a day, and it was long enough to know she's priceless. You'll get one million," Damian says.

"And you won't try to contact her or interfere in her life in any way," I add. "Do you agree?"

My father takes another large drink from the bottle he grips like a lifeline. Then he nods. As easy as that. I feel relief invading every tendon in my body. *Callie is coming home.*

Damian pulls the legal documents out of the manilla envelope he's been holding.

"I'll handle this part," he says. "Go speak to your mother."

I find her still in the kitchen with Willa, tears streaming down her cheeks.

"Mom."

"Oh, Zander," she says, wiping her face with shaking hands.

"You have a choice to make," I tell her, grasping one in my own. Rubbing my thumb in her palm does nothing to ease her. "He's agreed to give me guardianship over Callie."

She bursts out in sobs, but something tells me it's not all sadness. This decision needed to be out of her hands. I think she's realizing that, just as I am.

"You can come too, Ellen," Willa says. "That's the choice you need to make."

"I don't know…"

"You don't need to know just now," I say. "A trust has been set up for you. It only has your name on it and it's all yours the day you leave him. Or the day he dies. It's enough, Mom. It's more than enough."

Damian brings the documents in, setting them down in front of her.

"Until you decide, you need to sign these," he says. "Let us keep Callie safe."

"Promise me," she says through hiccupping gasps. "Promise me she'll be happy."

"The happiest," Willa says. "We'll take the best care of her."

"With everything I am, I promise. She'll want for nothing, Mom."

She presses her palm to my cheek, blinking through the tears as she takes me in. Takes in the honesty of my vow. Her sobs subside the smallest amount and then she picks up the pen.

Soon, we pull into Katie's driveway. I texted Callie before we left my parents' house to let her know I was on my way. She comes running out of the front door in her excitement to see me.

"Z!"

"Hey, baby girl," I say, catching her as she jumps into my arms. "I'm so sorry I wasn't here."

"You're here now," she says, looking up at me. Her hair falls back and I see the bruise, a nebula of colors on her cheek. It's healing some but that only makes it uglier. I'm proficient in bruises; I'd say she's got a few more days before it really starts to fade.

"I should have been here sooner," I tell her, choking on my own tears.

"You're here now," she repeats with more emphasis.

"I am, and I have news."

"Did you do it?" Her brow wrinkles, a trait we share it seems.

"Yes, Callie. I did it, with their help." I gesture to Damian and Willa. "Do you want to come live with me?"

"Really?" Her upper lip trembles.

"Really."

"Yes, Zan! Oh my gosh, I love you. When do we leave?"

Her enthusiasm is an even bigger relief since I was worried about pulling her away from her friends. Though I would love nothing more than to leave this town right now, we decide to stay two more nights. Katie's parents have graciously offered to have a slumber party for Callie and her friends to spend some time together before I take her to the far corner of the country.

I thank them both profusely and promise to get them the best seats at any Minnesota game they ever want to attend. I don't know how to repay them for what they've done, but I made it clear that if they ever need anything at all, they are to call me.

We also ask Callie to make a list of anything she wants packed up and send it to our mother, who has promised to take care of that for us. I'll be stopping by tomorrow to ensure that's happening without drama from my father.

It's not over yet, but this has all gone better than anticipated. And the hero worship on Callie's face every time she looks at me tells me this has all been worth the effort.

20

DAMIAN

B efore landing in Minnesota, I knew Alexander's father was an idiot. The number he threw out earlier today cemented that belief. I was prepared to pay five times that, at least. He has no idea, but the trust I set up for Ellen is much larger than what we paid him. He receives the smallest amount. It's enough for him to drink himself to death, though. Which I imagine is all he cares about at this point.

No matter what, Alexander's family is financially secure, and he can put that worry behind him. Callie also has a trust set up to pay for future schooling. Without much family of my own, this feels like a great investment. Not that I expect Alexander won't be able to provide this for them himself. I think he'll have a long career in the sport, barring any unexpected injuries. But what good is all my money if I don't help those I love? I can't take it with me when I die.

Love. An emotion I never expected to feel because I never understood it. In truth, I didn't believe it was real. It wasn't something I grew up with and then when I started studying cults and manipulative tactics used on groups of people, that belief grew. Love felt fake, like nothing more than a tool. Do this because you love me. If you love me, you'll do what I say. Time and time again, I'd see someone that ruined their entire lives because they believed they were in love and were loved in return, only to realize it was all a lie.

That taught me that love wasn't something to seek or achieve.

Then love fell into my lap like a heap of bricks and now it is a weight I never want to unburden myself of. It's all-consuming, overwhelming, but gratifying. Pride rushes through my veins like lifeblood. For Alexander, for Willa, but also for my own growth and self-awareness.

None of us say much on the drive back to the hotel. Tension is thick inside the rental car. If we make it out of bed for the next twelve hours, I'd be surprised. There's been too much stress in our lives these past handful of days. Stress tends to cancel out your sex drive. Now that it's subsided, there's that rush of adrenaline that we all need to release.

What better way than fucking?

Especially because I have the urge to touch. To feel. To give and receive.

The lady at the front desk gives us a weird look as we walk past, barely reacting to our polite greetings.

"What's with her," I ask once we're ensconced in the elevator.

"She asked me on a date once in high school. I declined because she wasn't a hockey fan, she's never forgiven me, I guess."

"I'd be sad if I'd missed a chance with you, too," Willa sympathizes.

"That looked much more like bitterness than sadness," I say.

"Maybe she regrets not getting into hockey so Zander might have gotten into her," Willa quips, and I pull her into me so I can laugh into her neck. She squirms and wraps her arms around me.

"Definitely something to be bitter about," I agree.

"Whatever," Alexander says with a laugh as the elevator doors open.

They both enter the hotel room before me. I set the Do Not Disturb hanger, then lock the door. Alexander is looking at Willa like she's his next meal, and she's oblivious to it while taking off the layers she wore to protect her from the low temperatures outside. She sits on the end of the bed and removes her shoes while we both watch like it's the most interesting thing in the world.

When she has her boots off, she falls back, letting her arms and hair spread out above her head. Only then do either of us start to move, removing our own clothes. She doesn't notice we're down to our boxer briefs only now.

"That went surprisingly well," she says.

"It did," Alexander says, kneeling at where her feet hang off the bed. He removes her socks and massages her feet. "Thank you for sitting with my mom."

"Of course," she says, then moans as the blood flows. "That feels nice."

I lie beside her, my fingers going to the button of her jeans.

"Hi," I say when she turns to look at me.

"Hello, Damian," she purrs. "What's your mood right now?"

Fuck, I love how cautious she is with me. With her pants unfastened, Alexander pulls them over her hips and down her legs.

"It's a new mood for me, love," I tell her. "One without limits."

I press a kiss to her forehead, the tip of her nose, then her mouth.

"Are you sure," Alexander asks.

"I'm sure," I reassure them both, not telling them all the ideas pouring through my mind. Wrapping my hand around the back of his neck, I pull him down for a kiss, too. Three mouths working together, not fighting each other as our bodies tangle. Hands, so many hands, touching. I dig one into her panties, only to find Alexander already there. We work in tandem to work her into her first frenzy of the night. She's so responsive it never takes long.

When she pushes at his boxers, his hard cock bounces on her thigh as it's set free. As much as I want it in my own mouth, I want to watch her swallow him more. I stand and remove my own final piece of clothing.

"Suck him down, Willa. Show me again how well you take him," I say, pumping his dick in one hand, mine in the other.

"Keep yours close too," she tells me as she moves to her hands and knees, her head hovering over him.

"Have I ever said how much I like it when you're bossy," I ask, swatting the ass she purposely lifts so high in the air. She doesn't yelp, she moans as she fills her throat.

"Fucking hell, your mouth, Willa," he says, full of appreciation.

Stradling Alexander, I let my own cock rest against the base of his. He fists it, working it in time to her bobbing. Her hand joins his and she starts to alternate between the two of us. He's right, her mouth is unmatched. When she has each of us as wet as she is, she brings us together in between her palms. Her mouth isn't big enough to take us both, but she twirls that talented tongue around both tips. I rock my hips the smallest amount, silk gliding against silk.

Fucking amazing.

Willa pauses to watch as we slide against each other, her face flush.

"I want that inside me," she says, her words softly floating over us.

"Goddamn," Alexander curses.

"Think you can take that," I ask her, my thumb tracing her lip.

"We won't know until we try," she answers, then sucks my thumb into her mouth. Ever the sexual adventurer.

"You are a fucking dream, Ms. Cole."

"Hmmm, no, but my life is," she muses as Alexander takes her pussy in his mouth and I kiss her passionately, lying down next to her. Willa meets me with the same fervor. I'm so wrapped up in it that I don't notice when Alexander stops pleasuring her until his mouth is on my cock. I groan into my kiss with Willa, overwhelmed by the sensation of having them both on me at once.

Willa's oral skills are better than any woman I've ever been with, but Alexander… sucks dick like he was born to do it, taking me down in his throat and sucking back with just the right force. My hand finds the back of his head and encourages more.

"I want to watch," she says, pulling away from our kiss. "It's my turn."

Maybe she has a little dirty voyeurism in her, too. She crawls up to the head of the bed, making a small nest for herself to watch as Zander continues bringing me just shy of the edge, then easing up. Before long, I'm fisting both hands in his hair and trying like hell to fuck his mouth to completion. He's a tease though, and won't let me get there.

"Fuck, Zander, I need to come."

"Me too," Willa says, her fingers deep inside herself, chest heaving.

"You like to watch, beautiful."

"Apparently," she says with a dramatic sigh.

Alexander relents and stops what he's been doing. Slowly, he climbs up my body, hovering over me.

"You taste good, March," he says, eyes glinting, before dropping his mouth to mine. Shit, so does he. Alexander drops his body onto mine. Our cocks nuzzle, and instinctively, I thrust upward. I lift my leg over his hip to keep him there while I reach for Willa. Her hand clasps onto mine and I feel… whole. For the first time ever, I don't feel the void in my chest that's plagued me for as long as I can remember.

My free hand roams over his body, every cut and ridge, of which there are so many. When I get to his firm ass, I'm rewarded by a low hum deep from his chest. So, I keep it there, massaging the large globe.

Willa whimpers, and we both turn our faces to hers.

"One of these days…" she says in barely a whisper, but she doesn't finish the sentence. She doesn't have to, we both understand. Someday she wants to watch us fuck each other. Someday, I'm sure we will, and she'll be there bossing the two of us around like we do her in the bedroom.

"Come here, Willa," Alexander says, rising to his knees above me. He guides her to straddle me, holding my cock at its base so she can lower onto me. Her heat sheathes me like a warm hug. Alexander gently presses a palm along her spine. She snuggles her face into my neck, nibbling and sucking and generally just driving me crazy. He inserts a couple of fingers inside her, alongside my dick, gauging her comfort.

"Please," she pleads, mewling excitedly.

He replaces them with the tip of his cock, gently nudging her entrance.

"Look at me, Willa," I say. "Keep your eyes on me."

She kisses me and doesn't look away. As Alexander pushes in a little further, her pupils glint with whatever she's feeling but it isn't fear. Pleasure mixed with an edge of pain that's overshadowed by the sheer desire for us all to be together. Or so I imagine.

I grasp one of her ass cheeks, pulling it aside, making more room for him to maneuver. She's relaxed under my palm, a good sign that she isn't in much discomfort. He moves in a little further.

Being in her is one thing, but having Alexander's cock next to mine, buried deep inside her is almost sensory overload. All three of us take a still moment to appreciate it. Willa practically vibrates, pressing kisses to my jaw.

"You okay, sweetheart," Alexander asks her.

"No. I'll never be just okay again. Now, I need you to fuck us, Zander."

I smile up at him, amused by her always. His expressions says he feels the same.

He slides out, but not fully, then back in. Starting easy and picking up the pace slowly. Biting my lip, I start moving too, out when he goes in. Fucking hell, nothing has ever fired all my nerve endings at once.

Running from this is the last thing on my mind. I want more, I want it always.

"Kiss me, Willa. Don't stop kissing me until we've both finished inside you."

A needy whimper escapes her just before her lips meet mine, her tongue diving in with the same passionate need that I meet her with. Alexander's hand rests on the side of my head and he whispers filthy sweet-nothings to us both. Telling us how amazing this is for him, how he can't wait to feel what it will be like to come this way.

"I want our cum dripping all over each other," he mumbles into her ear, and she quivers, grabbing my hair in one hand with all the strength she can manage. The sharpness of the pull and the tightening of her cunt are the perfect combination and I lose the small amount of control I was still holding on to.

"Now," I demand. "Come with me, Alexander."

"Oh, fuck," Willa gasps. "That feels… Oh my fucking god." She shakes in between us, and I get it. For the first time, I have an idea of what it feels like for her. The warmth of my release, and his, blanketing us.

Erotic, euphoric, the most pleasurable moment in my entire life.

Alexander leans over, kissing Willa's shoulders as she starts to calm down.

"I know I say this a lot, but you're fucking amazing."

"You can keep telling me, I don't mind," she says, resting her face in the crook of my neck. She can stay there forever, for all I care. Make a home there, build a fence around it, permanently connected to me.

I love her. I'm fully in love with them both. Maybe I'm the first of the three of us to reach this level of affection, or maybe I'm not. Maybe it's something we're all thinking about right now, none of us quite sure if this is the right time to speak the words to existence. Maybe, they don't need to be spoken because it's so felt in the way our hands all find soothing movements on each other until we're all soft, sleepy, and content.

Alexander is the first to move, climbing off the bed, he picks Willa up in his arms. Cradling her like she's the most precious thing, because she is.

"To the bathroom with you," he mumbles in the curtain of her hair.

"Yes, sir."

Our after-sex routine is always one of two things. We either end up bathing together, or Willa returns from the bathroom with warm washcloths. If they want to shower tonight, he's going to have to carry my ass in there too. Because right now, I'm not willing to leave this sanctuary that still holds their heat and their scent.

It feels safe here, like home. Another all-new feeling for me. I wonder if this is what it's like to hear sound for the first time or see color. I imagine my heart blooming, coming alive with new growth after it has sat inside me withered and dry for so long.

Love is a wondrous and powerful thing.

As it happens, they both come out of the bathroom. Alexander with a washcloth in hand. He doesn't allow me to take it from him, instead handling it himself. Another revelation, because I feel no awkwardness or discomfort in letting him.

Willa snuggles closer but keeps a small distance.

"I don't know if it will always be like this," I say, turning to her. "But come closer."

I stretch my arm out, and she moves into my chest. Alexander takes a position at her back, studying my face. Can he see the changes I feel? Are they powerful enough to permeate the very air? Of course not, but they're mighty enough to change the course of my life.

These aren't the first people I've cared about. There is Fig, his family, and Delilah. However, these are the first people I'd never question laying my life down for or giving my wealth to without question. I'd even leave, if that was what was best for them. But I'll never do anything to warrant that. I'll never cause them pain or harm, and I'll do whatever it takes to keep others from doing that as well.

If that's not love, then love isn't what this aching deep down in my soul is.

Alexander's hand comes to rest on my chest, over my heart. A sign that he's protecting me just as much as I am them. I feel something else new and rare for me.

Happiness.

21

ZANDER

The last four days have been an exhausting whirlwind. We're home, and after so many school visits, we've decided on one and she's finally enrolled. It's an all-girls school which I feel tremendous relief from. Callie was all for it, too. Maybe that shouldn't surprise me with our conservative background, but it did.

All I know is that this parenting thing is too new for me to have to deal with her trying to bring a boyfriend home any time soon.

She spent the first half of today shadowing another student. When I picked her up, she was all smiles. It's costing me a lot, but that should be easier when my contract is renewed after this season. Assuming I continue to play well. And here in Seattle.

One thing is for sure, we're going to need a bigger place. I've given Callie my bedroom, which leaves me on the couch. My ridiculously comfortable couch, of course, but it's not the same as a bed. Besides, I could use a little privacy, too.

Hers is more important just now, though. Callie's already had to give up so much by leaving her friends, family, and the only place she's ever known. Switching from a very small town to a very large city is a rush in itself. She's never taken public transportation or had to worry about walking anywhere safely.

Everything here is new for her. While she's excited, it's also daunting. She liked the girl she shadowed today, quite a lot. Hopefully, she'll make friends quickly. Having a sidekick will make me feel better. Especially with how often I'm gone.

My mother should be here. I silently curse her for not making Callie a priority over my drunk dad.

Callie doesn't feel the same. She wants no contact with him, but she's called our mother plenty of times since we flew out here. So, I keep my raw feelings to myself, she doesn't need to be influenced by my opinion. She'll have time to come to her own conclusions.

I grew up in hockey, a team sport. It's all I know. Now everything weighs heavy on just me. Callie's well-being, my mother possibly becoming my father's punching bag, keeping my burgeoning relationship with Damian and Willa quiet. Not only from the press, but from Callie until I can figure out how to broach that conversation.

All while maintaining my position on the team.

Pressure has always been a part of my life, just never this intense. Never with so much at stake. One wrong move and I risk losing so much.

Too many things are shifting in my life at a breakneck pace.

I just got Callie here and tomorrow I have to leave her for a six-day away stretch. It fucking sucks. I won't be here for her first week at her new school, or while she settles into this city. I'm heavily relying on Willa and Isla for support, which is equally shitty because they have their own lives and responsibilities. This isn't fair to either of them, or Callie.

She's doing her best to understand and be supportive, but at the end of each day, she curls up so close to me on the couch, I know she has doubts and insecurities.

The shining light is that she loves Willa, Isla, and Sadie. All three have been by regularly. We thought it important for them to acclimate to each other. Callie will be staying over at Willa's starting tonight, since I leave early in the morning. Callie wasn't keen on a four AM wakeup. Can't say I blame her. Since Willa doesn't have classes tomorrow, she's offered to take Callie shopping for everything she'll need for school. Other than the basics she could pack into a large suitcase, she didn't bring much with her.

"That's not how you do it, Z." Callie pushes my hands away and takes over seasoning the steak.

"How do you know, squirt?"

"Because Mom actually taught me how to cook," she says, rolling her eyes. "You can't call me that around other people, you know."

"I know," I reassure her. "It's my secret nickname for you whenever you're being a pain in my ass."

"Can I say that word, too," she asks, wide-eyed. Only my dad cursed in my house and only when drunk. Which was often enough, of course.

"Callie, you're almost fifteen. You say whatever words you want, but only at home with me. No disrespecting anyone."

"Okay. Do you at least know how to peel a damn potato?"

Her face reddens when she tries out her first four-letter word, so foreign coming out of her own mouth.

"Yes, *squirt*. I know how to peel potatoes."

"Well, get busy then. Willa will be here soon."

"Yes, ma'am," I say. "I didn't know you were so bossy."

"Sorry," she says.

"Don't be. Nothing wrong with you being assertive. Especially when you know what you're doing," I say. "And you get to put me in my place when I need it. Got it?"

"I'll try. It's weird though. You're my brother, but kind of my dad. And sometimes you seem more like a kid than I am."

"I'll try to be more mature from now on," I say, then stick my tongue out at her.

"No." She laughs. "I didn't mean it in a bad way. Only I think because you were always gone with hockey stuff, you didn't ever learn basic stuff. Like how to cook."

"For sure," I agree. "How about you teach me the stuff I don't know? In return, I'll teach you a thing or two. Like how to throw a punch."

"I could use that, I guess. But you don't owe me anything. You know that, right?" Her eyes water as she looks up at me. "I'm just glad to be…"

"Cal, I owe you the world because I love you. You're the most important person in my life," I tell her. "Don't ever forget it, and don't ever be scared to ask me for anything. Or talk to me. Okay? We're a team."

"I've never been on a team. Can we name it?"

"Sure. We can be Fane Fish."

"No! Fane Flamingos."

"Hard pass," I say, aghast. "Fane Flies."

"Better than fleas, but not by much," she says, filling a pot with water and starting the burner. We're making steak, mashed potatoes, and a garden salad. The salad I could probably handle on my own. But the kid is right, I don't have a ton of skills in the kitchen.

"Flounders?"

"Oh my gosh, you're so bad at this!" She giggles. Genuinely and carefree. Something I want for her always.

"Frogs?"

"Hmm, I kinda like that."

"Frogs? You like Fane Frogs," I ask with feigned outrage. "How is that better than Flounders?"

"Because frogs are cute."

"Frogs have warts."

"This isn't a fairytale, Z."

Touché.

But I sure do plan on changing that for her.

My childhood was filled with hope. I had goals and I systematically accomplished them. That was a privilege Callie wasn't offered. Extra money and resources went to me and my endeavors, not hers. If she ever had life dreams, they weren't something she shared with me.

Selfishly, I never asked. I've been absent for too much of her life and I'm ashamed I didn't make her a priority sooner. Until now, nobody ever has. Before I get the chance to ask her anything about her dreams, there is a knock on the door.

"I got this, you get the door," Callie commands.

"Yes, ma'am," I say. Willa wears a big smile when I let her in the apartment. She's excited to be keeping an eye on Callie for me while I'm gone. Says it's been too long since she had a kid in the house with her. There aren't a lot of women in the world like Willa Cole, I suspect. I'm eternally grateful she's in my life and that Damian pushed me into giving this a chance.

"Hi," she says, brightly. "Something smells delicious."

"That's all Callie," I tell her, pulling her in for a kiss.

"That explains it," she teases.

"Excuse me?"

"See, even Willa knows you're basically useless in the kitchen," Callie calls.

"I peeled the potatoes," I protest.

"Ah, good job, big guy." Willa pats me on the chest as she moves into the kitchen to see what Callie is up to.

"Wow," I say, mocking disbelief. Truth is, I don't mind being the brunt of the joke if it keeps my kid sister happy. While they finish up the meal preparations, I set the small table for the three of us. Willa was right, it does smell amazing and after I take the first bite, I know it tastes even better. "This is great, Callie. Thank you."

"You're welcome," she says, preening some under the compliment. Another thing I don't think she's gotten much of in her short life.

"Zander told me you settled on a school today."

"The Rodan school. I'll start on Monday."

"Rodan has a good number of arts and science courses from what I hear," Willa says.

"I think so. I won't get to pick many electives until next year, but Jana said that was their focus." Jana is the girl Callie shadowed and has been the center of a good amount of our conversation today. Jana this and Jana that. I'm not complaining though, it's good she liked her.

"Is that a good thing," I ask. "I hate to admit this, but I don't even know what your favorite subjects are."

"That's okay, you've been pretty busy my whole life," she says. Again, she's being genuine, but I still feel like an ass. "Math is my favorite, because it's easy. But I really like to draw, and I had been teaching myself to knit when I could get my hands on yarn. I guess art is my favorite subject. But I'm pretty okay at English, too. I like to read and write poems."

"She also likes some history," Willa says, and Callie nods in agreement. "We can hit up an art supply store and there is a yarn store a couple of blocks away."

"A whole store just for yarn?"

"A whole store," Willa confirms.

"Oh geez, I think I love Seattle."

"It's quite a bit different from Ely, huh?"

"For sure," Callie says.

"Did you bring any drawings with you," I ask her.

"No, those didn't feel like the most important things. But I have some pictures of them on my phone."

She pulls it out of her pocket and lets us scroll through them. This isn't just a hobby, these are amazing, and that's not my biased opinion talking. They're good enough that I recognize who every portrait is of, and her landscapes are gorgeous. I'm torn up that she didn't bring them with her. Even if I'm not ready to speak to our mother just yet, I will be calling to see if she'll ship whatever Callie left behind. These deserve to be in a portfolio for her, not sitting collecting dust in a drunkard's house.

"Fuck, Callie. These are beautiful."

"Thanks," she says, another huge smile on her face.

We finish our meals with more talk about art and hockey, then clean up the kitchen before Callie packs up the few things she'll need for an overnight at Willa's. Couldn't ask for a more convenient situation. It's still not ideal, but we'll make do until I can come up with a better option.

Damian hinted at Callie and I moving in with him. It's an attractive offer since he has the room, and his house isn't far from her new school. Seeing as Callie doesn't know the finer details of our relationship, it's not something I'm able to move forward with.

Hopefully, some day soon. Maybe even with Willa.

Saying goodbye, I remind Callie to text as often as she needs, and that I'll call her every day. I thank Willa, again, who says to stop it, but I won't. It means everything to me that she's willing to help me out. After they've left, I pack my own shit and then head to Damian's. He hasn't had as much time since we've gotten home, we've hardly seen or heard from him. Spending a few days away between New Orleans and Ely set him behind on school. He's been busy catching up but he's making time for me tonight.

It's been a while since we've had time, just the two of us. Plenty of time with the three of us. Willa and I see each other without him, and they spend quite a bit of time without me. Somehow, Damian and I can't connect the same way.

He's relaxing in his living room, watching hockey, of all things.

"Look at you becoming a fan," I say.

"I think it's the fighting," he says. "It turns me on. But holy fuck do you all spit a lot."

I drop my bag and sit next to him, kicking my feet up on the ottoman.

"You don't notice you're doing it until you see other guys doing it on television."

"How's Callie settling in," he asks, just as Lemming, a rookie who plays for Montreal, takes a slapshot that barely misses the net.

"Good, I think. The next couple of weeks will be the test, between me being gone and her starting at Rodan."

"She's likeable, I think she'll do fine there. Probably doesn't hurt having a big brother who plays pro sports, either."

"Sure," I agree. "But I want her to attract friends because of her, not me."

"Of course. She'll find her footing. We all will."

Damian's confidence in everything is like a balm to my worries. He's never one to wallow in negativity. The athlete in me appreciates it. Something that's been drilled into me as a kid is that we don't dwell. We analyze, we adjust, we improve. You make whatever changes need to be made and you move on.

Callie and I will be doing a good bit of that, I suspect.

I watch the game, half asleep, until Damian nudges me and shuts it off. With how crammed my days have been between games, practice, workouts, and handling whatever Callie's needs are, I'm dead on my feet every night.

"To bed, Alexander. You can hardly keep your eyes open, and you need to be up soon."

Doesn't seem fair that our schedules finally align, only for me to be too tired to fully enjoy it. Still, it's been nice to just sit here and exist without a hundred different things to do. Better still is falling asleep beside Damian, my hand on his back and his lips on my neck. He doesn't ask anything of me, there's no expectations other than companionship and closeness.

Yet I don't feel like I'm holding up my end or offering enough for proper balance. The worry that I'm the reason this will all go to hell is always there in the back of my mind. For so long I was worried I couldn't offer Willa what she needed. Now, I think it's that I can't give Damian what he deserves. This is all I have, short, stolen moments. How do we build a future on that? A life? A family?

Maybe we're bound to fail.

22

WILLA

It's my birthday. Which means family dinner. Luckily, Dad and the team are in town and have the night off. I invited Zander, Callie, and Damian, even though I didn't mention what tonight was for. We've never made a big show of holidays in my family. Maybe because Dad was gone for so many of them due to work. Now Cillian is, too.

We don't ignore them, by any means, we just try to keep them casual and low-key. Often, they're celebrated when convenient, not necessarily on the day. Tonight is a special treat.

While I should be excited, I'm nervous. It's been a couple of weeks since we brought Callie back from Minnesota. Everything with her is going great, she's settling in at school and she and Zander have found a routine.

It's taken a toll on our triptych, however. Other than our campus café meetups, I hardly see Damian. Zander sees even less. None of us has had sex since that night in our Minnesota hotel. Sex isn't what I miss the most, not even close. It's the connection, both emotional and physical, that I ache for.

My days aren't the same without Damian's playful flirting or the way Zan constantly pulls me in for bear hugs and deep kisses. He's kept our interaction fairly PG. Understandable since Callie is always around. But still. What's a girl gotta do to get a little nookie?

Wait it out, I guess. It's not my call on when or what he tells Callie. Besides, it hasn't been that long since we all started seeing each other. A couple of months is all. Regardless of how long I've known Zander, or how it feels like I've known Damian for just as long. Despite how I get butterflies every time I know I'll see one of them, or how I hate falling asleep without one, or both, in bed with me.

We're young and we have time. I hope, anyway. It would break my heart for this to all end before we ever really got started. Heartbreaking is too weak of a word. It would be devastating. I've never known romantic love before, but I'm sure this is it. What else could it be? I've never been so willing to orbit my life around another person. Or persons. Well, except Isla and Sadie, but that's a different situation.

"How are you so sure your parents won't freak out about you having two boyfriends," Kit asks as we walk up the path to the front door.

"They love me. It should be as simple as that. If it's not, we have bigger issues." Truly, that's how I feel. Sure, any dad is going to be a bit weird about something like this. But I'm an adult and he needs to trust that I know what is best for my heart.

"I hope you're right."

"Yeah, me too," I say with a laugh.

Isla, Cillian, and Sadie are already here. After Mom pours us each a glass of wine, we go search them out, and Sadie instantly rolls into her questions for Kit.

"I need facts on small dogs," she demands of my best friend.

"All small dogs, or a specific small dog?"

"Small dogs that get along with cats, pacifically."

"Specifically," I correct her. She's been asking for a dog for weeks. Isla is hesitant because they live in a floating house. Their yard is literally a lake. Not so conducive for dogs.

"That's a very subjective topic, I'm not sure I can give you facts on that, Sadie." Kit looks up at me for help, but I just shrug. I'm not getting involved in the debate on whether or not they get a dog. "Maybe we should pick something I know better."

Sadie breathes a long sigh while she thinks of another topic.

"Butterflies," she finally says.

"Oh, that's a good one," Kit says excitedly. "A group of butterflies is called a flutter, which is pretty fabulous if I say so myself."

"So fabulous," Sadie agrees, dramatically holding a hand to her chest.

"And they taste with their feet."

"No way!"

"Promise," Kit says.

"That's crazy!"

The butterfly conversation lasts a few more minutes before it turns to waterfalls, then oddly enough to Mothman. How my six-year-old niece knows anything about the Cryptid, I have no idea. But then again, she surprises me all the time.

"How are you doing," Cillian asks. He sits beside me, wrapping an arm around my shoulders while we watch Kit entertain his daughter. Cillian and I used to be great friends when he first started dating my sister as teenagers. I loved him like a brother. We lost him for a few years due to the stupid choices made by him and people around him. But since he's been back, we've rebuilt that relationship. He knows me as well as anyone.

"I'm good."

"You don't feel older?"

"No, funny man," I say, rolling my eyes. "Well, not because of my age anyway. Twenty-five today feels the same as twenty-four did yesterday."

"But," he prompts.

"But," I mimic. "I feel older because of life changes, I guess. I'm suddenly something of a step or co-parent. It's a lot of responsibility."

"It is," Cillian agrees. "Are you getting as much out of it as you're putting in?"

Am I? It's not a question I've asked myself. Callie is a pleasure to be around, and I do honestly love helping her find her way in this new life. I've taken her to get art supplies, yarn, and she's always down to stop off at a bookstore, too. All things that help keep her busy, which gives me the opportunity to get schoolwork done.

"You mean, am I letting myself be taken advantage of."

"No, Zander would never do that. Not intentionally, anyway. But I worry that you're going to burn out under all the responsibilities, and I want to be sure someone is there to help you back up. You tend to be the caretaker, you know?"

"Well, then it's a good thing I have two men that love to take care of me," I whisper, making him choke on his drink.

"Ah hell, tonight just got way more interesting."

"How dare you," I tease. "My birthday is always the highlight of everyone's year."

"It is. I apologize for implying otherwise." He laughs.

"You're forgiven only if you promise to never let it happen again."

"You got it, Willa," he says. The doorbell announces the arrival of more guests. Sadie goes running, excited to see her uncle and her new friend Callie. My niece loves people and animals. She constantly wants them around. It's been good for Callie, too, to have another kid around in the sea of adults she's been thrown into.

Callie has made friends at school. Three girls get spoken of often. But she's yet to make plans with them outside of school. I think she's shy because her background was so sheltered and limited to such a small town. With Sadie, she's the same easygoing girl she is with Zander or me.

Mom leads the three newcomers into the living room. Isla and my father are in the kitchen working on my cake. I'm not supposed to know that, but this family is shit at keeping secrets from each other.

"Is that the other man," Cillian leans over to whisper in my ear.

"Yes, isn't he pretty?"

"You're the pretty one, with that big old smile on your face. Happy looks good on you, Willa." He stands to shake Damian's hand as Zander introduces them. Cillian engages Damian in conversation with my mother, and Zander sits with me while Callie and Sadie play with Curly.

"Happy birthday," he says.

"Thank you," I say, leaning onto his shoulder. "Are you nervous?"

"About telling your parents? Not so much. I'm more scared of Isla, I think."

"That's fair, she's psycho," I say. She's not, of course, but she has a hair trigger temper. "It's nice you aren't scared of my dad."

"I didn't say that," he says with a wink. "Seeing how he is with Cill has helped lessen my worry, though."

My mom laughs at something Damian says, using his charm to win her over. He's relaxed tonight, like he so often is with me. Less and less, I see that reserved part of him that keeps a shield around himself. Mostly, I only see him at school, but he never hesitates to hold my hand or brush my hair away from my face.

Zander hasn't spoken with Callie yet about our relationship because she's had so much going on and he doesn't want to overwhelm her. But I'm past ready to tell my family that I'm in love with both men. Mom already thinks of Zan as family and I want her to know Damian, too. He's family to me now. Even if things don't work out with the three of us, Damian is a part of me. Just like Zander.

They're stuck with me in some capacity. Forever.

Plus, Damian deserves that tether. Callie already knows Zander and I are more than friends, just from observation. I heard her talking to a friend on the phone and she referred to me as her brother's girlfriend. But Damian doesn't have that, he doesn't have anyone claiming him.

I am going to do that. I'm claiming them both as mine. Even if only privately with my parents and sister. Isla suspects that Zan is dating us both, but not that I am, too. Zander and I have both been vague about it. It's our business, until we decide to share.

Partly, I'm trying to hold us together. The distance, the separation due to our current schedules, makes me sad. If there's one thing I hate, it's being sad. Especially over men. Love is supposed to be happy and comforting. Lately, it's felt like so much work trying to keep hold of my connections.

"Happy birthday, beautiful," Damian says to me, leaning down to place a kiss on my cheek.

"Thank you, Mr. March." I stand, taking Zander's hand to pull him up with me. "Cillian, can you keep the girls occupied for a few?"

"Sure thing, birthday girl," he says with a sly smile.

Beckoning my mother and Damian to follow, I lead everyone into the kitchen. No time like the present. Maybe I could have waited until after dinner, that way if it's awkward at all a getaway is eminent. But it's too late now.

"Hey, get out! We're not done," Isla protests.

"I think we'll stay, thank you," I say in a sugary sweet voice. "I already know what you're up to, and I have an announcement of sorts."

The cake they've been working on is a replica of Catherine de Medicis' garden at the Chateau de Chenonceau in France. It's a place I've long dreamed of visiting, dubbed the Ladies Castle due to how much of it was inspired by several famous women who lived there. I saw a picture of it years ago and it's become something of an obsession. I used to say it was the place I'd have my wedding at, even though they don't do that sort of thing there.

"You're a brat," Isla says, but she's smiling as she twirls on the last of the icing.

"So are you," my dad tells her. "Happy birthday, Willa."

"Thanks, Daddy."

"What's this announcement, dear?" Mom looks vaguely worried.

"I'm in a relationship," I say, bluntly.

"Figured as much when Fane brought you to the gala," Dad says. "You making it official?"

He poses the question to me, not Zander, because he taught me my life decisions are my own. Cillian still tells the story of how he first asked my dad if he could ask Isla out on a date. He wanted to clear it with his coach to avoid backlash. Dad basically told him Isla would chew him out for the move. He's not the type of man you ask for his daughter's hand in marriage.

"Yes, I'm making it official. But it's not just Zander and I." I wrap my arm under Damian's and gently tug him closer. Dad stills, narrowing his eyes. "It's Damian, too. Dad, this is Damian."

"You're dating them both?"

"We're all dating each other," I clarify.

The room falls silent, every single person staring at me. Dad's face is blank, just like when he's coaching a game. He gives nothing away. I'll take it as a good sign that he isn't hopping over the counter to land a fist in either of my boyfriend's noses though. Isla doesn't look surprised, perhaps a little concerned, but not much. Mom… well, she looks… pleased? Excited?

I expected eventual understanding and acceptance, but only after a long period of them throwing questions at us. My mother doesn't look like she has anything at all to ask. She just looks proud.

"Oh, I saw something like that on a television show a few weeks ago," Mom says. "Polyamory is getting quite popular. I think it's great, honestly, if you can keep jealousy out of it that is. There are so many benefits to it, much more than a traditional relationship."

"What benefits," Dad asks her, still with his poker face so I can't gauge his reaction.

"More love and affection is an obvious one. Especially in life like the world of hockey. With Zander gone so often, Willa wouldn't be left at home alone for days on end."

"Do you not feel loved when I'm away," Dad asks, not in a confrontational way but with genuine concern.

"Of course, I feel loved, darling. But there were plenty of times I felt lonely, especially early on before I had the girls."

"What other benefits," he asks, after studying her for a short moment.

"Diversity of interests. You don't always get fulfillment in every aspect of your life from your partner. She can talk hockey with Zander, but I imagine Damian is a better conversationalist with her studies, due to his own."

My mother must have really been drilling him for the whole ten minutes he's been in her house. I'm just in awe of her reaction to all this, let alone her knowledge on it.

"What studies," Dad asks Damian.

"I'm completing my dissertation this year to get my PhD in Sociology."

Again, silence falls across the room. I can practically hear Zander's heart beating wildly next to me. This is a coming out for him in a sense, too. He may have sounded assured of the outcome, but I wonder how much of that is that cocky athlete bravado.

They all have it, my dad, Cillian, Zander. They don't like to admit weakness any more than defeat. They say women are attracted to men that remind them of their dad. I always hated that, it sounds creepy and condescending. As if we don't have an imagination of what a man should be past the one who raised us, or we're looking for another man to protect and guide us after we're too old for our fathers to do it.

But maybe there is some truth there. Because more and more I see parts of Zan that remind me of my father.

"I'll need to get to know you more," he tells Damian. "But I trust Willa to know herself and what's best for her. So, welcome to my home, Damian."

"Just like that," I ask.

"Are you happy? Do they make you happy?"

"Yes," I say with a huge smile.

"Do they treat you with respect?"

"Yes, Dad. Of course."

"Then just like that," he says. "Don't think you get special treatment, Fane."

"I wouldn't dare, sir."

"You got a problem with your kid sister dating your best friend," he asks Isla.

"No, Zan is family. And Damian is great."

"I'm likely to have a lot of questions," he says. "Just know that it's because I want to make sure my daughter is getting the best in life. If I find out otherwise is happening, I'm not opposed to physical violence."

Damn hockey players, always ready for a fight.

"Neither of us wants anything but the world for her," Zander says. "I can promise you that, Coach."

"We'll take good care of her," Damian adds.

"Then let's eat some dinner, I'm starving," Dad says after a beat and a nod of his head.

"You're always hungry," my mom huffs.

"Callie doesn't know yet," I say, moving to help my mom take food out of the oven.

"Okay," my dad says. "I won't ask my questions at the dinner table then."

Dinner goes off without a hitch. Dad has Damian sit beside him so they can speak easier. He's known Zander since he was a teenager, but Damian is fresh blood. He's not uncomfortable under the barrage of questions, though. Several times, I try for eye contact to make sure he's doing okay, but he's engrossed in whatever subject they happen to be on at the time.

"Seems like Coach might like your new friend even more than you do," Cillian says to me.

"I should be happy about that, right?"

"Better they're insta best friends than your dad clocking him on the jaw."

"Ah, you still sore about that," I tease him. My dad once punched Cillian. Twice.

"Nah, we all know I needed it."

"Yeah, you did, Superstar," my sister agrees.

After dinner, Mom ushers us all into the family room for presents. Sadie gives me a card she made herself, it has a picture of a sun shining on flowers. She's written her name and mine under two stick figures. It might be my new prize possession, and I tell her smiling face just that.

Mom and Dad give me what is normal for them, a fat check safely tucked away in a new beautiful handbag that they know I'll love but would never splurge on myself.

Cillian and Isla gift me a new tablet.

"Easier to pack when you travel," Isla says.

"Thank you, I love it," I tell her. Though travel is rare for me these days.

"Careful, this one's heavy," Zander says, pushing a large box toward me. I open it to find a bright sparkly pink bowling ball nestled inside a matching bag emblazoned with my name.

"Shut up! This matches my outfit."

"Look at your IQ," Isla teases, so I stick my tongue out at her, making the girls erupt in giggles.

"The bag was Callie's idea," Zan says.

"Thank you, sweet girl."

"You're welcome," she says, beaming at me with pride.

"I'm spanking all your asses with this beauty," I tell them, to their answering laughter.

"Oh, Auntie Willa," Sadie says dramatically. "Language."

"Sorry, Sadie," I say, pretending to be distraught by my behavior.

"Here you go," Damian says, handing me an envelope.

Inside is a printed itinerary for two weeks in July. In motherfucking France to see the Chateau.

"Damian," I whisper. "This is too much."

"It's not," he says, dismissively. "You'll get a private tour of the grounds. I tried for an overnight stay, but they wouldn't budge. Still, you'll have all day with a guide."

"Oh my god."

"It's after the classes are finished for the year and any potential play-offs," Isla adds.

"You knew?"

"Of course," she says. "This family is the worst at keeping secrets from each other."

"You guys are the best fucking family, ever," I say, teary-eyed. "I take it back, Cillian. Twenty-five feels a lot different than twenty-four."

23

DAMIAN

The Coles are much like Fig's family. Accepting, loving, close. Spending Willa's birthday with them was better than I could have expected. They welcomed me in as if there wasn't another option, even after Willa told them she was dating us both. She'd tried to convince me that her parents would be supportive Admittedly, I didn't believe her. I've seen her dad on television enough to know that he's stoic and stern. Evidently that's reserved for his hockey life, he's far different with his family. He took a genuine interest in me, and not once did I feel like it was an inquisition. Instead, I found myself welcomed into their family time. It was nice to be around a family that knows everything about one another. There isn't a weight of secrets pushing you down as soon as you walk in the room. Not like with my family, where you are constantly alert of what can and cannot be said in certain company. The Coles are open and affectionate and their love for each other is palpable. They're trusting.

I've never wanted that type of family more than I did walking out their front door that night. I didn't want to leave it behind.

No longer am I stepping away from physical connection, instead I'm running headfirst into it. If it looks like it did that night, that is. I crave it, I'll fight for it.

Yet that whispering voice in my mind says I'm not worthy of it. That I never have been and that's why I never received it. Because I'm undeserving, I haven't earned it. And I never can, because I don't know how. What do I have to offer except money?

As a rational person, I know I can give more than that. Childhood trauma isn't easy to ignore, however. The cult I grew up in isn't a religious one, or sexual one. My family's cult, the one so many wealthy elitists belong too, is money, power, and perception. It still requires deconstruction to leave it all behind. And that is something I fear I'll struggle with for the duration of my life. Even paying off Alexander's father gave me an evil thrill. Knowing I had something he wanted so badly that he would give up his own flesh and blood for it. I didn't offer the money because I wanted to hold that over his head, I did it for Callie. But it was still thrilling. When I should have been disgusted.

No matter how grounded I feel with both Alexander and Willa, the insecurity is always there playing havoc inside my head. Especially since I feel the distance between him and me lately.

He's so busy, which I understand. But I think he's dragging his feet telling Callie about us. Specifically, his relationship with me. I don't know how not to be insecure about that. If I wasn't in the picture, he could be having a normal relationship with Willa as his girlfriend. Maybe that's what he needs now that he's raising Callie. A relationship that doesn't cause waves in his career or with his kid sister who was raised in a very conservative way.

I'm the thing standing in the way of that. Yes, his bisexuality is too, but he loves Willa enough to waylay that part of him. Of that I'm certain, even if he professes his unwillingness to compromise. The question is does he love me enough to take a chance? Or do I love him enough to not let him risk everything.

These are the questions that circle my brain whenever I'm idle. Instead of falling into it too often, I've thrown myself into my dissertation and am now further along than I anticipated being. It's not a bad problem to have, despite the circumstances that led me here.

Alexander has a home game tonight, and I'm meeting Willa and Callie there. I haven't seen much of either of them. Callie still looks at me with a glint of hero worship. From Willa I get longing, something I share. If it were up to me, I'd move them all into my house and we'd spend every night together.

As a fucking family. *My* family.

Not just Willa and Alexander but Callie, too. When I allow my thoughts to spiral toward fantasies, she's there. Needing my help with homework or teaching me some obscure hockey fact that I know nothing about. She's in the kitchen with us, helping us prepare dinner or Sunday breakfast.

I see it all so clearly in my dreams. It's a far-off reality.

Maybe I need a vacation to clear my head, rid myself of these morose thoughts. For now, I need to set aside and enjoy the game. Callie and Willa are already at the seats when I get there. Willa greets me with a hug, Callie an unusually non-enthusiastic smile.

"Hey, Callie. How's school?"

"It's fine, I guess," she says, not making eye contact with me.

"Did I do something wrong," I whisper to Willa, taking my seat next to her. She looks as confused as I am when she gives me an unknowing shrug.

"Mister Damian, can I sit with you," Sadie asks. "Uncle Zan says you're learning hockey and I'm the best teacher."

"Sadie, don't bother him," Isla says, but I wave her off.

"It's fine, I'd love a tutor."

"What's that mean?"

"Teacher," I tell her.

"Oh, yeah, I'm a real good teacher."

"I'm a real good student. I think we'll make a great team," I tell her, and she nods like she already knew this.

She rattles off information as if I've never seen a game before. I let her because she's entertaining as hell. Even when there's an exciting play happening, she never fails to let me know exactly what's happening. Her rambunctious cheering doesn't stop her. It's also contagious. Callie, who continues to be a reserved version of herself tonight, can't help but join in.

If ever there was a better example of a child with an old soul, I don't know of it.

"How's the dissertation coming along," Willa asks during the intermission. The first period was largely uneventful in the way of scoring. Both goalies managed to block all incoming shots and we're sitting at a score of nothing to nothing.

"I'm nearly done."

"That's amazing," she says. "I can't wait for the day when I know I'm nearly done with school."

"It comes quicker than you'd expect."

"I suppose it does. Feels like Sadie was born only a year a two ago even though she's nearly seven."

"Maybe there's a lesson there about not taking life for granted," I muse. A lesson I could use myself.

"What's wrong," Willa asks.

"Who says anything is?" Of course, she's picking up on my mood change. One of her many talents is how observant she is of others.

"I can tell. You can talk to me, Damian. I *want* you to talk to me."

"I'm fine, beautiful. Just in my own head a lot these days."

"Callie is too, it seems. I don't like it from either of you."

"For me, it will pass. As for the younger Fane, we should keep an eye on it. She's been through a lot."

"You'll tell me if it doesn't pass," she asks, worrying her bottom lip with her thumb. I want nothing more right now than to haul her back to my place and put that mouth to better use. I'd never have thought someone caring about me the way she does would turn me inside out, but here we are.

"Sure," I agree. "I think I need some time away. Get out of the city, maybe. Clear my head."

"That does sound nice."

"Well, you have two weeks in France coming up," I remind her.

"I do. Though I must say that itinerary you gave me is rather vague on who will be coming with me."

"We'll see how things shake out," I say as Isla, Sadie, and Callie get back from their bathroom break and snack run. Sadie immediately climbs on Willa's lap and begins sharing her popcorn with the two of us. I've learned it's her favorite game night snack.

The plan is for us to go to France together. The three of us, and Callie. Cillian and Isla expressed interest in going as well. That hinges on Alexander and Callie, at the moment.

Callie sits and immediately takes her cell phone out, vigorously typing away.

"Everything okay, Callie," I ask. She briefly looks at me and nods, not saying anything. It causes Willa's frown to deepen.

Callie's mood doesn't change for the entirety of the game. She cheers when the Blades score and whoops with the rest of the crowd when they make a great play or hit. But outside of that, she keeps to herself and only talks to Sadie when the younger girl demands some attention from her.

Alexander had another good game, earning two assists and only landing in the penalty box once for some scuffle on the ice that he didn't start, but sure didn't ignore. It seemed targeted by the other player who was chipping away at him over and over until Alexander reacted, and I can't help but wonder if it's the rumors about his sexuality at play again.

I don't have the luxury of sticking around and finding out. Me going to the family room to wait for him only adds fuel to the fire he'd rather extinguish. Instead, I say my goodbyes to everyone before I head home. By myself. Again.

If this has taught me anything about myself, it's that I'm an impatient motherfucker. Somewhat, anyhow. I waited for years for Alexander to be in the same geographical location as me. But now, my patience is thin. Which only makes me feel like a selfish bastard. Something I have never wanted to be.

As soon as I'm home, I book a flight home. My last trip was so short, maybe being back in The Crescent City for a few days will do me good. It will be nice to catch up with everyone I wasn't able to see anyway. I'll leave tomorrow afternoon and come back next week without all this baggage I'm carrying.

I'm asleep for about an hour when my doorbell rings, waking me. Groggy and confused, I open the door to find Willa.

"What's wrong?"

"I didn't want you to be alone tonight," she says.

Jesus Christ, this woman is too good. Too kind and too thoughtful for the likes of someone like me. I am so fucking in love with her.

"Get in here, Ms. Cole." I hold the door wide, locking it after she enters. "I was asleep."

"You just…you seemed sad. More than you were letting on."

Fuck, her being here is about the greatest gift I could ask for. Because I didn't have to ask. Willa's here of her own accord, because she wants to be here. Because she was concerned. Not that I want to worry her, but it makes me fucking hard that she is. "Just get undressed."

"Yes, Mr. March," she says with a quiet giggle as I drag her to my room. Pulling her shirt off of her, I tug the cups of her bra down and take one pert nipple in my mouth. "That feels good. I thought we'd talk, though."

"Come first, talk later."

"If you insist."

"I do," I say, moving to her other breast while my hands work the waistband of her jeans. She helps me push them down over her hips, wiggling to get them around her ankles. They stop there. "On the bed."

Willa sits on the edge, but I push her to lie back so I can pull her shoes and jeans off. By the time I'm done, she's discarded her bra as well and I stop to take her in. We're always so rushed and hungry, tonight I get to savor her pale skin and perfect curves. Her rosy nipples match the color of her lips. A berry stain that makes me want to eat her up. I've been with beautiful women; ones who drape themselves in expensive clothing and jewelry. None hold a candle to the natural beauty in front of me.

"Damian," she calls, pulling me out of my revery. "Come here. Be with me."

Dropping my own underwear, I climb up with her, stretching her arms above her head. Our fingers entwined. Her thighs cradle my hips as she pulls them up, making room for me. I peer down in her eyes with wonder and swear I can see everything there is to know about her there.

"How are you real?"

"What?"

"You're too good to be true, Willa."

"I'm just as real as you are. Just as real as that hard cock you're teasing me with."

I thrust in, making her gasp and throw her head back. It exposes her creamy neck. I lick the long line of it, moving my hips ever so slowly. Again, there's no rush tonight and being inside Willa isn't something to be wasted.

"This cock?"

"Yes," she breathes. "Whatever you're doing with those hips is pretty fucking fantastic, too."

She clenches something inside, hugging my dick as if she's trying to keep me from pulling out. I love it, but I do pull out only to ease back in. Her hips find the same rhythm, dancing with me as if we were born for this. Maybe we were and we're all just animals with a need to copulate. Forget the rest of life's bullshit; what we look like, what we do, and society's ridiculous nonsense.

We should all be fucking with animal abandon. Life would be so much easier.

I nuzzle under her jaw, right below her ear. A sensitive spot for her, I know because she bucks under me. Her ankles come to lock around my waist.

"Can you come, or do you need help?"

"Kiss me and I can," she says, turning her face to mine. I seal my mouth to hers and swallow down the moans as we both give way for our bodies to take over. She shatters under me and my head roars in triumph. As if I've accomplished a lifelong dream or won a fucking Nobel prize or something.

Long minutes after, when our hearts have slowed and we've cleaned her up, I still feel it. The new longing to cement whatever we have between us into something impenetrable. Sturdy and long lasting.

"I've never been in love before," I say to her as she snuggles into my chest, my arms wrapped around her. It may not be direct, but I'm certain she'll infer my meaning.

"I never had been either."

"Had?"

"I love you, Damian."

I feel the crack so profoundly that I can't understand how it isn't heard. Why it isn't echoing off the walls. The lock on my armor is broken and it all falls away. A weightless feeling takes over me, but she's here, tethering me like a cord that runs between her heart and mine. Our souls interlinked.

Those four words I've spent my whole life without hearing are turning me into a sentimental twat.

"I love you, too, beautiful."

"That's nice," she says, drowsily. "I like the sound of it."

"Do you want to hear it again," I ask, and she nods. "You first."

"I love you, Damian March."

"I love you, too, Willa Cole."

"I'm sorry things have been so weird lately."

"Don't do that, Willa. There's a lot going on, but it's nobody's fault," I say.

"Still, I've missed you. I've missed the three of us."

"I've missed that, too," I say. As much as I don't want to leave her and this new feeling, I won't abandon my plans. I need a touch of home, some gumbo and jazz music. "I'm going home for a few days."

"When?"

"Tomorrow afternoon. I'll be back next Thursday."

"I guess I have to miss you for a little while longer then," she says and snuggles closer, pressing a kiss to my collarbone. I'll miss her too, but suddenly, I don't feel as lonely as I did earlier today. Willa is marked on my heart now and I'll carry her with me wherever I am. "I hate all this distance, Damian. I wish I could fix it."

"We'll figure it out, beautiful," I promise.

I'm adamant on not giving up without a fight.

24

ZANDER

Something is up everyone's ass lately. Mine included. Callie throws a fit every time I try to talk about anything important. Willa is mopey. Well, as mopey as Willa can get, which isn't much but it's noticeable. And Damian is damn near missing in action. Sort of, anyway. He's answering texts, but I haven't been able to connect with him to hear his voice in days.

Not to mention I'm still getting the occasional snide comment from other players on the ice. I can't kill the rumors. Professional hockey is too small of a world, everyone knows everyone else. Per Coach's instructions, I'm ignoring it as much as I can. Focusing on the game, not the bullshit spewing out of random mouths. But even he knows hockey rules only allow me to take so much of it before I shut those mouths up.

Other hockey players I can handle, everyone in my personal life griefing me is a different story.

It's all really starting to wear me the fuck down. Everyone has a problem these days with something...

I suspect it's me. It's a strong suspicion. I'm the problem.

But what the fuck did I do? I'm having a great season on the ice, so much so that I think I've cemented a solid spot on the team. I got my sister out of that hell hole of a house. I've admitted to the two people I love that I want a relationship with them both. Fuck, I even told Coach.

So why is everyone still so goddamned pissed off?

To be fair, the only ones angry are Callie and me. But I'm angry enough for everyone. Mostly because my kid sister isn't acting like her normal adorable self. Instead, she's like a Demogorgon skulking around ready to scream at whoever comes around the corner.

It's enough to put anyone on edge. I don't know, maybe this is what all teenage girls are like. How would I know? But I can't take another few years of this shit, we need to get it handled.

What if this is because of her new friends? Callie is at a vulnerable age, easily influenced by others. It's possible she's learning bad habits from them or taking on their shitty-ass personalities. Or, fuck, maybe she's being bullied.

So help any little brat that's treating my sister like crap. I'll lose my mind.

Her tuition is non-refundable. If I have to pull her out and find her a new school, I will, but damn. It would be great to get through a couple of months without fires to put out. Seems like there has been a constant iron ball of drama chained to my ankle since I got called up.

After my game the other night, Willa waited with Callie until I came out of the locker room but then quickly left. She hasn't been herself since. I know she went to Damian's, and he left the next day for New Orleans. The abruptness of his trip is concerning. He's been working so hard lately, I'm sure it's just burn out that he needs a breather from.

Willa's birthday went over so well and now only days later nobody wants to talk to me.

"What's the frown for, Fane," Vaughn asks. "You've hardly got any weight on there."

"Fuck you, man," I retort. I'm pressing as much as I always do in the weight room.

"Just giving you shit; I can tell something's spinning in that tank of a head. Spill it."

"I don't know how to raise a teenage girl. For starters," I grumble.

"Dude, there's no manual on that," he says. "How old is she?"

"Almost fifteen."

"Ah, rough age. They're figuring their personalities out, finding their paths, you know? Except they're doing it while their bodies wreak a hormonal civil war inside them. Give her some leeway, would be my advice. But not too much."

"I'm not sure that's helpful," I grunt out through my next leg press. "What's enough but not too much?"

"Again, there isn't a manual, Fane. You're going to have to figure it out with her. Don't let her get away with too much, but also be sympathetic to what's she's going through. You know her best."

Do I though? I'm trying to, but I've been away for most of her life.

"How old is your daughter?"

"Nineteen, so it hasn't been long enough for me to forget how she was Jekyll and Hyde for a good couple of years."

"She's good now?"

"Nah man, she's feisty as hell," Vaughn says with laughter. "We fucked up though, we threw a divorce at her in the middle of all that turmoil. But she's easing up on us little by little."

Divorce must have been hard on them all. I haven't ever really contemplated marriage. How would that work with three of us in a marriage? Maybe a commitment ceremony or something. Obviously, nothing legal. But does that matter? Why do we need the state to sanction our commitment anyway?

I'm sounding more and more like Willa by the day.

"At least you had years of parenting experience to rely on by then. I dove right into the deep end."

"Zander, you're one of the hottest defensemen in The Show right now. If you can handle hockey, you can handle a teenage girl. Have a little fucking faith."

"Thanks, Vaughn. Honestly, I appreciate the pep talk."

"No problem, Fane. I'm always around if you need help. Not like I have a fucking life outside of this game, anyway."

Vaughn finishes his set and leaves the weightroom. At thirty-seven, he's our oldest veteran. It's unusual in this sport for guys that age to still be playing pro. I suspect he'll be retiring soon, but I understand why he hasn't. He's still good and fast. Still scores goals. Besides, he's good for team morale.

I do another rep on my legs and follow it up with twenty minutes of cardio before I call it a day. Callie will be done with school soon, so if I leave now, I'll beat her home and we can have a serious sit down before she sequesters herself to her bedroom. Or my bedroom rather.

That's just another one of the many fires to put out; getting us a place where we both have our own beds. And privacy. I travel enough that I at least get a real bed now and again, but sleeping on the couch when home has long gotten old.

There's just enough time for me to shower before Callie walks in. One of her new friends, Selma, gets picked up every day by her mother. They've been giving Callie a ride home for the past week. It's been nice not having to worry about that anymore. The kid's grades are good too, so that's another positive. My mother even sent Callie's artwork after I requested it. She was ecstatic when it arrived, a rare moment of elation from her lately.

"Hey, Cal," I greet her when she lets herself in the front door. "How was school?"

"It was good. Nothing eventful," she answers.

"Come have a seat."

"I have homework," she says.

"It can wait a few minutes. I want to talk to you." She huffs but sets her backpack down and comes to curl up on the end of the couch. Instead of looking at me, she picks at the polish on her nail. Isla took her to get them done with her and Sadie on a 'girls' day'. It was the first time she'd ever had a manicure. She loved it. "What's been going on with you?"

"Nothing."

"Callie, come on. Whatever it is, you can talk to me. We're in this together." She sucks her bottom lip in, tears springing to her eyes. "Callie?"

"I told Selma about you," she starts. "That you play for the Blades. She searched for you on the internet."

Ah, fuck.

"What did she find?"

"Some Seattle gossip site."

"And what did Selma have to say about that?" Just my luck, my sister finds a friend who is homophobic.

"Nothing," she blurts. "Well, she said it was wrong that some stranger on the internet would try to out you like that."

"So, what's the problem?"

"Is it true," she asks, looking vaguely horrified.

Well, fuck. It's my sister who is the homophobe.

"What if it were?"

"Zander! The Bible says," she begins.

"No, Callie. The Bible doesn't say anything of the sort. Not the original texts anyway."

"Is that true?"

"Yeah, baby girl. But you can look that up yourself. Come to your own conclusions about it," I say as she picks more polish off. "As for my sexuality, I'm not gay. I'm bisexual. Do you understand what that means?"

"It means you like both boys and girls," she says, wearing her skepticism all over her face.

"Men and women," I clarify. "But yeah."

"It's weird."

"It's not weird, Callie. There's nothing weird about loving people. It's just a new concept for you."

"Does Willa know?"

"Of course, she does, Callie." This is a conversation I should have had with her weeks ago. She shouldn't have been blindsided by it all. "Look, Cal. Willa and I are in a relationship together, and with Damian. It seems complicated, but it's a simple as all of us caring about each other."

She doesn't respond as she sits staring down at her lap. There's no way to know what is going through her mind, and all I can do is wait her out right now. Like Vaughn said, I must give her some space to make her own opinions, her own choices, and mistakes.

Though I refuse to let her be hateful toward people who are different from her.

"Why didn't you tell me?"

"Because you were already going through so much with the move here, I didn't want to overwhelm you."

"No," she says, sending me a seething glare. "You didn't tell me because it's shameful and you know it's wrong."

With that, she stalks to her room. *My room.* And slams the door shut behind her.

That went just fucking great.

The thought crosses my mind to go after her, force her to talk this out with me. Let me explain how I feel.

I didn't expect her to be as easygoing about it as Willa's mom, but I wasn't expecting a slammed door in my face either. All I ever wanted outside of the NHL was to be accepted for who I am. Be *loved* for who I am. Maybe I underestimated the influence her upbringing would have on her, because I truly believed she'd be more open to understanding the life I'm trying to build here.

On the other hand, she's not entirely wrong. I do feel ashamed. Nearly every day I think about how unfair it is that I can't openly love the people I do. More accurately, I have to risk so much to be open about it. The kicker is I'm now back to being uncomfortable with my sexuality in my own home.

Fuck.

———

Two days later and it's not much better with Callie. She's polite enough during meals and when I ask about school. Beyond that, I get little out of her. Today, I leave for another road trip.

I miss him. I miss Willa. I miss holding them both and the laughter we always share. Nothing could make me give up Callie, she's worth every sacrifice I make. But I didn't expect it to be this lonely.

"Good morning," she says, finding me in the kitchen finishing up toaster waffles. I drop them on a plate and hand it to her.

"Morning, Callie. Remember you're at Willa's tonight."

"I remember," she says after a long sigh.

"I don't love the situation either, kiddo. But for now, it's the best I've got."

"I could go stay at a friend's house," she suggests.

"You could if I knew any of those families, but I don't. And we can't rely on strangers every time I have to leave town. This is the last road trip for the season anyway." The very last thing I'm going to do is send Callie to stay with people I've never met. The best solution would be to move into a house with Damian and Willa and not have to worry about Callie every second I'm gone. She's nowhere near ready for that. Maybe she'll never be and will be another three years before I get the family I dream about at night. "In the off season, we'll figure out a better living situation. I miss my bed."

"It is a great bed," she says, even giving me a small smile. It's more than I've been getting so I'll take it as a good sign. "Sorry you didn't make the playoffs."

"It's okay. The team was plagued with injuries early on," I say. "We'll make it next season."

The team made a great push, we barely missed it. The Stanley Cup is the goal every year, but it's also nice for some of the more seasoned players to get a head start on their vacations. Everything with family is planned around the season, engagements, marriages, birthing babies. There are a lot for players to look forward to when the season ends.

For me, I have a grumpy sister to look forward to. Though, as soon as she's done with school, I plan on taking her to Disneyland. I want to experience that first with her. Then maybe we'll head somewhere tropical.

Hopefully she likes me again by then.

"When are you back again?"

"Saturday," I remind her. "Be nice to Willa, please? She is picking up my slack because she cares about you. So be kind, regardless of what you think of our relationship."

It's the first time I've brought this up since our original discussion. I can't leave without making it clear that she doesn't get to treat Willa the way she's treating me. It's not fair, especially when Willa is putting so much of her own life aside.

"You think I wouldn't be kind," she asks, her nose wrinkling in concern, or maybe distaste.

"You've always been before," I reassure. "But you haven't been that great to me lately. I'm just reminding you that she doesn't deserve that sort of treatment."

She looks down at her plate, not saying anything as she eats her waffles. I don't deserve her treatment either, but I'll take the brunt anyway. It's my job, I guess. We have a big roadblock to get past, I have to believe we will. At least she isn't rushing off and slamming doors this morning. For as much as I don't know Callie, I do know she's not hateful.

Her views on sexuality aren't anything she formed herself. They're taught. They're doctrine told to her by our parents, the small community we grew up in, and the church we were forced to attend. She can learn that life doesn't have to be so rigid.

After breakfast, we both pack up the things we need before I walk her down to the street to meet her friend.

"Love you, Cal," I tell her, pulling her in for a big hug.

"I love you, too, Z." She may sound a little sad, and I wish I could change that for her. All I can do is press a kiss to the top of her head and squeeze her a little tighter.

"See you in a few days, I'll call."

"Okay, good luck."

With that, she's off to school and I'm off to end my season. First stop is Los Angeles, then two days off in Houston before our final game.

On the flight to California, I handle some long overdue business. First, I send a message to Isla and then I email the Human Resource contact. I can't predict if Callie is going to change her opinion of my lifestyle. Nor how long that might take. Yet, in the same way I'm not compromising by giving up either of the people in my love life, I'm not compromising who I am for her benefit. I love her for who she is, and she's going to have to do the same. She's stuck with me, whether she likes who I am or not.

I'll give Callie everything I have. In return, she's going to have to at least respect me and the decisions I make for myself.

Just as I send off my last email, something hits the side of my head and falls into the aisle of the plane. Looking down, I see a foam bolt from a Nerf gun.

Motherfucking Wallin.

"Shots fired!"

"It's on, fucker," I say, grabbing my own nerf gun from the empty seat next to me. He started this nonsense a few road trips back. A childish game that takes over the cabin for a handful of minutes but eases some of the strain from traveling. Most of the team has embraced it.

When it finally settles down and most everyone has lost all their ammo under the seats, I feel lighter than I have in days.

25

DAMIAN

I've never agreed to anything so quickly. The text came in before I woke up this morning, my last in New Orleans. My trip has been good, exactly what I needed. It forced me out of spinning around in my own head.

Seeing Fig, Brie, Cookie, and Delilah was grounding. I remember who I am again, that I'm more than the sum of my childhood. More than my anxieties constantly tell me I am. Being with people that love me for who I am, knowing all they do about me, it was a reminder. A much needed one.

I had dinner at Fig's parents' house. Shopped the vintage stores with Cookie before we had an impromptu baby shower for Brie. Walked City Park with Delilah, followed by Pimm's Cups at her favorite new bar. Even had dinner with Delilah's grumpy partner, Pope.

The etouffee and gumbo may have helped my attitude some, too.

It was a taste of the good things from my childhood. The parts I loved about my upbringing. Seattle may be my home now, but New Orleans will always hold a special place in my heart. Maybe it will forever be the place I come to check myself, to reset, to gain some perspective on my life.

Opting to drive to Houston, I rented a car first thing this morning. The drive isn't bad, and it is less than six hours. Giving me plenty of time to build up the anticipation of seeing Alexander, privately, and at his last game of the season. But not so long as to be exhausting.

The stretch between New Orleans and Lafayette has always been one of my favorites to drive. I had a grandmother in Lafayette as a child and we made the trip often enough. I'd entertain myself by making up stories while driving through the bayou. Sometimes it was about our car breaking down and being overtaken by gators while we waited for rescue. Other times it was more mystical, and I was stolen from my parents by legendary creatures that lived in the swamps. My favorite creature was the Rougarou who resembles a werewolf; he'd kidnap me, and I'd be rescued by Alligator Annie. This area is very conducive to stimulation of the imagination, besides it being a gorgeous landscape.

When I texted Alexander back this morning to let him know I could easily change my plans, he called me, told me where to be and when. Asked if I'd stay with him tonight and tomorrow after his game. I couldn't say no. I *wouldn't* say no. For weeks, all I've wanted was a little time with him so I can get a sense of what's happening, where his head is at, and where we stand. A bit of reassurance and validation to ease the amount of missing him.

Wow, that makes me sound needy as fuck.

It is not an attractive trait, but at least I can be honest about it. The first step to fixing it is admitting it.

When I stop off in Beaumont for a coffee, I send Alexander a text letting him know I'm about ninety minutes out.

ALEXANDER:

Drive safe, love you.

For a few long minutes, I stare at the text, half expecting it to disappear or for the letters to shuffle around into new words. When they don't, I smile and get back in the car. As I'm about to start it up and finish my drive, my phone rings.

"Hey, Willa," I greet, putting it on speaker so I can get back on the road while we talk.

"Did you know?" I'm not sure what she's talking about, but she doesn't sound like it's any sort of emergency. More wonder than anything.

"Know what?"

"That Zander was going to add me to the Wives and Girlfriends group?"

"No," I say, trying not to laugh at her shocked tone. "That's good, right? Makes you official and gives Isla a wingman in the group."

"He added me to his health insurance, too."

"Again, a good thing. Yes?"

"It's surprising. He didn't tell me he was going to do it."

"Maybe he's feeling generous," I tell her. "I can ask him, I'm on my way to Houston now."

"You're not coming home today," she asks. "And also, hi, how are you? Sorry, I skipped over that when you answered."

"It's fine, beautiful. I'm good and I'm happy to hear your voice. And no, I'm not coming home just yet. He asked me to change my plans."

There's a brief pause before she speaks again.

"That's so fucking sweet," she says, and I can hear the emotion she tries to control.

"Are you crying, Ms. Cole?"

"No," she lies. "Okay, maybe a little. It's just that I know how much you've both been missing each other. And I'm happy. Shut up."

"You, my love, may be the most ridiculously adorable human I've ever known," I tell her. "How's it going with Callie?"

"I don't know, good enough, I guess. She's not as chatty with me as she used to be, but she isn't being rude either. I wish she'd be open with me about whatever is going on with her."

"Sorry to hear that. Hopefully, Alexander can get it sorted in the off season."

"I hope so," she agrees. Willa doesn't stop the conversation right away, instead she keeps me company for the next half hour of my drive. She asks me a hundred questions about New Orleans and my friends there. I can't wait to take her with me on a trip home, show her all the spots that mean something to me.

"Someday I hope to see the city with you," she says, mimicking my thoughts.

"You just tell me when, Willa. I'd be happy to take you home."

More than that, I'd be proud to have her with me. She's accomplished, smart, kind, and determined. Not to mention drop-dead gorgeous with her honey curls and freckled nose. Only a stupid man wouldn't want a woman the likes of Willa Cole. I'm many things but not that.

By the time I pull up to the valet at the hotel, I'm feeling more like myself than I have in weeks. Whatever has had me so morose the past few weeks has passed. I'm ready to see my boyfriend.

The first I've ever had. The first I've wanted. If I'm lucky, it will be the last.

Alexander opens his hotel room door with a wide smile, but I notice the concern on his brow, too. He's not feeling as light as me, but I can try to get him there.

"Hi, big guy," I say.

"Oh God, you too?" He laughs and his shoulders drop some of the tension he's holding. "Get in here."

"Good game in LA," I tell him, dropping my bag in the corner of the room.

"You watched?"

"Of course, I did. You're playing a lot like a fourth forward," I say, my words met with surprise as he realizes all I've learned about his chosen sport. My eyes drag over him, looking for new cuts and bruises. Seems he can't play a game without tallying a new one. Underneath all that, I see a body nearly shaking with the same anticipation that's been building in me since I read his text this morning. "Get undressed, Alexander, and I'll let you work that adrenaline off on me."

"You'll let me, will you?" He steps up to me as he grabs his tee at the bottom of his thick neck and pulls it up and over his head. His muscles pull and stretch over his body in the most mouthwatering way.

"Only because you're so goddamned good looking."

"You flatter me, March. It's also incredibly hot that you learned hockey for me." His strong hand finds my nape and pulls me closer. "Kiss me, Damian. I've missed that fucking mouth of yours."

I oblige, meeting him in the small space that exists between us. He's warm and tastes like I remember, like lust and something sweet. He nips my lower lip, stalling the kiss as he pulls it a small amount. With Willa, we always take more care, we're not as… feral. Digging a hand into the waistband above his ass, I find him bare underneath. Of course, he is. Gripping one cheek hard, I get the reaction I wanted when his chest rumbles with needy approval.

"Are you going to let me take this ass tonight?"

"No," he says. "And I'm not taking yours. When that day comes, we'll share it with Willa."

Alexander doesn't want to deprive her, and I love him for it. For so many things. Like being twenty-three and taking on the responsibility of raising his kid sister. Or how dedicated he is to his career, to his health and body. I've loved him for some time, I realize that now. Telling him during a sexual encounter might not be the best timing, but I don't care anymore.

"I love you," I tell him, looking into his dark eyes and cupping his cheek in my palm.

"I know, Damian. I've *known*. I love you, too."

"Yeah, you let that slip earlier."

"It wasn't a slip," he says. "Pull that cock out now, I'm ready to make you come."

"Have I ever told you how much I like your filthy mouth?"

"No, but you can make it filthier if you lose those pants," he says, and I swallow down my grin.

"Kiss me again first."

We're all mouths and hands as we peel the rest of our clothes off each other. Once they are discarded to the floor around us, we take a similar position to the one in Seattle some months back. That first night in his hotel room when the possibility of us felt more real than it ever had. Face to face, cock to cock. He licks his hand, then drops some saliva to our tips that bounce against each other.

"I want your eyes on me, Damian," he says, his hand wrapping around us both as he starts pumping at a slow, easy pace. "When you come all over my cock, I want to see your face."

"You'll come first."

"Fucking make me."

My pleasure, I think. Though there is little I need to do since he's handling all the work. I let him, instead focusing on running my fingers along his defined abs, down the vee than runs above his hips. The closer my hands get to where he's working us both into a frenzy, the more blood rushes to his chest.

He's closer than he wants to let on. Alexander can't hide how his body reacts to me, or to Willa. I've watched him enough to know. I'm not ready for this to end just yet though. I step back, taking my dick in my own hand but keeping my eyes on him.

"Don't make it easy for me, Fane." Alexander narrows his eyes at my taunt. I send him a sly smile, then drop to my knees before him.

"Open that mouth then, smartass."

I do, taking him down as far as he needs all while keeping my eyes upturned to his glazed ones. Alexander likes a mouth on him, I'd go as far as saying he likes it as much or more than sinking into a pussy or ass. The rush is different, so I understand it, even if I don't quite agree. Then again, maybe it's only my and Willa's mouths.

Whatever it is, he enjoys the position. The control. He grabs my hair on both sides of my face and takes everything he wants. When I taste the saltiness of his pre-cum, I pull off and lick the length of him, swirling over the tip to catch every drop. Alexander watches with rapt attention. Then he plunges back in with more force, unrelenting until he's completely spent and I'm coming in my own hand right along with him.

Might not be exactly what he had planned, but the result is the same. We shower and order room service and then settle in for the night, relaxed, lazy, and content with each other's company.

"I heard what you did for Willa," I say after we've eaten and found some mindless wilderness survival reality show on the television.

"It was past time," he says. "It felt right."

"It is right." Willa shouldn't be kept in the shadows just because Alexander's sexuality must. Or because I must. She deserves the spotlight. She earns it by putting up with the two of us.

"Callie knows."

"About Willa?"

"About all of us," he clarifies. "She… doesn't understand."

"Understand or like?"

"Both, I guess. It's why she's been acting differently. Her friend found the blog post and the pieces started coming together for Callie. She's worried it means I'm going to Hell or something."

Well, shit. I expected her to not understand, at least right away. I should have expected religion to have some influence here, but it honestly hadn't crossed my mind. Truthfully, I don't know her well enough to know how much the church affects her life.

That's a higher hurdle to clear than just not understanding something new to her. It isn't easy to overcome years of an indoctrinated belief system.

"That's unfortunate," I hedge, uncertain about Alexander's intentions moving forward.

As much as I'd hate it, I couldn't blame him if he decides to take a step away from me even as he takes a step closer to Willa. He has a whole other human to consider in this situation. Callie's at a tumultuous age as it is, not even considering all she's already been through. If I had a sibling, I imagine I would do everything in my power to ease life's turmoil for them.

In the same way I want to do that for both Alexander and Willa. If that means I have to stay away until Callie comes around or becomes an adult and moves out on her own, it's a sacrifice I'd make for them all.

I love them, but maybe love isn't always enough. Or maybe the timing isn't right. We're meant to be together, of that I'm certain. Only maybe just not quite yet.

"Yes, but I have to believe she'll come around," he says. "Because I'm not giving up on any of us."

"No?"

"No. I love you, I love Willa, and I love Callie. That's fucking that," he says in a deep, reassuring tone. This is the Alexander I first met. The man that refused to fully suppress who he is for a league with rigid standards. His fierce determination may have dimmed for a short time, but it's back now. While it won't be easy for us, I have faith we'll make it.

The next day, Alexander is busy with the team, while I stay back at the hotel working until it's time to go to the arena for his game. He steals the show, having the best game of his career, scoring two goals and wracking up two assists. Most of the crowd around my seat are Houston fans but even some of them comment on how well he's played tonight. He's fast, clean, precise, and intentional.

It's exhilarating to watch him, so bulky and large in life, but looking almost elegant and graceful on the ice. The Blades take it in a five to two win, and the loss for Houston means they are out of playoff contention.

Most of the crowd exits the arena in various forms of disappointment all while I'm riding a high on my walk back to the hotel to wait for Alexander in our room. I shower, get a few hundred more words written on my dissertation, then order some late-night room service, expecting he'll be hungry when he finally gets back to the room.

A few hours later, everything I'd been feeling today crashes down and burns in flames.

26

WILLA

The call comes in the middle of the night. My phone ringing wakes not only me but Kit and Callie as well.

"Damian? What's wrong?"

"Alexander is at the hospital," he rushes out.

"What happened?"

"We're still figuring it all out," he starts. "There was a group of drunk assholes waiting for the team to leave the arena. They jumped him and it turned ugly quickly from what Cillian and your father told me. The entire team stepped in."

"How badly is he hurt," I ask, my voice shaking.

"Maybe a broken rib or two, they're taking images now."

"Is this because we won?" It's not just because he played so well and knocked them out of a playoff run. Sure, that's probably part of it. But it isn't the entirety.

"Cillian said the men were slinging slurs at Alexander," Damian answers, confirming my thoughts. "Some local press is here."

That changes things. Denial is still an option, as is not commenting at all. But the speculation will swirl more than it has before. It may only be local journalists there now, but national sports broadcasts will hear about it quickly.

"You're at the hospital, too?"

"I am, so are a few of the other guys. Your father too, he's going to make a statement when one is prepared by team management. Alexander spoke to the GM before they took him for the X-ray."

Callie is in tears now, not knowing what's going on but understanding enough to know it isn't good. Kit wraps an arm around her, comforting her until I can explain to them further.

"Shit, okay. You'll call me when you know more?"

"Of course, beautiful."

"I'm going to fill Callie in."

"Okay," he says. "She knows, by the way, about all of us."

"Oh." Zan hadn't told me, but we haven't had a lot of time to talk away from Callie. "Okay, good to know."

"We'll be home tomorrow," Damian says. "I'll keep you informed. Love you, Willa."

"I love you, too."

I take a long, deep steadying breath.

"Where's Zan," Callie asks, tears clogging her throat.

"He's at a hospital in Houston getting some X-rays. He may have a broken rib," I say to her. "Some men attacked him after the game. Damian and Cillian are staying with him." I explain what little I know and tell her Damian is going to keep us informed until they all get home tomorrow. She's inconsolable though, breaking down into a fit of sobs. All I can do is guide her to the couch and pet her head until she cries herself back to sleep.

I'm not so old that I don't remember what it's like to be her age. Everything is extra emotional, and your nerves are on high alert. With everything she's been through with her parents and the move, this is the iceberg that sunk her ship.

I switch my phone over to vibrate in the hopes it won't wake her as easily when I get more notifications, and I pull a blanket up over her to keep her warm while she sleeps with her head in my lap.

Damian texts to tell me it's only one bruised rib. Cillian texts to let me know the rest of the guys are only bruised and cut up. Except Blom, our goalie, who Cill says went absolutely feral. He has a broken nose but says it's a trophy for breaking one of the attackers' jaws.

People underestimate how unhinged goalies are.

Cillian also tells me all seven men who attacked have been arrested and the league attorneys have been apprised of the situation. He and Damian are staying at the hospital until Zander is released, then they'll try for a few hours of sleep before catching the flight home.

I try to do the same, curling up as best I can on the sofa with Callie. My bed sounds great, but I don't want to disturb her.

She wakes me up early in the morning by gently shaking my shoulder.

"Z says they are about to board the plane."

"Oh, good. Did you talk to him?"

"He sent a text, I saw it when I woke up," she says, shaking her head. "Why did they do this, Willa?"

Tears still pool in her eyes, now bloodshot from a night of crying. Her hair is a messy brunette nest atop her head, and she wraps a blanket around herself like it will offer some kind of security.

"Come here, kiddo," I say, holding my arms out for her to come sit with me. When she's settled, I tell her the truth. "I think it was mostly because their team lost. But they targeted your brother because of the rumors of his sexuality."

"I was mean to him because of it," she cries. "I'm just like those men."

"No, Callie." I pull her head to my chest as she starts to hiccup. "You're nothing like them. You weren't mean to your brother because you wanted to hurt him." I let her work it out of her system, again just holding her and soothing her however I can. It's a long handful of minutes before she's calmed down enough to talk more.

"I've been reading some about it, bisexuality," she says, her cheeks flushing.

"There's no reason to be embarrassed, Callie. It isn't shameful," I say. "Do you have questions about what you've read?"

"I'm not sure. Z said that the Bible doesn't say it's sinful," she says. "I've never read the Bible. I only know what I was told at church or by Mom and Dad."

"That's probably the case for a lot of people. You go to church because you trust the teachings, but that doesn't mean whoever is teaching them is always right. Do you think Zander is a bad person because he loves both Damian and me?"

"No," she says immediately. "Zan isn't a bad person at all."

"Do you think I'm a bad person? Or Damian?" Callie shakes her head vehemently. "I didn't grow up with religion, so I can't really relate to your struggle there. But I'd be happy to help read about it with you or find some people to talk to. For now, maybe, knowing we aren't bad people and we're not causing anyone harm by loving who we do, is what matters the most. We don't all have to fit into a box, or change who we are, to deserve love."

"I do love him," she says, her lip trembling. "I know I told him before he left. Do you think he believed me?"

"Oh, sweet girl. Yes. He knows how much you love him." Teenage guilt is no fucking joke. "Nothing you could have said to him would change that."

"I haven't been very nice to Damian, either."

"He's noticed that," I tell her sympathetically but honestly.

"Mom said," she starts to say, but stops to chew on her bottom lip while she rethinks things. "Damian paid my dad, didn't he?"

"He did. We thought that was the quickest way to get you here with Zander."

"I shouldn't have been rude to him," she says. "He's been really nice to me, more than I deserve. I blamed him, you know?"

"For Zander being bisexual? He's always been that, Callie. It's only that he likes Damian enough to nurture a relationship with him."

"Yeah, I'm kind of understanding that now," she says with some relief. "I should apologize."

"You'll have a chance to."

Her stomach growls and I offer to make breakfast if she'll find something for us to watch while we wait for Zan to get home. I'm tempted to scroll through the internet and see what, if anything, is being said about the brawl between the Seattle Blades and some drunk hockey fans. But I know it won't do anything good for my own state of mind. Instead, I focus on blueberry pancakes.

It won't do Callie any good if I fall apart with worry over Zander's physical state or worry about his career. His rib is bruised, but there was no fracture. Which means far less of a recovery time. While it's now officially the off season, it's next to impossible to get a professional athlete to chill the hell out and let their body heal from injuries.

When breakfast is ready and I bring a plate stacked high to Callie, who, to my surprise, has landed on watching *Queer Eye*. We eat and cry some more whenever Jonathan or Karamo imparts some tender wisdom. Six episodes later, Callie idolizes Antony and wants to learn how to cook a wider variety of recipes. More importantly, she's gotten a taste of a lifestyle outside of conservative small-town Minnesota.

By the time we get a text saying they've landed and are almost home, you can hardly tell Callie has spent so much of the past twenty-four hours in tears. Of course, that changes as soon as her brother walks through the door.

She runs into his arms, crying through her apologies and telling him how much she loves him. I can see his own eyes water as he looks for me above her head, but I pretend I don't see. What I can't ignore is the black eye, the cut high on his cheek below it, or the wince he hides when his sister squeezes him tight.

Damian moves around Zan and Callie, dropping both his luggage and Zander's before coming to greet me.

"Hey," he says, pulling me in for a hug.

"Hi. I'm glad you were with him."

"Me too. Now I'm glad we're home."

"Me too," I mimic.

"Did she get any sleep," he asks about Callie who is still distraught in her brother's arms as they speak quietly to one another, and she gently touches the bruising on his face.

"Not enough. She's been pretty low energy all morning."

"Do you think there's any possibility of getting her to agree to come to my house tonight? I think he'd prefer to keep everyone under one roof tonight."

"She might be okay with that," I say. "She's made some strides today."

Turns out that's true. After she apologizes to Damian through yet another curtain of tears, she agrees to go wherever Zander wants to go. Perhaps some of it is an attempt to make amends with Damian. It's not necessary, but it shows her true character.

I don't get a moment to talk to Zander alone until we've made it to Damian's house, and he takes Callie to show her the three different guest rooms she can choose from. Only then, do I get to take inventory of all Zan's injuries in a way I wouldn't do with his sister in the audience.

"Let me look at you," I tell him, tenderly raising his tee up to inspect his torso. It's a landscape of bruises on his left side. "Fucking hell."

"It looks worse than it is," he says, and I look at him skeptically. "They had a few seconds of surprise and got some lucky shots in before security and the guys jumped in."

"Assholes."

"Yeah," he agrees. "Stupid way to fuck up your life. The league is pushing hard on charges."

"Good, fuck those guys," I snap. He laughs, making him flinch in pain.

"I'm going to make a statement. I've been talking with management."

"What are you going to say?"

"Not sure yet, but probably the truth." He searches my face for a reaction while he says the words.

"That might lead to more of this," I say, hesitantly. I'll stand by whatever decision he wants to make. I'll be proud of him regardless of his choice. "And end your career."

"I'm being told that as long as I don't push it as a platform, they'll support me."

"Do you believe that?"

"Maybe. I have a couple of days to decide," he says, pulling his shirt back down so I stop obsessing. "It might be the start of something good, too. This sport needs diversity."

On that, I can wholeheartedly agree.

"I'm with you, whatever you decide."

"I appreciate that."

"It's what you do when you love someone."

"You love me, Willa?"

"You know I do, big guy."

"I love you, too," he says, leaning down to kiss me. Not deep or lustful, but sweet and caring. "Thank you for taking care of my sister."

"I love her, too," I tell him. "She's family, no need to thank me."

Damian and Callie come back downstairs and she's all smiles, lighter than she's been in weeks now that the burden she's been carrying is laid out on the table and she understands we're all here to help her.

"Z! Damian says I can do whatever I want in one of the bedrooms. He even said I can paint a mural on the wall!"

"That's very generous of him, kiddo," he tells her.

"I know, you guys are the best," she cries, emotions getting the better of her once again. *You gotta love puberty.*

"Hey, remember what I said," Zander asks her, wrapping his arm around her.

"We're all going to learn how to do this together and I shouldn't feel bad."

"That's right," he confirms.

"Did my fight turn you on," Zander asks me later. After we've spent the afternoon lazily watching a movie, had pizza delivered for dinner, and Callie passed out like the dead.

"No, it scared the shit out of me," I admit, crawling up into the middle of the bed.

"I can handle a few drunks."

"Your hockey bravado is hot as fuck, but I'd prefer your fights be one on one and on the ice."

"I'll keep that in mind." He grunts as he gets comfortable in bed, adjusting pillows until he's at an angle that makes his injuries tolerable.

"Besides, you're out of commission for awhile anyway," I remind him.

"I'm not," Damian reminds me with a sly smile.

"Me either," I tease. "But we wouldn't want the big guy to get worked up and then not be able to take care of him."

"I was told no sex," Zander grumbles. "Not that I couldn't watch."

I scoot to one side of him, Damian takes position on the other, and our hands meet over Zander's chest.

"We can wait a couple of days," Damian says. "We have the rest of our lives."

Zander brings our entwined hands to his lips and kisses them before closing his eyes. He's content. Happy. No matter where we go from here, we go together, the three of us and Callie. The family Damian has always wanted, the one Zander has always wanted to protect. The one I'll fight tooth and nail for every day of my life.

27

ZANDER

Three days after returning home from Houston and I've never been more confident in the decisions I've made.

Callie is lighter than she's been since moving to Seattle. Not only has she bonded with Willa in a purely sisterly way, but she has been gravitating to Damian more and more as well. She's charmed by him, like everyone is, now that she sees that the love we all share isn't shameful. We've spent more time at his house, and she is enjoying having her own space again. And the freedom he gives her in it. He's nurturing in a way that is so unexpected in a man that grew up the way he did. You'd never know he came from a cold home when he's made his so welcoming and warm.

She saw the three of us hug each other before Willa left for classes yesterday and there was a genuine smile on her face. We didn't grow up in a loving household either. She's experiencing it for the first time just like Damian and I are. And learning that it doesn't have to look like she expected.

Willa has been something like a nursemaid to me. Hockey is in her blood as much as mine, she understands what I need to heal, but also doesn't coddle me. After I worked out for the first time this morning, she assessed my cuts and bruises, applying some ointment her dad recommended without commentary on the fact that I'd re-opened one of the gashes on my left hand.

It'll heal and it felt amazing to get back into a routine.

I've spent a lot of time talking to Coach, the GM, the PR team. My decision is firm. I'm certain it's the right move as I step into the press room and take center stage. The team has been very supportive, not just management but the players too. Many have reached out to check on me and offer kind words. We truly define the word team.

Whether I'm walking into a total shit storm, and let's be honest, I probably am, I know they have my back. If the league forces me out at some point for this, I'll still have made friends. Coach takes a seat on one side of me, Cillian on the other. He didn't need to be here, but as team captain, he wanted to be. It's a show of support and I appreciate it more than I can say.

"Fane is going to make a statement about the incident from the other night in Houston, then we'll open it up to some questions," Coach says, nodding his head at me.

Crash and burn or fly free; it's now or never. I scan the room and see Willa and Damian standing in the back, both smiling proudly at me.

"After our last game in Houston, leaving the arena, I was attacked by a group of men. While it may have been partially due to my performance in the game, I believe it was more than that, based off the slurs they yelled. The truth is, I'm bisexual. A fact I will no longer hide, nor will I stand for any ill treatment because of it. What happened in Houston was a hate crime. I was targeted because of rumors about my sexuality. I'm putting that to rest today.

"My personal life is nobody's business and is off-limits. I will not entertain any questions asked about my personal life that you wouldn't also ask of any other member in this league. I'm not a sideshow, my love life is not fodder for anyone's entertainment or ire," I say clearly and directly. "I've known little of life outside of this sport. Hockey is my life, it's my first love. I won't be giving it up because some people are more preoccupied by my personal life. I work hard, I take my position and profession seriously. This team and the opportunities it's given me mean the world to me. I don't take it for granted and I promise to always work as hard for them and the fans, as they have for me."

Cillian pats me on the back as I finish up and hands raise in the small crowd of press gathered in the room. The first few questions are softballs asking about injuries and if the men had all been arrested.

"Are you saying you have a boyfriend," one reporter asks.

"He already told you yahoos his personal life is off limits," Blom says from the side of the room where he leans against a wall. "Next question."

Most other reporters laugh, and I shoot him a smile.

"Do you hope this is going to start a chain reaction in the NHL," a female reporter asks.

"Do I hope that? Yes. Do I expect it to happen right away? No," I say. "Realistically, it doesn't make sense to believe that every player in professional male sports is straight. Statistically, I think it's something like two and a half percent of men identify as gay or bisexual. Why wouldn't that translate over into the world of sports? More importantly, why isn't it accepted in sports like it has become in other areas of life? Or even in women's sports. It's a lot to contemplate, and an important conversation that should be had."

"Is it a conversation you'll be spearheading," she follows up with.

"No," I say bluntly. "I'm a private person, I'd like to keep it that way. As I've said, I'm here to work hard for the Blades and I'll keep my focus on the team. Also, I think there are others who are more articulate than I, and who are better qualified to lead that conversation. That doesn't mean I won't throw my support behind it though."

"Surely you expect people will be curious," another reporter asks.

"People can be as curious as they want to be. That's on them. But again, I'll say, if it isn't something you would ask a straight player, then you have no business asking me. My personal life will not be fetishized."

"Do you worry about your place in the league?" This is from Jonathon, a journalist at one of the bigger sports magazines.

"I always worry about my place in the NHL. We all do, it's part of having a profession where everything changes very quickly." It's not the answer he's seeking, but it's what he's getting. Changes in the NHL won't happen by a tidal wave, they'll start with a small ripple. I'm just the first of what I can hope will be more and more. If I'm lucky enough to have the opportunity to retire from the league someday, it would be nice to leave it a better place than what I found it in.

A league that celebrates diversity instead of one that all too often fights to hide it.

Coach is asked a series of questions and then someone asks Cillian if he's here in support of my decision to come out.

"I am," he says. "Zander is an important part of this brotherhood. He's proven himself in each game and he works harder than most to excel and improve. I love the guy; I've never been prouder to call someone my teammate."

His statement is followed by a round of whooping from the guys that made the effort to be here today instead of off with their families as they normally would be. Beside Blom, stands Wallin, Vaughn, and Letty. I'm no longer the rookie to them, I'm one of them.

Part of a team. Something I've been for as long as I remember, but it's never felt this profound. Men I've only known for a few months are standing shoulder to shoulder with me while I make a move that could have lasting effects on us all.

That's not something I'm taking for granted. Fucking ever.

For so long, I've hidden who I am for fear of backlash. That weight isn't gone, but it isn't as heavy now either. Because I'm not carrying it alone. The guys are with me, Coach is with me, Damian and Willa are with me.

It's more family than I could have ever dreamed of.

WILLA

I t's graduation day.

For Callie. She's done with high school and ready to start at the Cornish College of the Arts in the fall. Our entire family was there to watch her walk and throw her cap. So was her mother, who finally left their dad about a year ago. She moved here, but Callie stayed with us. Leaving the sanctuary she built herself in the room she picked in Damian's house wasn't an option for her. We were happy about that, just not ready to let her go yet.

She doesn't have to move out for college, but she's expressing a desire to be on her own. At least she'll still be close.

Damian has published his second book and is working with a documentarian on a cult that is being run out of British Columbia. He's busy but thriving.

Zander is still playing for the Seattle Blades. This city has embraced him. The first season after what happened in Houston was grueling on his mental health. He was hated in so many places they played. That only fueled him though, and the rest of the team, determined to show up all the homophobes in the world of hockey.

They've dominated the league the past couple of years because they play with continuity and none of them are in it for themselves. Oddly enough, them knowing about our relationship has bolstered them rather than hindered them.

Often, it's our house they all gravitate to. We regularly host the guys and their wags for various events or quick holiday get togethers between road trips and games. Nobody finds our situation weird anymore. We're just us, the Cole/March/Fane family.

And we're growing by the day. I gave birth to our first son sixteen months ago, in the midst of setting up my charity organization that works with the women's and domestic violence shelters in Western Washington. I'm doing exactly what I had planned on, helping women learn a livable skill that gives them the independence to walk away from the horrible circumstances they can all too often find themselves in.

Kit asked me when I was pregnant with Jasper if I had any idea if the father was Zan or Damian. I didn't then. I do now because he looks so much like his daddy. On paper, he is Jasper Cole-March, the next heir in line to the ridiculously large March fortune. Whether he shares blood with Damian or not has never mattered to any of us.

The baby I carry now, the tiny girl growing so quickly, will be Lilly Cole-Fane, and she'll be our last. I don't particularly enjoy pregnant life. I thoroughly believe I was meant to be these babies' mama, but my body hates the process and I'm sick more than I'm not. I will never be one of those women who waxes romantically about what it was like growing a human inside of me. This shit is rough.

Damian has already gotten a vasectomy and Zan has his appointment next month. There wasn't a question in either of their minds about other options.

"You did all the hard work, we can handle the rest," Damian had said.

Pregnancy has been the only tough part of motherhood for me. The rest has been great, but I'm lucky and have more support than most. Two husbands definitely help.

I'm not legally married to either man, but we held our own commitment ceremony. Hugo Blom officiated in a light-hearted and joyful celebration of the love we share. Instead of rings, we wear matching tattoos on the inside of our ring fingers, a simple script reading *CMF*. I know who I belong to, and at the same time, I know they belong to me.

We're in this for the long haul. For life.

Together, the three of us together as one.

MORE FROM ALISON RHYMES

Subscribe to Alison's Newsletter for Early News and Bonus Scenes

RAINFALL

I met the love of my life at ten years old.

At sixteen, I gave him my heart.

Three years later he was drafted to the NHL and moved across the country.

Five years after, he's back. And he's meeting his daughter for the first time.

I still hate him.

Even if my heart says that's a lie.

At ten years old, she changed my life.

At sixteen, I told her I loved her.

Three years after, I left and broke her heart.

Five years later, I'm coming back home to the surprise of my life.

I hate her for it.

Even though my brain says this is all my fault.

BROKEN PLAY

They have ties that bind.

June grew up in the shadow of her brother and his best friend, Drew McKenna. She stood back while Drew dated his way through high school and college, watching and waiting. Waiting for him to realize he loved her as much as she loved him.

When he did, it was the happiest she'd ever been. Until she found him with another woman only five years after their marriage.

Leaving her husband was a simple decision, but there was no easy way to cut him out of her family.

When June receives a fresh start to her career, she also finds what could be a new lease on love. Reality hits Drew with a vengeance.

He wants her back.

She wants to make him suffer.

BRUTAL PLAY

Mistress.

Whore.

Lorelai has been called every name in the book. Except for the ones she's always dreamed of.

My love.

Mine.

Noah Anders is the only man to have ever owned her heart. But it's her soul he wants.

Theirs is a battle of wills, tempers, ego, friendship, and loyalty.

He wants retribution.

She just wants to survive.

BITTER PLAY

Reed Turner has loved his sister's best friend, Leighton, for damn near a decade. He's given her space to grow in her career and her life. Now he's ready to claim the woman he's always believed was his. It's too bad another man in her life keeps getting in the way.

Leighton Ward has never been in love. Now, just as so many things are changing in her life, she finds two men vying for her heart. Both hold strong ties to her future and making the wrong decision comes with heavy consequences.

He knows what he wants.

She's as confused as ever.

DECONSTRUCTING DELILAH

A modern-day retelling of Samson and Delilah…

As the son of a preacher, Pope Blackwell believed he learned the difference between good and evil early in life. After all, it was beaten into him regularly. Now as an adult, he's traded in his life of abuse for one where he holds all the power.

When a young woman strolls into his life full of more bravery than she should possess, he becomes consumed by her fire.

Delilah believed escaping her family's abusive ways would be the hardest challenge of her life. Then she met Pope Blackwell.

One sinner and one saint. A world of differences between them.

Faith. Experience. Age.

His obsession only grows as she challenges him until he's ready to topple any pillar that stands in her way, and she'll fight every demon to be by his side.